INTRODUCTION

A Carolina Christmas by Jeri Odell
Charity Bradford longs for excitement after growing up within the confining walls of an orphanage, though her new job as laundress at the Biltmore Estate promises little adventure—except for her frequent trips to the stables. There she captures the attention of young Malachi Claybrook, known to her simply as Clay. More and more, Charity dreams of her handsome stable hand, but will reality prove that appearances can be deceiving?

A Proper Christmas by Sylvia Barnes
Selma Bradford's second day as chambermaid at the Biltmore Estate is decidedly not off to a good start when she stumbles upon a guest in his room. While Selma begs for forgiveness—and prays she'll keep her new position—handsome bachelor Jacob Sinclair can't help becoming enamored by the lovely Selma. But in a world where maids and aristocrats do not mix, will love thrive at Christmastime?

A Honey of a Christmas by Rhonda Gibson
Peggy Bradford loves being an assistant cook at the Biltmore Estates. She enjoys being close to her sisters and has become what she thinks is an old maid. Will the arrival of beekeeper Mark Ludman prepare Peggy for a honey of a romance? Or will she feel the sting of impossible love?

An Accidental Christmas by Diane T. Ashley with Aaron McCarver
Melissa Bradford can't do anything right. At least nothing most young ladies can. She has followed her sisters' leads and gotten a position at Biltmore, but unlike them, she is inept at every task assigned. Ned Robinson travels to Biltmore to seek support for his dream of opening an automobile factory, but an "accidental" meeting could cost him everything. Is the captivating servant with an affinity for mechanics the key to his future and his dreams?

A BILTMORE CHRISTMAS

FOUR-IN-ONE COLLECTION

DIANE T. ASHLEY with AARON MCCARVER
SYLVIA BARNES
RHONDA GIBSON
JERI ODELL

BARBOUR
PUBLISHING

Cover design: Kirk DouPonce, DogEared Design

Published by Barbour Publishing, Inc., P.O. Box 719, Uhrichsville, Ohio 44683, www.barbourbooks.com

Our mission is to publish and distribute inspirational products offering exceptional value and biblical encouragement to the masses.

 Member of the
Evangelical Christian
Publishers Association

Printed in the United States of America.

Prologue

Wʜᴀt will become of us, Miss Elsie?"

Ten-year-old Peggy asked the question. Elsie Caps hugged the nearest of the four little girls to her. She swallowed hard and bit back the tears that stung her eyes. "You will stay here with me."

Three-year-old Melissa pulled away from the group. Worry and grief lined her young face, a face that should have been wreathed in smiles and innocence. Instead, a glazed look of hopelessness shadowed her wide-set green eyes. "I don't want to be 'dopted. I want my mommy," she wailed.

Elsie pulled her back into the circle of her arms. She looked steadily into each set of eyes desperately pinned on her and spoke with quiet firmness. "You will never be adopted out. I love you. Your mommy and I were best friends, and I promised her I'd take care of you. I will never allow you to be separated, much less live with strangers."

Melissa's lips quivered. "You promise?"

"I promise." She forced a confident reply that masked the insecurities threatening to overwhelm her.

Charity looked at Elsie. She spoke in a broken whisper, "But where will we live?"

"You will live here with me."

"Here at the orphanage?" Six-year-old Selma looked at

her oldest sister, Peggy, for confirmation that Elsie spoke the truth to them.

Elsie sighed. Only actions would eventually take away the unease and restore stability in the lives of these four children whose mother and father suddenly had passed away. "Yes, we will all move into the orphanage." She'd have to give up her small apartment to stay with the girls. Looking at their sweet faces, Elsie knew she'd never regret the decision.

As if they understood, the little girls huddled closer to her. "We'll help you, Miss Elsie." Peggy patted her back.

"I can make my bed," Selma proclaimed proudly.

Peggy leaned back and looked her straight in the eye. "I can cook some. Mama was teaching me." A sob cut off the offer. She dug her small face deep into Elsie's shoulder.

"Thank you, girls. I'm sure we'll all get along fine. You'll see." Elsie prayed that she'd been honest with the children.

A CAROLINA CHRISTMAS

Jeri Odell

Dedication

I dedicate this book to my Lord and Savior, Jesus Christ.
You opened the door for me to write, and my prayer
is that each and every book in some way honors you.

Chapter 1

October 1896

Charity gazed from one sister to the next, having no idea how hard saying good-bye would be. They huddled together in a tight hug, each face as somber as the next. A lump tightened her throat.

Each of them—the four Bradford sisters—was an interesting combination of Mama and Papa. Charity hated how their images had faded in her mind. She never wanted to forget them, but a dozen years had effectively erased many of the memories. So grateful for the photograph tucked away in her Bible. Otherwise, she might not remember their faces at all anymore.

"What a pathetic sight you are." Mama Elsie wrapped her arms around Charity and Melissa. "You'll only be three miles away, child."

Charity smiled at the woman who'd become like a mother. "I know." She brushed a tear from her cheek. "But I've never spent a day apart from Selma or Melissa, and we see Peggy often. An hour away by foot seems terribly far."

"You don't have to go," Mama Elsie reminded.

"I do." Charity couldn't explain the burning desire within

but knew she must leave. She'd been in this orphanage since she was eight. After reaching her adult years, she'd taken a job here to remain close to her sisters, but now at twenty, she couldn't bear these walls any longer. She had to get out and breathe the fresh air, feel the sun on her face, and live life beyond this gray existence.

She stepped back, breaking the hug. "You've been good to us and loved us as your own. Now I must make my own way in this world, and someday perhaps I can care for you." She held Mama Elsie tight and kissed her cheek.

"Ah, Charity, my little dreamer." Mama Elsie returned the kiss. "You've always been the most like your father, a bit of wanderlust in you, child."

No truer words were ever spoken. Charity dreamed of a different life, a life filled with travel, perhaps helping others less fortunate than herself.

She turned to Melissa, taking her into her arms. "I can hardly believe it. My baby sister is fifteen!" She tugged at the cap Melissa wore. Melissa had shoved much of her auburn hair inside the hat. "Someday you'll outgrow your desire to be a boy. You'll meet a man who'll make you want to be every bit a woman."

Charity spoke with authority, though all her knowledge came from books not life.

"Like Mr. Darcy?" Selma teased, and her three sisters giggled.

Charity raised her chin. "Make fun if you will, but I shall one day have my own Mr. Darcy." She'd read *Pride and Prejudice* so many times that some of the pages had come loose from the binding. "He is the epitome of a man."

In truth, for twenty-year-old Charity, spinsterhood was looking more probable with each passing day, which was one reason she'd taken the job at the Biltmore. Free room and board and a chance to save some of her salary for the future. She wanted more than she'd known as a child.

Charity released Melissa from her long hug and moved to Selma. She and Selma shared the same light brown hair, the color of their mother's, or so Mama Elsie said. Both Selma and Melissa inherited their papa's striking emerald eyes. "You're almost eighteen. It won't be long until you join Peggy and me out in the real world. Prayerfully consider the future God has for you. If you're lucky you'll be like Peggy and know exactly what you love, finding a way to do it each day."

"Baking makes me happy." Peggy said those words often.

"I do not love laundry, but it is a means to an end." Charity smiled to soften the truth of her words. "What that end is, I am not so sure, but God will direct my path. I claim that promise daily."

She and Selma hugged. Selma hung on tightly and sniffled. "I will miss you terribly."

"And I you. Do remember that I have one day off per week and a half day every other Sunday. I will walk home often. I promise." Kissing Selma, she moved on to Peggy.

Charity took Peggy's hand. "If you grow tired of your job at Reynolds House, maybe you could work in the kitchens at Biltmore. Wouldn't it be fun to be there together? Though with our work hours starting at six and ending at nine in the evening, we would not garner much time together. Maybe our two hours off in the afternoons would coincide." Charity shrugged.

"I will give it some thought," Peggy promised. "Though I'm quite content with my present position. I'm treated well."

Charity wrapped her arms around her older sister. "You, my dear sister, would be content anywhere, as long as you found dough to knead and ovens to bake in." They both giggled.

Charity believed Peggy's deep love for kitchen work stemmed from feeling connected to their precious mama. They often had worked together preparing family meals before the Good Lord took Mama and Papa home to be with Him.

"I do wish I had a passion for something that rivaled yours for baking." She stared into light-blue eyes the exact shade as her own. "You have no idea how blessed you are."

"God has a plan for you, and when you find it, your passion will ignite." Peggy's words held promise.

I certainly hope so. She knew God said it. Her head believed it, but her heart feared she'd never discover God's purpose for her.

"I must leave now." Charity let her gaze roam over the four dearest faces in all the world. She picked up the satchel and walked out the door, turning back to face the group who'd followed her outside into the crisp autumn air.

"Wait," Peggy called. "I'll walk with you a ways. I need to get back to work myself. I only came to say good-bye."

She hugged the two girls and Mama Elsie. "I will see

you soon," she called to them as she rushed to catch up with Charity. Both looked back and waved once more.

"I feel as if I'm two people," Charity said. "I'm filled with excitement as I embark on this new life; yet I'm sad leaving behind the known and familiar. Did you experience such emotion when you left home?"

"I did," Peggy assured. "But as I said earlier, I'm very pleased with my life and the happiness I feel when I cook."

"Imagine, I shall not only have my own bed, but own room. A private room. Even as a laundress, I will have all the amenities the house has to offer. Indoor plumbing! Can you imagine such a luxury? Forty-three bathrooms in one house."

Peggy giggled. "That's more than the entire village added together. Seems ostentatious when most homes don't even have one, and I would hate to clean forty-three bathrooms."

"Me, too, but would not mind using them, not one bit. When Miss Bohburg hired me, she showed me the servants' quarters. She is Swedish, speaks with a heavy accent, and is in charge of the laundresses." Charity sucked in a breath. She'd been talking so fast, she'd nearly forgotten to breathe.

Excitement built as she shared with her sister and dearest friend. "The rooms are comfortable with nice beds. Mine has a white iron head- and footboard. Covered walls. A wooden rocker, a dresser, even a rug on the floor, making it feel very homey. I shall enjoy my room very much and should I grow lonely, there are twenty other bedrooms on my hall filled with other servants. We will all live together on the fourth floor."

"Maybe someday I shall come for a visit and see for myself."

Charity spun around, raising her eyes to the sky. "Guess what is the very best of all Biltmore has to offer?"

Peggy shrugged and shook her head.

"A library with more than ten thousand books in eight languages!"

"Since you only read and speak English, the other seven languages may prove worthless to you." Peggy poked her in fun. "Are servants allowed to borrow books?"

"We may check them out one at a time! That is more books than the library at Biltmore Village houses."

"And you do love to read!"

"I will keep you informed if I find any that you must read."

"Thank you. What will your job entail?"

"They use handmade French linens in their guest bedrooms and intricately embroidered damask linens on tables and dressers. I will work in brown laundry in the basement. That is where the kitchens are as well." Charity stepped over a rock. "Anyway, they use wooden washboards and after the linens dry, we also press them. From everything I saw, it's an intricate operation. Miss Bohburg says though Biltmore is a private home and the largest in the United States, it is run like a hotel."

"So you will work in the basement and live on the fourth floor. Where does the kitchen staff live?"

"They have rooms in the basement near the kitchen, but all the servants eat together in the servants' dining room, which will give me a chance to meet people. Can you imagine not knowing a single soul?"

"Maybe Mr. Darcy lives there," Peggy teased.

"Mr. Vanderbilt does. He is very rich and very single."

Peggy's mouth dropped open. "And strikingly handsome. But surely you don't think he's your Mr. Darcy."

"You never know. I've read about him. He's shy and reserved and loves reading. What a pair we'd make. We could spend quiet evenings in the library together, travel to Europe and New York on holiday."

Peggy's cheeks pinked as Charity shared her deepest dreams. "Your life station is quite different than his. The two of you marrying is not only highly unlikely, it would be frowned upon."

Charity noted the worried expression on her dear sister's face. She laughed. "They are only dreams. I will not count on them coming true, but will do my best to make his acquaintance. Perhaps my beauty will capture him, and he will not be able to chase me from his mind." Charity did not believe she possessed any outer beauty, so all her words were in jest.

"Honestly, being a servant at Biltmore is as close as I'll ever get to wealth. Do you wonder why some are born with everything and some with nothing?"

"I guess the good Lord puts us where He wants us. Perhaps if we had wealth, we'd not have time for Him."

Two gentlemen on horseback passed. They tipped their hats. "Good afternoon, ladies."

Both girls said hello in unison.

"Now that was a fine specimen," Charity whispered and

grinned at her sister.

The familiar pink hue returned to Peggy's cheeks. "Which one?"

"Either." Though she favored the one with raven hair and black eyes.

"You, my little sister, must do a better job corralling your thoughts. A woman with men on her mind can only fall into trouble."

Charity enjoyed toying with Peggy. Sometimes she was far too serious. "I only say those things to glean a reaction from you."

Peggy rolled her eyes. "Charity, you have craved adventure since I can remember, and now you embark on the biggest one of your life. I remember when Papa would leave, you'd cry to go with him. You wanted to preach to the Indians, too."

"And here I am at twenty, finally starting my own life. Do you think Mama ever resented Papa being gone so much?"

Peggy shook her head. "Papa preaching the Good News to all who would listen made her time alone with us easy to bear. After all, she had a stake in his ministry, too."

"You and Mama were so close." Charity's quiet words held awe.

"I think in some ways she relied on me, since Papa wasn't there much of the time."

"Isn't it strange that the first time she left us behind to travel with him, they were killed? I wish she'd stayed home. At least we'd have one of them." Charity gazed at her sister, remembering.

"But God did provide Mama Elsie and the orphanage. We have never wanted for a thing, and we were always well loved."

That was all true. "But how nice it might be to own more than two day dresses."

"Two is twice as many as one," Peggy reminded her. "I'd better turn back now. I think this is about the halfway point. You have another mile and a half or so to go."

Charity set down her small suitcase and hugged her sister tight. "I love you."

Peggy smiled and Charity recognized the expression on Peggy's face. She was about to expound some older sister wisdom. "Don't get so caught up in dreamin' that you miss what God has for you in the here and now." With that, Peggy turned and headed back toward Biltmore Village.

Charity watched her walk away, repeating her parting words again and again in her mind. Peggy walked the opposite direction for several minutes, then spun around and waved once. When she was nothing more than a speck on the horizon, Charity pivoted and headed toward her future.

The majestic Blue Ridge Mountains rising in the distance beckoned her onward. She'd read many a travel book, savored the pictures, but had never laid eyes on a place prettier than western North Carolina. No matter where the Lord led, she hoped this area—her favorite place in all the earth—would always be home.

"Thank you, Lord, for the promise of a new beginning and for my job at Biltmore. Even if I hate laundry, I shall cherish every moment of my stay there."

17

Chapter 2

Joseph Malachi Claybrook followed his older cousin Elizabeth to the fourth floor observatory.

"You must stay here at the Biltmore while building your own home." Her request sounded more like an order.

"This is your family, not mine," Clay reminded her.

And in truth, Clay knew she and George Vanderbilt were much more distant in relationship than Elizabeth cared to remember. She called him cousin, but actually their grandfathers were cousins.

"I spoke to Cousin George, and he welcomes you. If you recall, his father, your father, and my father were all dear friends back when we were children." Elizabeth sat erect at the edge of a chair, pushing her bustle off to one side. "I shared your plans to build a mansion near the Biltmore estate, and he was most interested. He'd love to sit with you and hear of your plans."

Clay paced to the window. The magnificent view drew his gaze across fields and outbuildings to the mountains in the backdrop. "I'm not building a mansion but a modest home."

Elizabeth gave him a pouty look and poured them each a cup of tea. "Why ever would you settle for modest? Grandfather Claybrook's death left us and our siblings a tidy sum of money. You surely can afford a step or two above modest." Elizabeth liked flaunting the family money. He did not.

She raised a disapproving arched brow. "What sort of parties could one throw in a modest home?"

"You know me. . . ." He settled on the chair across the small table and faced her, picking up the delicate china cup and sipping the warm tea. "I've always been restless in New York City. I hate the crowded feeling it brings. High society and parties leave me discontent."

"You're foolish, Malachi. The world could be your oyster. Why would you throw away your station in life?"

"Because none of that truly matters. I had no peace in my life until I came to North Carolina for a holiday with family. We attended revival meetings with my mother's family." He wandered back to the window. "A tent revival led by The Reverend Abraham Bradford, and he led me to salvation in Jesus Christ that very night. I was thirteen at the time and found peace with Jesus here in the Blue Ridge Mountains. Sadly, that was his last tent meeting. He and his wife were killed the following day in a tragic train wreck." He faced his cousin. "Do you have peace, Elizabeth?"

His question apparently startled her. She stammered, "Frankly, I've never thought about it. But I do have money and can do whatever I want, whenever I care to. That gives me peace."

Clay felt sorry for her. "I remember to this day the good reverend speaking on money being God's tool to use, not just for our comfort, but to help those less fortunate. I plan to invest heavily here in the orphanage in Biltmore Village. It is where Reverend Bradford's children are growing up, and in his honor I wish to give them a fine facility, rather than spending all I have on me."

Elizabeth rolled her eyes. "Waste your share of the family's money, if you like. I shall hope that when you meet with George, he will redirect your thinking on this whole matter."

Clay only smiled. "The matter is settled, Elizabeth. I followed my heart and have returned here, as was my plan since age thirteen, to build a home on the land adjacent to Biltmore."

"Well, no matter. George wishes you to make yourself at home here while you build."

The thought tempted Clay. He'd be much closer to oversee the project than if he stayed at the boardinghouse in the village. Plus he'd heard the kitchen staff here was top-notch.

"Would there be room for my horse in the stables?"

"I'm certain of it."

"Then perhaps I will consider George's most generous offer." He'd left his horse with a stable hand. "If you'll excuse me, I'd like to go down and check on Buck now and get him settled. We've traveled a long journey."

Elizabeth's mouth hung open in a most unbecoming fashion. "You rode from New York?"

Clay again grinned at his snobby cousin. "What better way to see God's beautiful creation?"

As an aristocrat, he could afford hotels and nice stalls for Buck. He didn't really travel like the true pioneers did, with a bedroll and a saddle under his head. He and Buck did spend one night under the stars, but only one.

"I'll see you at dinner," Elizabeth called after him. Sounded more like an order than a request. He shook his head as he started down the grand staircase. *She always was a bossy thing.*

He exited through the back and found Buck tied to a tree. He led him down toward the stable area. "Do you want to live here with these high-class, pretentious people?" he asked the large buckskin.

Clay scratched between the animal's eyes and up under his black forelock. "I'd rather sleep in the barn with you than under the roof with my showy relatives. What do you think, big fella? Would you share your stall?"

I'll sleep and eat in that monster of a house, but all my awake time will be spent with Buck or working on our new place.

❄

When Charity arrived at Biltmore, she scarcely could take it all in. Everything about the house—down to the smallest detail—testified of wealth beyond her wildest imagination. She rang the bell at the delivery door. A butler answered. "Miss Bohburg is expecting me."

"Your name?"

"Charity Bradford."

"Miss Bohburg is otherwise occupied at the moment. I will show you to your room." She followed him up three flights of stairs, and he led her to the same room she'd been shown last week when she was hired. He turned to leave.

"Excuse me, sir, but may I visit the stable during my breaks?"

His turned-up nose spoke loud and clear. "If you wish."

She heard the unsaid: *But why in the world would you want to?*

Charity felt the need to explain. "I have always loved horses."

His shrug said he couldn't care less.

She ended her explanation, and he quickly departed.

Charity opened her bag and hung her other day dress next to two uniforms already there. *I hope the rest of the staff is nicer than that old curmudgeon.* After unloading the rest of her things and placing her Bible and well-worn copy of *Pride and Prejudice* on the bedside table, she made a beeline for the stables.

The beautiful grounds boasted perfectly manicured lawns and flowers of every size, shape, and color, plus formal gardens, which she'd visit later. For now she wanted to see and pet each horse.

When she entered the barn, she didn't spot another living soul. Hoping to garner permission, she lurked in the entrance.

"Afternoon."

Charity startled as the rich baritone rang out a greeting from behind her.

"Good day." She turned and faced the man, believing him to be one of the riders that passed her and Peggy on the road earlier in the day. Not that she recognized him, but she'd know that big, beautiful buckskin he was leading anywhere.

"You look a little lost. May I help you?" He stopped next

to her. His horse nudged him.

"He's beautiful. May I pet him?" she asked, reaching toward the black velvet nose.

"You may. Nothing Buck likes more than the attention of a pretty lady."

Charity's face grew warm. Usually Peggy was the one who blushed at the drop of a hat. Charity ignored his comment and kept stroking the soft face, admiring the animal's earnest eyes.

"Say, weren't you walking on the road earlier today?"

"Yes. I'm Charity Bradford, a new laundress here at Biltmore. Is he yours?"

"Buck?" He rubbed the horse's neck, up under his mane. "He is mine."

"So they allow servants to own animals?"

The man hesitated and then smiled. "Only the ones who work in the barn."

"Am I permitted to visit the barn during my off hours?" She lifted her eyes from the handsome gelding to his equally handsome owner.

"I believe you are. You apparently have a love for horses."

"I do." She looked straight into eyes black as coal. "I plan to own one in the not-too-distant future."

"Do you ride?"

"Not yet, but I will. Isn't it wonderful that women can now do such things!"

His grin nearly stole her breath. Oh my, but was he handsome. She'd best be careful or she'd find herself swooning, and she was not the type of woman to do such silly things.

"I'll tell you what, Charity. If you come down to the barn on your afternoon hours off, I'll teach you to ride."

"You would do that? And would that be permitted by Mr. Vanderbilt?"

"It would be my pleasure to teach you, and I will gain permission so you need not worry."

❄

"Are you in charge of all the animals in this barn?"

He again hesitated. "Just some." *Forgive me, Lord. Just one.* But somehow he sensed if Charity knew who he was, she'd not give him the time of day. Knowing George, there were probably rules about this sort of rendezvous. But for some reason, he wanted to get to know this pretty little thing. Any woman who loved horses had his attention. Most declared horses smelly and unsavory at best.

"Shall we start tomorrow afternoon, then?"

"I'd love to, sir, but tomorrow is my first day, and I have no idea when my break time will be."

He wished they could start today, but he hadn't garnered permission to borrow a horse. Then he looked at Buck. "How about now? You could take a few laps on Buck."

Her face lit up like a Christmas tree. "Oh sir, may I?"

"Clay. My name is Clay."

"Is that appropriate?" Even though she'd grown up poor, she'd obviously been well schooled in propriety.

"It is for riding buddies. So what do you say, Charity? Your first lesson on Buck?"

She let out a little squeal then covered her mouth with her hand.

"I assume that is a yes. Step over here and I'll lift you up."

She looked down at her muslin day dress. "I don't have the proper attire to ride."

He nodded. "Well then, for today I'll let you brush him and get acquainted."

They led Buck farther into the barn, Charity talking to the horse as they walked. He took him to the stall the barn manager had assigned earlier that afternoon. While he removed the tack, Charity scratched Buck's face and whispered sweet nothings to him. Buck seemed to be enjoying the female contact as much as Clay.

Chapter 3

Charity headed to her room during her afternoon break to change into her day dress. She'd best not wear her laundress uniform to the barn. Others might not appreciate her smelling like a horse. She giggled, climbing the last flight of stairs. She loved the smell of hay and horses but knew others did not share that sentiment.

Opening her door, she spotted a box sitting on her neatly made bed. She stopped just inside the room but saw no one. She slowly moved toward the box. Would Mama Elsie have sent her something? She gingerly lifted the lid, and there ensconced in tissue lay riding attire.

She lifted from the box an interesting garment. The soft brown velvet material felt good against her skin. The pants were concealed under the skirts of the riding habit. She held them up and spun around, a grin nearly splitting her face in two.

Charity hurried through the clothing change and at the bottom of the box discovered a pair of riding boots that were a bit too big, but the rest of the apparel fit well. On her way to the barn, she spotted Clay holding Buck and another horse under a tree. Two saddles waited on the ground near his feet. She ran the rest of the way, not wanting to miss a moment of her lesson.

"I see you found some more appropriate clothes."

She stopped short. "You did not place these in my room?"

He grinned. "I would not be allowed in your room."

"Ah, but you must be responsible. Certainly they did not appear on their own."

He chuckled and handed her the reins to a small sorrel mare. "This is Trixie. She is yours for the duration of your lessons."

"Thank you. She is beautiful." Charity touched the small white star between the horse's gentle eyes. "And thank you for the riding habit—however it got into my room and whomever you borrowed it from."

"I have a sister about your size, and she is not as enamored with horses as you. She wore that only once, was thrown, and vowed to never ride again. With her blessing, I'm passing it on to you."

"Send her my regards and deepest appreciation. I shall give them the best of care and hopefully spend many hours in them atop Trixie." Charity was deeply moved by this near stranger's kindness.

"There is so much more to owning a horse than simply riding, and since your hope is to one day own one of your own, I feel it is best if you learn to care for her as well as feed her."

Charity nodded. "That would only make sense."

"So while Trixie belongs to you, you will have to come down to the barn in the mornings to feed her and provide clean water for her."

Charity nodded. That meant a very early morning

because her duties in the brown laundry began at six. But it would be worth it, she assured herself.

"Let's start with morning care." After tying both horses to a tree using their reins, he led Charity back into the barn.

"Trixie's stall is right next to Buck's down this first row here."

Charity followed Clay. He showed her how to measure Trixie's morning food and rake the stall, as well as where to haul the manure. "Normally the stable hands do all this, but since you want your own horse, I think it best if you know the amount of work you'll be in for."

"I most certainly will not be affording a stable boy," Charity agreed. "I'm not afraid of hard work, especially for someone as beautiful as Trixie."

After the morning chores were taken care of in the stall, he grabbed a bucket of grooming supplies and led her into the afternoon sun.

"Daily hoof care is a must." He bent over, lifting Trixie's, and with a bent metal tool, he scraped out horse droppings. Charity leaned close to see exactly what he did. She caught a whiff of his clean masculine scent. *I should not be aware of such things!*

He set the hoof back on the ground and led Charity around the front of the horse. He held out the tool he'd used. "Your turn."

She sidled up next to Buck's shoulder, facing the opposite direction, and slid her hand down his foreleg as she'd seen Clay do. At the ankle, she lifted the horse's foot, bending it back toward his rear legs. She rested it on her slightly bent knee and reached for the instrument. Trying to mimic what she'd seen Clay do, she loosened the hardened dirt and droppings from his foot. Then she returned it to the ground, dusting off her riding britches with her palms before straightening. She looked at Clay, waiting for his response.

He smiled when her eyes met his. "Well done!"

She returned his grin. "Really?"

"Like you've been doing it for years."

"I have in my dreams. Having read so many books on horses and equine care, I feel like I've already done some of the chores firsthand."

Seeing approval in his eyes, her stomach fluttered. How handsome he was.

"I will teach you more on her care tomorrow." He quickly brushed Trixie's back then threw a saddle up on the mare, cinching it tight. "But if you want to ride today, you don't have much time." He glanced at the timepiece he'd pulled from his pocket.

Placing his hands at her waist, he sent a tingle up Charity's spine. Lifting her like she weighed no more than a feather, he sat her on the saddle. "Take your right leg and lift it over the saddle horn and the horse's neck."

She did as he requested. At last, she was astraddle a real-live horse.

❄

Clay waited under the old cottonwood tree for Charity. She usually got her break about now. He had both horses saddled and ready to go. In the two weeks since her first lesson, Charity had become a solid equestrian. She fed and cared for her mare in the mornings, groomed and saddled her in the afternoons. Clay did the evening feeding, since Charity worked until nine each night.

Today was her afternoon off, so he'd ordered a picnic basket from the kitchen. They'd take a nice ride and eat on the banks of the French Broad River.

He saw her coming. She looked cute in her riding attire. He was glad he'd remembered that Rebekah had left those behind at his grandparents' farm. He'd taken his weekly ride out to their place and picked up the clothes while there. Trixie also had been purchased for his citified sister, so he'd brought the mare as well. She was older now and very calm, which made her the perfect horse for Charity.

He spotted Charity on the path from the big house. As always, when her eyes met his, she ran the last little way like an excited child. His heart swelled with building emotions as he waited, watching her. "You ready?"

She swung up into her saddle like she'd been doing it for years, not just a couple of weeks.

"Where to today?"

"I thought we'd head off over those hills." He pointed west. "Circling around back to the river."

She lifted her face to the sun and closed her eyes. "I'm riding a horse! I still can scarcely take it in. Riding has made my job here most wonderful in every way. I thought doing laundry would be pure drudgery, but I enjoy caring for the fine linens. They require extra love and tenderness."

Seemed when Charity was around, all he did was smile. How he loved her enthusiasm. They often enjoyed a peaceful silence as they rode, which he greatly appreciated. Some women he'd met filled every moment with chatter—unfortunately much of it useless. But not Charity. She appreciated silence as much as he.

They rode a couple of hours. He'd never get over the beauty of this area. Then he led them to one of his favorite spots along the bank of the French Broad River.

"How is this area for our meal?"

"Beautiful."

He tethered the horses to a nearby tree, untied a blanket from the back of his saddle, and rolled it out. Then he loosened his saddlebags and unloaded fried chicken, biscuits, apples, boiled eggs, and oatmeal cookies. Charity settled on one end of the blanket and he on the other.

"I love the sound of the water. Papa took us to the Atlantic Ocean once when I was about five or six. I still remember the crashing noise the waves made."

After Clay prayed, she took her first bite of chicken. "Most delicious."

"Thank the kitchen."

"I won't be able to ride on my next day off. I need to go home and see my sisters."

He nodded, still chewing his bite of biscuit. "Where's home?" he asked after swallowing.

"Biltmore Village."

"Why don't we ride together? I'll drop you off and come for you after I've taken care of some business."

Excitement danced in her eyes. "I'd love that! My sisters could meet Trixie."

He laughed. "For a moment I thought you were going to say meet me, but no, all that's on your mind these days is that silly horse."

Her face darkened to a pleasant shade of pink. "And you, too, of course. It's just that my youngest sister, Melissa, has the same love for these four-legged creatures as I do. She will be green with envy at my current life circumstance. Why, I almost have a horse of my own."

Maybe that's what he would give her for Christmas. Trixie, a big red bow tied around the mare's neck, would make a fine gift, especially for his horse-loving Charity.

❄

Several afternoons later, she and Clay rode to Biltmore Village. If he was surprised by her home being the orphanage, he never let on. She did not want his pity and was thankful he showed none.

When they arrived, she threw open the door. "I'm home. Melissa? Selma?"

Both girls bounded down the stairs, Melissa just ahead of Selma. They ran into her arms. "I have a surprise to show you!"

Holding their hands, she led them out the door to where Clay waited with the horses.

"These are my sisters, Melissa"—she held a hand in her direction—"and this is Selma." She gestured toward Selma.

"My dear sisters, this is Mister. . ." She realized she didn't know his last name. She paused, but he said nothing, so she added, "Clay."

"Good day, ladies." He kissed each of their hands like a

true gentleman. Charity's most silly wish was for the same treatment—a touch and kiss on the hand.

"And this is Trixie."

Both girls gushed about the mare, but especially Melissa. "May I ride her?"

"I must get to the bank, but when I return for your sister, I promise you a ride."

Melissa clapped her hands and spun around. "Thank you, thank you, thank you, kind Mr. Clay."

He bid them good-bye with the tip of his hat, leading Trixie away behind Buck.

Both her sisters chattered at once, firing questions in rapid succession. Charity finally caught one of Melissa's questions. "Do tell us how you have landed yourself a horse."

"And a man. And oh, what a man!" Selma teased.

Charity gazed into Selma's twinkling eyes. "It's not what you think. Clay is only a friend."

"Your words say one thing, but your face says quite another," Selma said.

"All right. Truth be told, if I were a different kind of woman, I'd simply swoon over that man, but he truly is a dear friend. We ride together almost every afternoon. He is also a servant on the Biltmore estate but works in the barns caring for the livestock."

She filled her sisters in on the past two-and-a-half weeks, one thrilled about the man and the other about Trixie.

"When we are together, the time is joyous. We talk, we laugh. I do like him very much and hope he is spending as much time dreamin' of me as I am of him. But I do not think it to be true." She dropped her gaze to her lap.

Chapter 4

Stanton Courtland is here?" Clay felt the pulse in his jaw throbbing.

"Not at this moment, but he is arriving later this afternoon." Elizabeth reminded him of a cat with her eye on the prey. He could envision her licking her chops as she spoke of the scoundrel.

"I can barely look at the man. You know he broke Rebekah's heart. How could you invite him, knowing what he did to your own dear cousin?"

"Stanton regrets his own immature behavior toward your sister, but how unchristian of you! 'Twas several years ago. You should have forgiven and forgotten by now."

Those were true words. He should have, but the thought of that rascal being here under the same roof, at the same table, made Clay mad. And that Elizabeth would fraternize with him was all the worse.

"I will ensure he is on a different floor than you. Will that make his presence more sufferable?"

"Only slightly. How long is his stay?"

"Two months. He will stay through the holidays and leave with the New Year."

"I feel like you're betraying Rebekah."

"She's on holiday with your parents in Europe and is none the wiser."

It's still betrayal. "They return in two weeks. She will surely hear of this. How do you think she will feel, knowing you are interested in her ex-fiancé?" If he were honest, Elizabeth was interested in any man who showed the slightest amount of attention. Two years older than him, she'd well passed the mark of spinsterhood.

"Stanton Courtland and Rebekah Claybrook are very old news. Unlike you, I'm certain she's moved on."

"You are completely disrespecting both my sister and myself." He turned on his heel and headed for the barn. Horses were easier all the way around and just as loyal as dogs, in his estimation. Perhaps more than some people.

❄

Since November had arrived, the autumn days were now dark and cold in the mornings. Clay had taken over the morning care and feeding of Trixie, which made Charity all the more eager to see the mare—and the man—each afternoon.

As she hurried down toward the barn, a dandy, as Miss Bohburg would have called him, traveled the opposite direction in a fancy buggy. The dappled gray pulling the rig did a high-stepping trot and was quite beautiful.

He stopped when he reached Charity. Tilting his hat, he said, "Good afternoon, miss."

Good manners forced Charity to stop. "Good day, sir."

He glanced around the area before his gaze returned to Charity. "Beautiful day for a drive through the country." His golden hair reflected the sun, and his nut-brown eyes danced with mischief.

"That it is. Now if you'll excuse me, kind sir, I'll allow you to be on your way."

"My dear, I'm in no hurry at all. But you, on the other hand, seem to be. Have you no time to enjoy the afternoon? Perhaps a ride with me in the buggy?"

Charity wasn't sure if he toyed with her or if the invite were sincere.

"Maybe another time. Good day, sir." Charity headed toward the barn. Much to her dismay, he turned the buggy and drove next to her.

"Might you consider a ride in my buggy tomorrow?"

Charity stopped. Clay already had told her he couldn't ride with her tomorrow on her day off. He had business in town that afternoon.

The man's brown eyes pleaded. She hesitated, and he cocked his head like a begging pup. "If I say yes, will you depart and let me get to my business?"

His wide grin not only exposed a set of perfect teeth, but two dimples as well. "I'll meet you here tomorrow."

"Tomorrow," Charity agreed, throwing caution to the wind. Anything to get him out of her way this afternoon, so she could ride with Clay. It dawned on her that she didn't even know the man's name, and glancing down at her attire, she realized he had no way of knowing she was only a servant. That might change his mind entirely.

When Clay spotted her, he waved, gathered the reins, and walked toward her. "What took so long?"

For whatever reason, she didn't want to mention the dandy, not wanting Clay to believe the wrong idea. "A guest."

"Those guests can be quite the distraction," he teased.

She mounted her horse. Thankfully they headed in the opposite direction as Mr. Dandy and his fancy buggy. Tomorrow she'd wear her servant's uniform and quickly change his mind.

"Charity, I've been meaning to ask since our trip to the orphanage last week. Do you know any of the Bradford children? My understanding is they are living in the same house where your sisters reside."

Her stomach knotted at the mention of her own last name. What could he want with her family? "That is my family name."

Clay stopped Buck and turn to stare at her. "You are Charity Bradford?"

"Yes." She drew back on Trixie's reins, stopping next to Buck. "How do you know of my family, and why do you ask?"

"Your father was a reverend?"

She nodded.

"Abraham Bradford?"

"Yes, but he has been gone at least a dozen years. Did you know my father?"

❄

Somehow this news endeared Charity to him all the more. How ironic that he'd met and was strongly attracted to Reverend Bradford's daughter.

"What? What is it? You look as if you've had the shock of your life."

"Your father led me to the Lord."

Her expression glowed at his news.

"I attended his last crusade before he died. I met your mother. You have a strong resemblance to her."

Her smile grew wider. "Do you think so? I've always hoped, but Mama was so beautiful."

He knew by the way she worded it that she had no idea she was, too. "As are you, Charity, quite beautiful, indeed."

The familiar soft pink tint spread up her cheeks. She nudged Trixie forward, and Buck stayed right beside her.

"I see that you do not believe me, but you are every bit as pretty as she."

"Thank you, but enough about me. Do share with me every detail of that revival. I was only eight when they died and am hungry for every snippet of information about them that I can gather."

Clay understood. He thought back to those very special days and began to share. He recalled portions of the messages and how they touched him. He told her of his walk to the front of the big tent and how her father prayed with him. She listened intently, like a sponge soaking in every detail. By the end of his recount, a few stray tears had rolled down Charity's cheek.

"It is a beautiful story. Thank you for sharing." She patted her cheeks dry. "I struggle to understand why God let him die, when he was doing such good work. And Mama, too. We needed her so." Charity voice cracked on that last sentence, so they rode awhile in silence. Both pondering. Both remembering.

Clay knew Charity had embedded herself deep in his heart. He longed to pull her from the horse into his arms and whisper sweet promises in her ear. He'd been trying to figure out how God wanted her to fit into his future.

✳

The following afternoon Charity walked out to meet the nameless man with the fancy horse and buggy. She grinned, wondering how surprised he might be by her servant's garb. His buggy waited in the same spot where they'd met yesterday. She saw shock register in his eyes, but he quickly recovered.

"Good afternoon." He stepped down from the buggy. "Another fine day."

Charity raised her eyes to the sky. "Yes. Yes it is." Then her gaze settled on the gentleman.

"Where would you like to go this afternoon?"

Charity decided to be direct. Raising her chin a fraction, she plowed forward. "You may bow out, and I shall not hold it against you. I realized yesterday that you most likely had no idea by my clothing that I actually am employed here at Biltmore."

"No. No I did not, but I did promise you a ride. Shall we?" He bowed slightly from the waist, his arm outstretched toward the small black buggy.

Charity accepted his help and settled onto the black leather seat. Such luxury. Mr. Dandy went around to the other side and climbed aboard.

"Where to, miss?" He paused. "What poor manners I have exhibited. I failed to formally introduce myself. I am Stanton Courtland."

His name sounded quite distinguished. Charity should

be impressed, but she found herself comparing him to Clay at every turn, and Mr. Courtland fell short.

"Charity Bradford. And I'd like to go into Biltmore Village for a brief visit with my sisters." She'd been missing them so much and, since yesterday, could hardly wait to tell them Clay's story about Papa. "Do you have some business to attend to? I would hate to bore you with a family visit."

He chuckled—a deep, hearty sound. "I shall drop you at your family home and find a way to amuse myself while you tend to your sisters."

How shocked would this man be to discover her family home was the local orphanage? Charity nearly giggled aloud at the thought.

"What brings you to Biltmore?"

"I'm on holiday for the next few weeks. My older brother oversees the family fortune, while I jaunt around the world spending it." He clearly amused himself. "I could use a pretty lady by my side to help me with my spending."

His flirting held no appeal. The Bible spoke of laziness time and again. One day this man would come to ruin, if he didn't change his ways.

She could, however, imagine many women falling for his charm, and he was quite personable. Here he sat in this fancy contraption, exuding wealth, with a servant girl at his side. Instead of treating her as an inferior, he was conversing with equality and ease. She did appreciate that about him.

He dropped her at the orphanage, hiding well any shock

or surprise he may have felt. "I'll return for you in an hour."

"Agreed." With that she entered the building, not glancing back.

While sharing afternoon tea with her sisters, she told them Clay's story.

"Did he bring you today?" Melissa cocked her head to the side, studying her sister.

"No." She then informed them about Mr. Courtland.

"You have two suitors?" Selma's mouth dropped open.

Charity giggled. "I have no suitors. Clay is a good friend. Mr. Courtland is far too pompous to even consider. Nor, I am certain, would he ever consider a woman of my social standing."

"Because he's rich, some might find his arrogance tolerable," Melissa said.

"In our station, none of us will marry rich. What we need are fine hardworking men." Charity's tone had grown firm, almost stern.

"Like Clay?" Selma grinned.

The words caused Charity's heart to contract. "Yes, like Clay. He is God-fearing. May we each meet a Clay someday."

"But you've already met him," Melissa reminded.

"This Clay doesn't see me in that way. We are only good friends." But she often dreamed he felt otherwise.

"Are you certain?" Selma asked. "When he looks at you, his eyes light up."

"And his face softens." Melissa raised her pinky as she lifted her teacup to her mouth.

Charity's heart pounded. "I don't think so." But how she

wished. "Sometimes I think he forgets I'm a girl."

The hour passed quickly, and Mr. Courtland returned. On their way out of town, they passed Clay in front of the bank. She smiled and waved. The scowl on his face made her wonder if they were even truly friends.

"And who might you be waving to?" Mr. Courtland asked.

"Clay. He is another servant who works with the livestock. We often ride together."

"Hmm. Clay. And he's a servant?"

Charity nodded. How strange Mr. Courtland acted.

"And what might Clay's last name be?" He squinted as if inspecting her.

Charity lifted a shoulder and let it drop. "You know, I've never asked."

"Maybe you should sometime."

Chapter 5

Clay agreed to join Charity for a dinner and celebration at the orphanage the Sunday after Thanksgiving. Servants were not, of course, permitted to take holidays off, so Charity awoke, excited to have an entire Lord's Day without work responsibility. She dressed in the one Sunday go-to-meeting dress she owned. She brought it from home on her last visit.

Slipping the powder-blue dress over her head, she knew it complimented her eyes, deepening the shade. She'd found herself thinking more and more about Clay. How she wished he saw her as more than a tomboy.

He met her in a buggy—every bit as nice as Mr. Courtland's—at the servants' entrance. He climbed down and lifted her up into the seat. The expression in his eyes nearly stole her breath away. *Maybe he does see the woman within.*

"Miss Charity, you are even more beautiful today than usual."

She cocked her head to the side. "And you clean up nicely." He wore more formal attire than she'd ever seen him in.

"Amazing what a little soap and water can do." His black eyes sparkled.

"I haven't been to church since I started this job nearly two months ago. I shall enjoy being back in the house of the Lord."

"As shall I." He tapped the reins against the horses' hindquarters. "Charity, I wish to speak to you about a couple of things."

His serious tone drew her attention and her gaze to him.

"The man I saw you with a couple of weeks ago—"

"Mr. Courtland?"

Clay nodded. "He isn't a nice man."

Charity frowned. "Pompous, yes, but certainly nice. He was very kind to me and has offered to drive me to the village anytime."

"People may seem kind, even be pleasant, but are not Christian in their dealings with others."

His somber expression made her wonder what sort of encounter he'd had with Mr. Courtland. "Is there bad blood between you and Mr. Courtland?" Concern wove itself through her question.

"Not me personally, but others I know. He once courted a woman close to me and was a two-timing scoundrel."

Charity knew her mouth gaped in a most unladylike fashion but had no power to close it. Did Clay think she was interested in Mr. Courtland in that way?

"He and I are barely friends and have no interaction other than his escorting me on an occasional buggy ride." Her voice took on a defensive edge. "I am not interested in him in a romantic manner, so he'd have no opportunity to take advantage of me in that way."

Clay nodded. His brows were drawn together in concern. "Just be careful."

"Is that why there is a strong tension between you and him?"

"What do you mean by *strong tension*?"

"I saw the two of you down by the barn a few days ago. It looked as if you argued."

Clay neither admitted nor denied that.

"I asked him about it, but he clammed up, just as you are now." Charity searched his face. "There must be something more between you, but neither of you will discuss it."

"As your friend, I am asking you to please consider my request and avoid him in the future." Clay's tone sounded more demanding than usual.

Charity nodded, still not understanding. "I find him fascinating. Not as a person, but all his escapades sound exciting. He's been all over the world and has told me some interesting tales."

"I'm only concerned about you."

Charity wondered if Clay could be jealous but immediately dismissed the idea as preposterous.

"Here we are." Clay pulled up in front of the church. He found a spot for the buggy and helped Charity down. She led the way to a pew where her sisters and Mama Elsie waited. She slid in next to Peggy. While they hugged, Clay slid into the pew next to her. Melissa and Selma leaned forward, both smiling and waving to him. He winked at them, and Charity heard quiet giggles.

The pastor spoke on the tares among the wheat. He

referred to wolves in sheep's clothing. Mr. Courtland popped into her mind. Was he truly an unkind man who only pretended to be a Christian? Clay's warning echoed through her thoughts. Her mind reeled back to the day Mr. Courtland had asked about him. She sensed animosity, even though he claimed not to know Clay. He'd obviously lied.

As soon as the sermon ended, while they were turning to "Amazing Grace" in the hymnal, Charity leaned over. "How long have you known Stanton Courtland?"

"Since childhood," he whispered.

An uneasy feeling knotted in her stomach. Perhaps she'd best avoid Mr. Courtland in the future. She had little patience for a liar.

After the song, they made their way to the back of the church. They each shook the pastor's hand. "Mr. Clay—"

"Clay, just Clay." Clay's rude interruption surprised her.

The pastor wore a puzzled expression. "Good to see you again." He shook Clay's hand. "And Miss Charity, I have missed your smiling encouragement from the pew."

"And I have missed being here. If I have a Sunday off, it's only the afternoon."

Once out in the windy weather, Clay offered them a ride in the buggy. They had to squish together, but all fit. Charity was pushed tight against Clay's side. His clear, clean masculine scent taunted her. The warmth of his body against her arm made her tingle. When he turned to speak, his breath mingled with hers in an intimate way.

Her cheeks grew hot as the awareness of him grew. She remained quiet as her three sisters chatted around them.

Clay asked Peggy about life at Reynolds House. The conversations swirled around, but all her focus was on this ruggedly handsome man whose arm burned into hers.

Then the truth hit Charity like a January chill. She, Charity Bradford, loved Clay. Clay, the man whose last name she didn't even know.

Soon they arrived at the orphanage, and he lifted her down. "Are you feeling well?" he asked.

"Quite."

❄

Charity's face glowed in a most beautiful way. At times, like now, it took all his strength not to pull her against him and kiss her soundly. Instead, he set her on the ground and helped Miss Caps from the buggy.

The orphanage bustled with activity and noise. Clay joined Charity in setting the table. As he watched her the rest of the day, he realized there was nothing about her that he didn't like. He loved her gentleness with the small children, her love for her sisters and Miss Caps, her adoration of the Lord. The list went on.

"I feel like you're staring at me. I'm not guilty of having straw between my teeth, am I?"

He laughed. "Just amazed by your beauty."

"I'm certain that is it." Shaking her head, she rolled her eyes.

Lord, I have no idea how to cross the barrier of our stations. How do I convince her that to me, she is the most beautiful woman ever? Am I running ahead of You?

Suddenly Clay knew what he must do. He had to return

to New York City and speak to his family about Charity. He knew they were a pure people without class prejudices. His father would guide him through this. Then he reminded Charity, "Sunset lingers."

She nodded, setting down the book she read to the tot on her lap. They said their good-byes and left. He covered Charity's lap with a warm blanket before starting down the road.

"Thank you for including me today."

"How could I leave my dear friend to fend for himself, without so much as a Thanksgiving feast?" Then she continued, "Do you know this is my favorite time of year? I love the weeks between Thanksgiving and Christmas. It is a magical time, thanks to Jesus."

"So is Christmas your favorite day of the year?"

"Most certainly. What about you?"

He'd never thought much about a favorite day. He decided Christmas would be from now on, though. And this Christmas would be most special of all. This Christmas he'd ask Charity to marry him.

They rolled up to the barn. He lifted Charity down. She ran in to check on Buck and Trixie while he unhooked the buggy and removed the harnesses. He returned the team to their stalls and joined Charity. "I'm going home to New York City."

Charity turned to face him. Happiness evaporated from her expression, and sadness filled her eyes. "Forever?"

He shook his head. "Only a couple of weeks." He reached up and brushed a wisp of hair out of her eyes.

Relief flooded her expression. "I thought for a minute that you meant forever. I cannot imagine my life without you in it."

He placed a hand on each side of her waist. "Nor can I." Slowly he drew her to him. Slowly she came. Her eyes, round and large, reflected questions. Hopefully his kiss contained the answers.

His lips gently settled on hers. She responded with sweet innocence. He unhurriedly lifted his head and gazed deep into a pair of blue eyes.

"I'd like to marry you. How do you feel about the subject?"

Joy filled her countenance. He knew her answer before she spoke.

❄

"I feel wonderful about the subject." Her heart skipped with glee.

"Really?" His ruggedly perfect face wore every emotion she'd felt for him during these past weeks, endearing him to her all the more.

"You are the one for me, Clay. My heart has known it from the start."

He gently kissed her again, turning her aforementioned heart into a pile of complete mush.

"Will you wait for me?" His expression overflowed with adoration.

"I shall. How long will you be gone?" She already missed him.

"I'll return by Christmas," he promised, kissing the tip of her nose.

"Where will we live? The servants here are all single."

He wrapped her in his arms. "Don't worry, my darling. I have saved and own some land. We will be fine." This time he kissed her forehead, above her right brow. "Just fine, indeed."

She wished she felt as confident as he did. She would have to trust him and the Lord that their future would all work out. "Hurry back." This time she boldly kissed him, amazed at the courage that came with knowing she was cherished.

"Quick as I can."

She wanted to hold on to him and never let go. Instead, she kissed his cheek, turned, and headed to the big house. Though she wanted to glance back at nearly every step, she forced herself to keep her eyes focused straight ahead. Only once did she turn and wave. Fighting the urge to run back to his strong arms, she entered the house, saying a silent prayer for Clay's journey.

Chapter 6

I saw you with her," Elizabeth accused in a not-so-quiet voice.

Clay closed the library doors then faced her. "So?"

"You kissed a servant girl!" Her red face accused him of a deed worse than treason. "You are a Claybrook, for goodness sake. We are a family of affluence, greatly respected."

"People are people, Elizabeth. Where has all this snobbery gotten you? Charity is a lovely young woman."

"Listen to yourself! Do you realize the cost to our family should you have a scandalous relationship with a servant?"

"First of all, as a Christian man, I'd never participate in a scandalous anything."

"You were kissing her. What would one think?" She tossed her head.

His anger hit a peak. "Cousin, you have more to worry about than a tawdry outrage. I plan to wed Charity Bradford."

Elizabeth sat down. Her red face went pale. "No. No. It cannot be. . ."

Clay grinned, enjoying her dramatic reaction. "Just think, Elizabeth, you and she will be cousins by marriage. Cousins and perhaps even good friends." He knew that would never happen.

She rose. "I assure you, my dear cousin, that shall never

happen. And I will do everything in my power to stop this ridiculous union."

He saw an idea forming as her eyes lit up. Elizabeth was a schemer.

"Eunice Hopewell regrets breaking your engagement. She's traveling here for the holiday, hoping to make amends. She asked for my silence, but in light of this news, I believe she'd forgive my breaking that promise."

Clay waited for the usual stab in his heart when Eunice Hopewell's name arose; however, the pain didn't come. He was finally free from the dregs of heartbreak! He'd healed. "I wish Eunice well, but no longer carry the love for her that I once did." He moved toward the closed doors, the new realization making his step lighter.

"You'll be making the biggest mistake of your life if you choose that little servant mouse over Eunice Hopewell."

She said the words with such force that Clay half expected the windows to shatter, and her description of Charity caused him to clench his fists. "No, you have it backward. For me, Eunice would be the mistake. Charity is a godly, kind woman, and most importantly, God's choice for me." He opened the door, and Stanton Courtland nearly fell into the room.

"Did you get an earful?" Clay asked with disgust.

He headed up to his room, needing to rise long before sunrise to catch the train; however, sleep eluded him. Between his cousin and Stanton Courtland, the two of them might attempt to sabotage his and Charity's plans. *Lord, protect her. Protect us.*

Sometime in the night, he rose and penned a letter to his beloved.

My dearest Charity,
I love you most deeply. You are the music in my life,
the sunshine in my days, and the very beat of my heart.
I shall miss you terribly and will count the days until
my return.

He'd thought about canceling his trip altogether, but felt he must go, desiring his parents' blessing on this union. Their approval was most important to him, so he would stick to his plan, hoping they'd return with him to celebrate his engagement.

Without being able to explain things to you fully, I need
you to be on guard until my return. There are people,
guests at the Biltmore, who wish to come between you
and me. No matter what is said by Stanton Courtland
or Elizabeth Claybrook, please disregard. I will explain
it all upon my return. Please trust me and wait.

All my love,
Clay

✲

Charity read the letter several times. Her stomach knotted. Why would wealthy guests try to destroy what she and Clay had found? None of it made a bit of sense, but Charity would wait and hope for the best. She gazed out her fourth-story window at the fresh blanket of snow shimmering in the moonlight. What she wouldn't give to see Clay one last time.

As she dressed for the day, she relived the delight of his kiss, the feel of his palms against her cheeks, and the touch of his whiskers against her face. While at work that day, she dreamed of him often.

"Excuse me, Miss Bradford?" The unfamiliar woman's voice pulled her back to the present.

Charity raised her gaze from the wooden washboard and looked into black eyes, similar to Clay's. "Yes, ma'am?"

"I'm Elizabeth Claybrook."

Charity nearly fainted when she heard the woman's name. *She's the one Clay warned me to avoid.*

"Mr. Vanderbilt has put me in charge of the house this Christmas season, since I am his cousin, and there is no lady of the manor. As a matter of fact, he will be traveling this holiday and may not even make it back for Christmas."

Charity nodded, wondering what this had to do with her.

"I am pulling you from your duties in brown laundry until the holiday season passes."

Charity nodded again, not sure exactly what that meant.

"However, that will not happen until next week. This week you shall be in charge of laundering and pressing all the special table linens that will be used throughout the rest of December." Miss Claybrook clapped her hands, and several maids carried large stacks of hand-stitched linens into the laundry. Charity swallowed hard. How would she ever get all of those piles done in a week?

"You will finish all of this by Saturday?" Though worded as a question, Charity knew it was truly, in fact, an order, and somehow this had something to do with Clay and his warning to her.

Charity fought the urge to cry and once again only nodded.

"It is most important that you do." With that, Miss Claybrook turned on her heel and was gone.

Charity systematically divided the linens into six equal piles. This woman would not break her or drive her away. She would come early and stay late, if need be, but she would finish this task.

The week proved to be long and hard, but Charity did conquer the piles of laundry and even penned several letters to Clay. She told him of her new slave-driving boss and the tales she heard at her mealtimes with the other servants. But she had nowhere to mail them.

❅

After a formal dinner with his parents on Clay's first night back in New York City, he asked if he might have a word with his father. They stepped out onto the porch.

His father lit a cigar and took a puff. "You still don't smoke?" He held out the box of expensive cigars.

Clay held up his hand in refusal. "No thank you, sir."

"What is this I hear about you and a servant girl?" His dad flicked an ash into an old milk can.

Clay's heart dropped. He'd hoped to reveal the information gently. "News travels fast."

His father stared at the cigar for several seconds. Then

he focused his coal-black eyes on Clay. "Telegraphs beat trains every time."

"Cousin Elizabeth?"

"Who else?" His father settled into a cane rocker. "You know this decision will wreak havoc for your mother and me? At least as far as your uncles and aunts are concerned."

Clay wasn't sure how to read his father. "Will you mind terribly? You always taught us that people were people, no matter their race or station in life."

"If you are certain, I will stand by your decision and rather take pleasure in the rest of the family's reaction." His father guffawed. He, the nonconformist, enjoyed ruffling the rest of his siblings occasionally. "Most should already know. I'm certain mine wasn't the only telegraph sent."

Relief flooded Clay. "Thank you, sir. She is a Christian, which matters the most to me, certainly more than status."

"I thought you'd outgrow that religion of yours, but you have not."

"Nor will I, Father. Jesus is my lifeblood. He is not a part of my life. He is my life."

Clay knew by the confused look on his father's face that he did not understand. He prayed for his father and mother daily. After these many years, he at times had to fight discouragement that they still had not responded to the Lord.

His father snuffed out his cigar. "I shall look forward to meeting your lady."

"Will you and mother travel back to North Carolina with me for Christmas?"

"I believe we shall." He rose from the rocker. "Let's go

inform your mother. She will need days to pack."

Clay followed his father into their grand home—humble home when compared to the Biltmore house, however. He whispered a prayer of thanks to his heavenly Father. He had business to take care of in the city and things to order to complete the house he was building. He wanted to secure the finest of rings for Charity. That allowed his mother several days to finish her packing.

> *Dearest Charity,*
> *I miss you terribly. I shall return the week of*
> *Christmas. Though I'd most certainly prefer your*
> *company, it is good to be with my family once again.*
> > *Love,*
> > *Clay*

✳

Occasionally Charity received a short note from him. If only she'd thought to request his address, she could return the correspondence. Taking a few minutes right before climbing into bed each night, she wrote to him, only instead of mailing them, she tucked the letters into a drawer, planning to give him the entire stack upon his return.

As silly as it seemed, she often slept with his latest communication. Somehow he felt closer that way.

A small contingent of servants were pulled aside the following morning after breakfast. Charity was the only one from brown laundry.

"I will be hosting the event of the century here at Biltmore this year," Elizabeth Claybrook announced with glee. "My cousin Joseph Malachi Claybrook. . ." She paused, her gaze fixed on Charity.

Charity suddenly took great interest in the floor, breaking the intense stare. *Why is she scrutinizing me so?*

"As I was saying, my dear cousin will wed my dear friend Eunice Hopewell. The engagement party shall take place here on Christmas Eve, a formal affair to rival the parties in New York City."

Sounded dreadful to Charity. How awful, to pretend everything must appear better than it was. Charity gave thanks she'd been born less fortunate and could live more honestly.

Charity drew her thoughts back to Miss Claybrook. "The gardeners shall provide you with fresh cedar and pine for the mantels, making the house smell heavenly. Miss Bradford, you shall oversee the entire main floor. Please make certain each room is taken care of."

Charity nodded.

Miss Claybrook assigned a servant to each floor of the house. "Tomorrow we'll begin unpacking the ornaments for the trees. Each will need to be hand-polished before it is ready to hang. By the end of the week, the house will be filled with Christmas." And with that, she turned and headed upstairs to the main floor.

Charity felt rather glad she'd been assigned this duty. She loved Christmas, and the thought of touching and cleaning each precious ornament excited her. She wondered if Miss Claybrook knew the true meaning of the holiday. Did she know Jesus? How Charity loved Him, hoping the same for her.

She finished her task, but very late in the day. Each mantel was dressed up with fresh greenery, and the smells delighted her senses. It reminded her of her childhood.

Though not wealthy, her family celebrated big. Mama and Peggy made special cinnamon rolls on Christmas morning. Papa always sneaked in a toy he'd made for the four sisters to share and placed it under the decorated tree he'd chopped down for them. He'd bring out the big family Bible that Mama kept next to their feather bed and read the Christmas story. Charity strained to remember the rich timbre of his voice. Then they'd spend hours around the piano, singing Christmas songs and hymns. A pang of longing hit her with blunt force. She still missed Mama and Papa every single day, even after all these years. But now that she knew how it felt to be in love, she understood what a blessing it was that they passed together.

Chapter 7

C harity slipped out of the house, just as the sun lit the eastern sky. How she hoped to avoid Mr. Courtland. Running into him at every turn made heeding Clay's warning most difficult. She often wondered if he purposely sought her out, but why would that be so? Any number of wealthy single women guests clamored for his attention. Surely he'd not think twice about her.

Making her way down the snow-covered path to the barn, Charity missed Trixie almost as much as she missed Clay. Last week she'd not taken a day off, needing to wash and press all the beautiful Christmas linens trimmed in mostly reds and golds. They must spend more money on some of their finest linen pieces than she earned in an entire year. If wealthy she'd give it all away. *Easier said than done, I'm quite sure*. She hadn't intended to judge.

She stood at Trixie's gate, scratching the mare's ears. Clay arranged for the other stable hands to care for both horses while he was away. He didn't want her sledging through the snow on cold, dark mornings. She hadn't ridden in nearly two weeks and ached for the chance.

"Miss Bradford, how good to see you today. I shall ride into Biltmore Village this fine morning. Would you care to join me?" Mr. Courtland continued past like he couldn't care less one way or the other, stopping a few stalls down, where his dappled gray resided.

Perhaps Clay was wrong about him. And she did have the entire day off. Mr. Courtland offered a chance to exercise Trixie and see her sisters. Charity argued with herself. On the one hand, she'd promised, at least in one of the letters that lay in a drawer. But on the other, a golden opportunity called her. Surely Clay would understand.

When Mr. Courtland finished saddling his horse, he led him down the wide corridor, stopping next to Charity. "Well, Miss Bradford?"

Charity's gaze danced between good and evil, Trixie and Mr. Courtland.

"I suppose. A day away shall prove nice."

"A bit restless, are you?" His face split into a broad grin that said he understood. "The snow makes one feel entirely too cooped up. Would you like help with your mare?" He handed her the reins to his horse and made quick work of bridling and saddling Trixie.

Once they were riding together away from Biltmore and toward town, he asked, "What are your thoughts on Malachi's impending nuptials? Aren't you and he close?"

She shook her head. "I've never met him, only his cousin Elizabeth."

"Really?" Somehow her confession caused Mr. Courtland pleasure. He reminded her of a sinister man with a devious plot. Perhaps she should have heeded Clay's advice a bit more closely.

"Why would you think otherwise?" She studied the man intently.

"I thought I'd seen you together a time or two. Perhaps I'm mistaken." His eyes roamed across the snow-covered peaks. There it was again, that mischievous spark in his eyes.

They rode a mile or so in silence. "Who is the man I see you riding with on occasion?" He leaned in, studying her with an uncomfortable intensity.

"Clay?"

"Umm, yes, Clay. He resembles Malachi Claybrook."

Did he hope to upset her? "I could not say." She refused to play his silly game. "Clay is far from an aristocrat. He is a simple stable hand—a Biltmore servant, as am I."

Mr. Courtland nodded, rubbing his chin. "You seem quite fond of this *stable hand*."

Heat rose in her cheeks, and she averted her gaze to the snow-laden mountains. "They are most beautiful this time of year." She had no intention of admitting personal feelings to a stranger.

"That they are, as is Miss Hopewell. She arrived late last week. Have you been granted the opportunity to see her yet?"

"No, I never see any of the guests. If I were a maid, perhaps, but I'm in the basement all day, either that or the fourth floor." She returned her gaze to the handsome rogue. "Except this week, as I have been decorating the main floor."

"Well, my dear, you are missing a treat. Keep your eyes open for a stunning redhead with ivory skin."

Charity wondered why he spoke of people she did not know. How odd. "Are you and Mr. Claybrook friends then?"

He paused. "I'd not say that, though we do travel in the

same circles and have common acquaintances."

"I see." Maybe Mr. Courtland carried a torch for this Eunice Hopewell woman. They arrived at the orphanage at a perfect time, ending their conversation.

In two hours Mr. Courtland called for her. The visit with her sisters and Mama Elsie proved to be wonderful, as always. She joined them for breakfast. The food at the orphanage tasted far better than the offerings at Biltmore. Of course she doubted all would agree.

As she mounted Trixie, Charity hoped for a quiet ride back. If she had her wish, there'd be no more babble about people she neither knew nor cared about.

"Perhaps it's best that you don't know Mr. Claybrook." Mr. Courtland pulled his horse even with Trixie.

She wanted to ask why that was, but to end the conversation, she only said, "Perhaps."

"He is a dishonorable man."

Charity squirmed under Mr. Courtland's scrutiny, longing to run Trixie all the way to Biltmore.

"He leads a double life, pretending to be a man he is not. He has his fiancée and a woman he sees on the side."

Charity could keep quiet no longer. "How sad for Miss Hopewell." Her curiosity drew her deeper into the conversation. "Does she know of the other woman?"

"It's not clear, but she loves the scoundrel nonetheless." He shrugged one shoulder, sadness pulling his small mustache downward.

"What about the other woman? Does she love him as well?"

"Hard to say. She's a servant girl, so scraps of attention from a man of his looks and caliber may have been more than the poor thing could resist."

Charity nodded. "Perhaps." Though she felt certain she'd not fall into such a situation. *Thank You, Lord, for Clay. I feel blessed to have found such an honest, hardworking man.*

She knew the Lord brought her and Clay here for such a time as this. Their paths crossed for the Lord's purpose. Charity smiled as she thought of the man she'd one day marry.

❅

The largest of all the Christmas trees at Biltmore was placed in the living hall. While hanging Christmas ornaments just so on the monstrosity, Charity realized this evergreen stood at least twice as tall as any tree she'd ever seen and was possibly three times as wide. Excitement raced through her veins, as she'd been assigned the task of decorating this grand tree—at least, as high as she could reach. Considering the honor, Charity took great pains to place each ornament with care.

She chose a carved wooden red cardinal from the box packed with many Christmas treasures.

"She has no idea. None."

Was that Mr. Courtland? A man's voice similar to his sounded close, though she saw no one.

A high-pitched chuckle followed. "Well, won't they both be surprised. My cousin shouldn't play such naughty games. The poor little twit dreams of a simple man, not an aristocrat! His little servant friend's heart shall break before he arrives. See to it."

Charity tried not to listen, but their words floated in unencumbered. She didn't want to overhear the conversation, which was obviously between Stanton Courtland and Elizabeth Claybrook.

That poor girl that they speak of. Lord, I pray You bring her through the heartbreak and humiliation.

❋

Finally Clay was on his way back to Charity with his parents at his side. He'd telegraphed Elizabeth to plan a simple but elegant engagement party. Though she'd originally objected, she finally agreed and, in her last telegraph, seemed excited about the prospect.

Thank You, Lord, that it is all coming together. Thank You for working out the details, including my parents agreeing to come. Most of all, thank You for Charity. How he loved her.

He'd shipped a beautiful red velvet ball gown by Worth to Elizabeth, asking her to make certain the box and note were delivered to Charity on Christmas Eve morning. He also asked her to make certain Charity had that day off.

Yes, tomorrow he'd be betrothed. Tomorrow would be the most incredible day of his life to date. Tomorrow Charity would know his true identity, and they'd be free from all pretense.

He now regretted not telling her sooner. Not intentional, but the lack of information had grown into a lie. Conviction fell over him like the snow blanketing the ground outside the train window. *I'm sorry, Lord. I wanted to get to know her and her, me, without restraints between us. Forgive me for lying.*

I have sinned against You and Charity.

Until now, he'd not thought of it that way, but deception was a lie. He'd led her to believe he was someone he wasn't. As he talked it out with the Lord, he knew God forgave him. Now he must confess to Charity at the first opportunity. He hoped she was as forgiving as their heavenly Father.

❋

On Christmas Eve morning before she left her room for breakfast, a large box was delivered to Charity. Was it from Clay? She lifted the lid. Recognizing Clay's handwriting, she picked up a note off a satin-trimmed dress.

> *My dearest Charity,*
>
> *I am requesting the honor of your presence at tonight's Christmas Eve Ball. Enclosed you will find a gown chosen just for this occasion, along with a pair of shoes.*
>
> *It will be a great honor for me to have you on my arm. Please meet me in the library at the Biltmore precisely at six in the evening.*
>
> *Missing you terribly,*
> *Clay*

She lifted the gown from the box, feeling overwhelmed. Never in her twenty years had she seen anything so beautiful. *I've certainly never worn anything nearly this magnificent.*

Holding the rich flowing red velvet against her, she spun around the small amount of open space in her room. *What will Clay think when he sees me in this? I hope in his eyes, I shall be the most beautiful woman at the party.* Stopping in front of the mirror, she smiled at the glorious dress, a perfect color to accent her complexion and brighten her eyes. She'd be sure to give her cheeks extra pinches tonight.

Suddenly she stopped. *Why is Clay attending a party honoring Malachi Claybrook?* It made no sense. Servants did not receive such invitations. Certain Clay would solve the mystery this evening, she pushed the questions from her mind. Barely touching the stairs on her way to breakfast, Charity collided with Mr. Courtland. She would have fallen backward had he not steadied her.

"Charity! Where are you off to this fine morning?"

"Breakfast." Now that she stood quite well on her own two feet, she wished he'd release her elbow. "I'm rather surprised to find you here in the servants' stairwell."

"I was actually coming for you." His eyes danced.

Her stomach knotted, wondering what he might be up to now. She sucked in a sharp breath. "Me? Whatever for?" Did he know she'd overheard a private conversation between him and Miss Claybrook?

"I understand you are on the guest list for tonight's ball."

How could he possibly know that? She'd only just discovered it for herself.

"I thought you might want to come to the library early, say about five. I will go through a quick etiquette lesson with you, answer any questions you might have."

Uncertainty fell on Charity like a ton of bricks. She had no business going to such an affair. What if she embarrassed Clay?

"I'm certain you'll do well. I only hoped to put you at ease."

His desire had the adverse effect.

"If you'd rather not. . ."

"No. I'm sorry and did not intend to be rude. Of course I'd most appreciate any assistance you might offer."

Mr. Courtland removed his hand from her elbow. "The library at five then. Good day, my dear." With that he descended the stairs.

Charity no longer floated. What had she gotten herself into?

Chapter 8

Feeling beautiful in the red gown, Charity glided down the stairs and into the library. Never had she felt more like a woman fit for a Mr. Darcy. And she, indeed, found her own Mr. Darcy in the form of Clay. How odd that she still did not know his last name. Every time she'd asked, they'd been interrupted in one way or another.

The library had been well decorated for the Christmas season, as had the entire main floor. Musicians played carols in the main hall, the music wrapping her with the joy of the season. The sights, sounds, and smells of Christmas touched her in a magical way.

She glanced up at the large clock upon entering the library. In one hour she'd meet Clay in this very room. Her heart pounded. Like an excited child waiting for that one special present, she anticipated Clay wrapping her in his well-muscled arms and whispering words she longed to hear.

Charity let her gaze roam around the room. Two new portraits had been added above the settee in the corner. Several early guests admired them, and a banner hung above them. *Congratulations Malachi Claybrook and Eunice Hopewell.*

Charity's gaze roamed over the large hand-painted face of Eunice Hopewell. A large man in formal attire blocked her view of the groom.

"Hello, Miss Bradford. You are beyond beautiful." Mr. Courtland's voice came from just behind her, the tone suggestive, inappropriate.

She glanced over her shoulder. "Why thank you." His black jacket enhanced his looks as well, but she chose not to express those thoughts. The man, quite cocky in his own right, needed no encouragement. "You were right when you spoke of Miss Hopewell's loveliness. She is far prettier than I had imagined."

"That she is." His voice held an awe Charity had not heard before. His expression, one of longing. *Poor man apparently loved a. . .*

Charity's air supply stuck in her throat. Her heart forgot to beat. Her mind froze as she stared into the painted black eyes of Malachi Claybrook. No wonder Clay always failed to mention his last name.

She willed herself to breathe. Raising her skirts, she ran from the room. Tears blocked her vision as she made her way for the front door. Be it ever so improper, she ignored Mr. Courtland's calls.

Running into the cold night with no wrap or coat, she was too numb to feel. She moved toward the orphanage, ignoring the stares as she passed guests along the road. Her foot hit a patch of ice. She fell. An elderly gentleman and his wife stopped to help her. They asked no questions, other than where she was going in such haste. Helping her into the buggy, the kind graying woman covered her with a blanket. They drove her to the orphanage and helped her to the door.

"Miss Caps, she claims she's one of yours." The man apparently knew Mama Elsie.

"Charity!" Mama Elsie pulled her into the orphanage. "She is. Thank you for helping her, Mr. Wright. I shall tend to her now." She nearly shut the door. "Forgive my manners. May I offer you something warm to drink?"

"No thank you. We'll be on our way." The gentleman tipped his hat, and Mama Elsie shut the door on the cold, cruel world.

Charity crumpled into a heap of tears on the sofa in the parlor. Selma brought her hot tea. Melissa wrapped her in a warm blanket. Between sobs she relived this evening's heartbreak.

"Charity, something doesn't add up." Selma's brow furrowed. "Why would he invite you to the party, only to humiliate you? It makes no sense."

"Why did he lie to me about who he is? Was I only a toy to entertain him until his true love arrived?" She let the warm liquid trickle down her dry throat. "Whatever the truth may be, I could not stay and face an engagement celebration between Clay and another woman." She sniffed.

"I cannot see how this is possible. Something is amiss. I saw love in his eyes when he looked at you."

"Selma." Mama Elsie wrapped an arm around her shoulder. "Sweet, sincere, sensible Selma. Love doesn't always make sense, dear."

❄

Clay could hardly stand the slow pace the driver took with the horse and buggy. Had the season been summer, he'd have climbed from the buggy and sprinted the last mile. When they finally pulled in front of the Biltmore house, his timepiece read a few minutes past six.

He dashed from the buggy, stopping a few steps up the walk. "Mother and Father, might I beg your forgiveness? I must find Charity. Please make yourself at home, and we shall meet up with you within moments, I hope."

"Go." His mother's smile said she expected nothing less. "Go to your love. We will be fine."

He rushed to the library, nearly running over a party guest. "Please excuse me," he called back without even slowing his pace. He searched the library, but no Charity. On his way out, the banner caught his attention. *Please, Lord, tell me this isn't so.*

In the main hall he found Elizabeth, chatting with a group of guests.

"Elizabeth, I must see you now." Grabbing her arm, he pulled her into a quiet, uninhabited corner. "What have you done?" Though he longed to yell at the top of his lungs and shake his cousin until her teeth rattled, he did neither.

"Please refrain from wrath. This is for your own good." She appeared unaffected by his anger.

"Where is Charity?" he asked through gritted teeth.

"I have no idea. Last I saw her, she ran from the library like a hunted deer."

Charity had seen the banner and must have gone home to the orphanage. It was, after all, her safe haven.

"I am going to find her." He enunciated each word with care. "And when I do, we will return for our engagement party and every trace of Eunice had better be gone. This party is for me and Charity, so you have a lot of apologizing and explaining to do while I'm gone. Do you understand?"

His parents joined them, each kissing Elizabeth on both cheeks. "Son, what is going on?"

In a very abbreviated version, Clay updated them.

"Please talk some sense into him," Elizabeth pleaded. "Or you soon will have a servant as a daughter-in-law."

"We want whomever Clay wants." He knew his mother believed in true love and appreciated her defense.

"My father said you'd respond that way. Foolish choice." Elizabeth huffed away.

"I'm going after Charity," Clay informed his parents.

"We'd expect nothing less. After all, you're a Claybrook, and we fight for the important things in life." His dad slapped him on the back.

"Family, honor, love." His mother quoted those often-heard words. His own version of the motto started with God, and he prayed one day theirs would, too.

Clay returned to the buggy with the hired driver who brought them from the train station. He'd rather take Buck, but it would be hard to accommodate Charity in that full red dress. "Lord, please go before me and prepare the way. Give Charity a forgiving heart." He whispered pleas all the way to the orphanage.

Miss Caps answered his knock.

"There has been a terrible manipulation of circumstances by my cousin. May I see Charity and explain?"

By the set of her jaw, Clay wasn't sure she'd let him in.

"Are you engaged?"

"No, ma'am, but I hope to be tonight." He pulled a ring from his pocket, touching his index finger to his lips.

Miss Caps nodded and stepped aside.

Clay entered. She motioned toward the kitchen. Sitting at the table with her two sisters, Charity wore an unfamiliar day dress and ate a bowl of soup. His heart constricted at the sight of her. He knelt beside his beloved. Those beautiful blue eyes reflected uncertainty and mistrust.

"I'm sorry."

She rose from the seat, moving away from him. Would she ever forgive him? Her gaze accused him of unpardonable sin.

"Girls." Miss Caps motioned for Selma and Melissa to leave them alone.

"No, please stay. All of you." His gaze settled on Charity. "I ask you to hear me out before you make any decisions. And the first thing you must know is that I am not engaged to Eunice Hopewell, nor do I plan to be."

"Were you?"

"Several years back, but it has long since been over."

Charity said nothing, and he couldn't read her expression.

"The second thing you must know is that though I did lie about who I was, I never lied about anything else. The Lord dealt with me about the lie and has forgiven me. I hope with time, you shall as well."

Again, nothing but silence. She'd folded her arms firmly in front of her. *Lord, please soften her heart.* One word kept repeating itself in his mind. *Honesty, honesty, honesty.* So no matter how hostile she felt, Charity would hear the whole truth from his lips.

"I come from a wealthy family but do not enjoy the fancy parties and high society. When I moved here to build a house and escape New York City, I sought a certain amount of anonymity. I only desired to be a normal person, not dishonest. When I met you, I knew the difference in our stations would frighten you away."

Charity nodded. *Well Lord, that is a good sign.* Hope swelled in his heart.

"You intrigued me." He saw the red hue climbing up her neck. "I wanted to get to know you without my money getting in the way, as it always had in the past. I never knew if women cared for me or only my money. With you, I never doubted."

Her gaze had softened. She glanced at her sisters and Miss Caps. They each gave her a slight nod and smile. Boy was he grateful.

Taking a deep breath, he continued, feeling more relaxed. "I did ask my cousin Elizabeth to plan an engagement party—for you and me. I've not seen Eunice in several years."

"How did you know I'd say yes?" The raised eyebrow challenged him.

"You said you loved me," he reminded.

"I loved Mr. Clay No Last Name. I never loved or knew a man called Malachi." Her mouth turned down, and her sadness hurt him.

He took a step toward her. "Charity, you know me

better than anyone on earth, even my own family. I'm still that same man."

"A very rich version of your former self."

He obviously never had to worry about Charity being swayed by his money. It repelled instead of drew.

"I love you. Only you. I have no intention of marrying anyone but you. If you say no, I'll go on alone."

Her arms dropped to her sides. "You have no feelings left for Eunice?"

He shook his head, taking another step. "They died a long time ago. Elizabeth hoped to revive them. Frankly, she is a snob and has a problem with you being a servant."

Charity raised her chin the tiniest bit.

"A problem I do not share." He took another step toward her, wondering if she could hear the pounding in his chest. "I think she hoped that if you were gone and Eunice waited in the wings, I'd see it as fate."

"But you don't?" This time Charity took a step toward him.

Reaching out toward her, he stroked her cheek. "I'll give all my money away, if that's what it takes to have you."

Her gaze never left his. "You'd do that?"

Nodding, he said, "I love you that much."

She stepped into his embrace. Holding her close, he kissed her mouth, her cheeks, and her lips again. "Does this mean you forgive me?"

"I do." Her smile stole the air from his lungs.

He bent one knee and lowered himself to the ground. "Charity, will you marry me?"

She nodded. Tears glistened in her eyes.

❇

Clay pulled a ring box from his pocket. She fought more tears. Holding her breath, she watched as he opened the box. A beautiful gold band with tiny diamonds winked up at her.

"It is perfect." He did know her. She preferred simple to ostentatious. Slipping the ring from its satin cushion, he slid it on her finger and pulled her close. Laying her head on his chest, she loved him more than she knew was possible.

"Charity, we are going to an engagement party." Joy filled his tone.

Her two sisters jumped and clapped.

"There is an engagement celebration tonight," he announced, waltzing Charity around the kitchen. They only bumped into one chair. His huge smile matched the one that nearly split her face in two.

"We can't go to such an affair." Mama Elsie shook her head. "We have nothing formal to wear."

"Ah, but my cousin does and owes me one very large favor."

She tied an apron over her dress. "You two must go on and enjoy your big night."

"I can't wait to introduce my future bride. And much to Elizabeth's dismay, the bride will be of my choosing, not hers. Eunice Hopewell will have no part in this party." He kissed Charity again. "You, on the other hand, will be at my side the entire evening."

He touched the tip of her nose. "Where is that dress I sent you? I can't wait to see you wearing it."

✳

Charity and her sisters scampered up the stairs. He smiled at Mama Elsie. She came to him and hugged him. "Clay, you are a fine man. Thank you for loving my Charity."

He hugged the older woman. "She's easy to love."

"That she is." She stepped out of his embrace and began clearing the table.

"I'm sending the driver to pick up dresses for the three of you." He moved toward the foyer. "Do you have a favorite color?"

"That's not necessary." She paused with Charity's soup bowl in hand. "It will take far too much time. The evening is ticking away."

Clay smiled. "You are a selfless woman. I'd like you to meet my parents."

"We will. Just another time. Perhaps dinner tomorrow? I'll be cooking, anyway." She shrugged, but her eyes twinkled with joy. "After all, what are two or three more mouths?"

"That sounds lovely. I will accept your invitation for the three of us."

After she'd finished tidying up, Mama Elsie said, "If you'll excuse me, I'll go check on the progress upstairs."

He stoked the fire in the parlor and paced around the small room. How long might it take one woman to dress? Finally he heard their feet on the stairs and headed for the foyer. The sight of Charity in her red dress nearly stopped his heart. Her eyes met his. Their gazes locked.

He met her at the bottom step, taking her into his arms. "You, my darling, are beautiful."

Charity blushed and tucked her head into his shoulder.

He glanced up the staircase at her sisters and Miss Caps. "I will indeed be the most envied man at the party."

❄

Charity barely noticed the cold as she snuggled under blankets next to Clay in the buggy. With a slap of the reins from the driver, the team of horses lurched forward at a good pace. Charity shivered, though she thought it was more nerves than chill.

Clay lifted her hand from under the blanket and kissed it. "You don't need to be anxious. I will not leave your side the entire evening."

"Thank you. I was just thinking of the irony. I am the same girl who pressed the linens for the party and decorated much of the main floor. Now I shall be the guest of honor?"

"And you will never have to press linens ever again or anything else, for that matter. You will have your own servants to do that chore, if you choose."

Charity had not considered the ramifications of marrying a wealthy man. The reality hit her at that moment. She'd be lady of the manor. It all felt like a dream.

Glancing out the window, she caught sight of the Biltmore. The moonlight settled over the snow, and it glistened like a fairy-tale scene. "The house is ever so beautiful. I've not seen it at night from this vantage point before."

"It's a lovely home. Ours pales in comparison."

"For me, that is a huge relief."

As their buggy drew near, Charity heard the faint sounds of music drifting from the house. Every window shone bright with light and cheer. The whole evening felt dream-like and far beyond anything she'd hoped for.

Clay helped her from the buggy. He held her arm tight against his side and she felt safe, secure, loved. No one could hurt her. Just inside the entry, a handsome older couple came to their side.

"Charity, this is my mother and father. And this"—he smiled deep into her eyes—"is my future bride, Charity."

Mr. Claybrook hugged her. "We welcome you." His father kissed each of her cheeks. "She is even more stunning than your description."

Heat burned her cheeks.

Mr. Claybrook stepped aside, and his wife hugged her. "My dear, it is so good to meet you." Her sincere smile and eyes put Charity at ease. "I look forward to the years ahead. We shall be the best of friends. Of that I'm certain." And somehow Charity was certain, too.

Clay placed his hand on his father's shoulder. "They traveled with me from New York to meet you and share this celebration with us."

Charity's heart overflowed with surprise and gratitude. She reached for each of their hands. Unshed tears blurred her vision. "Thank you both for coming. It means the world to me."

Clay's voice broke a little. "Father, would you do me the honor of announcing our engagement?"

They moved toward the main hall. All eyes were on them, but most especially on her. She kept her gaze straight ahead and a slight smile on her lips; after all, she hoped to appear pleasant. As they passed the library, she glanced in. The portraits and banner had vanished. Clay obviously wielded some power himself.

Mr. Claybrook spoke to the conductor of the orchestra, asking for a drumroll. "Ladies and gentleman, my wife and I. . ." He reached for her and pulled her close.

The simple gesture warmed Charity. Clay had a good role model.

Mr. Claybrook cleared his throat. "We would like to introduce our son and his fiancée. This is Joseph Malachi Claybrook, who prefers the simplicity of Clay. And his beautiful bride to be, Miss Charity Bradford. His mother and I could not be happier."

The crowd applauded. Charity saw no sign of either Eunice Hopewell or Elizabeth Claybrook. The next hour went by in a haze of names, faces, and well-wishers. By this time Charity's cheeks hurt from smiling. Clay kept her tucked against him through all formalities. This truly was a different world. She wondered if she'd awaken tomorrow and find it all to be a dream.

As the crowd dwindled, Clay whispered near her ear. "I have one more surprise. Your Christmas gift."

Charity had nothing for him. Then she remembered the small stack of tender letters she'd written, sharing the deepest part of her heart.

"It requires a coat, though."

"A coat?" She wondered if this wonderful night could hold any more happiness.

He nodded, wearing a wide grin.

"I must run up to my room. Will you grab my coat? I shall meet you at the side entrance. That way we can avoid a thousand curious eyes watching us leave."

"See, you are learning already." He placed a quick kiss on her cheek. "I'll meet you in five minutes."

She ran upstairs, nearly tripping on the hem of her skirt. Once inside her room, she retrieved the letters from her drawer. Taking one of her ribbons, she wrapped them and tied a pretty bow. Not an expensive gift, but in them she offered her love, her heart, her future.

At the designated meeting place, he helped her into her coat. As he opened the door, a blast of frigid air hit her in the face and she shivered. He wrapped his arm around her, and they headed to the stables. Dare she hope? Her heart danced in anticipation.

They stopped at Trixie's stall. The mare, a giant red bow tied around her neck, welcomed Charity with a nudge. Charity couldn't speak for the lump in her throat. Nor could she see well for the extra moisture in her eyes.

"Thank you." Her voice was raspy. She hugged him tight then held out the packet of envelopes.

He untied the ribbon and carefully opened the top one. His eyes glistened when he looked up after reading it. He pulled her into his arms. "Thank you." His voice sounded as funny as hers had. They laughed and hugged and kissed.

"Let's keep our engagement short. As soon as the house is done, we shall marry."

"When might that be?" She raised her head from his chest to gaze into his coal-black eyes.

"Another month." His words held assurance.

"Until then, I'll be dreamin' of the day we'll become one forever," she promised.

"What more could a man want? A Carolina Christmas with his very own dreamer."

His mouth found hers. The kiss sent tingles all the way to her toes. When he raised his head, love poured from his expression. "Thanks be to God who blesses us with so much more than we deserve."

Charity's heart echoed the sentiment. "Thanks be to God, indeed."

Jeri Odell is a native of Tucson, Arizona. She has been married thirty-eight years and has three wonderful adult children, a daughter-in-law, son-in-law, and five precious grandchildren. Jeri holds family dear to her heart, second only to God. She thanks God for the privilege of writing for Him. When not writing or reading, she is busy working in the finance office of her church.

A PROPER CHRISTMAS

Sylvia Barnes

Dedication

To my husband and children for their loyalty and
support, to the Bards of Faith for their encouragement,
and especially to Aaron McCarver for taking me under
his wing and flying me to a place I never thought
I would be. Love you guys.

Chapter 1

Biltmore Estate, Asheville,
North Carolina, November 1897

Selma Bradford hurriedly worked the small buttons at the back of her neck. She wondered why the seamstress didn't put fasteners on the front of the gray gingham dress provided by the housekeeper, along with an apron and cap.

Gazing at her reflection in the mirror, she grimaced at the blush in her cheeks and hoped she could calm her nerves before entering the servants' dining room. This was her first day on the job. She had been told by the housekeeper that she would eat breakfast at five and gather with the other upstairs maids in the servants' hall on the fourth floor to await her call to duty.

Her shaking fingers squeezed the last button through the hole before pushing the fallen light-brown wisps of hair under her cap. Her hands cradled her face as she looked in the mirror. Emerald-green eyes stared back with apprehension.

I can do this. I can.

Selma realized how lucky she was to join the team of

nearly eighty servants at the Biltmore mansion. At nineteen, Selma had her first chance to be a part of the most talked-about event of her lifetime. The estate's housekeeper, Mrs. King, had visited the village mercantile where she worked and, before leaving, offered her employment. She told Selma the holidays were going to be busy, and help was hard to find. Shaking off her thoughts as she heard the bell ring for breakfast, Selma donned her freshly starched apron and closed the door behind her to embark on her new journey. She entered the dining room in the basement just as the food arrived. She sought a vacancy by a friendly face and sat, trying to focus on the chatter around the table as others served the fragrant meal. She wondered at servants waiting on servants. Wide-eyed, she tried to understand her new surroundings.

A nudge by a neighboring elbow drew her attention. She turned to a small redhead who asked, "Did you come from down here?"

"Pardon?"

"Were you one of the servants downstairs?"

"Oh no, this is my first day."

"How did you acquire a position upstairs so soon? Most new servants begin downstairs and move up."

"I'm sorry. I do not know. I only know that the house-keeper took me to my room on the fourth floor. She told me I would be in training today under a lady named Maggie McAllister. I'm Selma, by the way."

"Rosie." She reached to take Selma's hand. "Maggie is sitting at the head of the table. The way she acts, she thinks she's the main housekeeper."

Selma, a Christian girl brought up by the teachings of the Bible, ignored the nasty comment. "Should I meet her now?"

"Certainly not. She will call you in the servants' hall." Rosie looked down at the plate just served to her. "Don't eat yet. We have to say the standard how-thankful-we-are blessing."

Selma was startled at the cynicism in Rosie's remark. She folded her hands in her lap and said her own little prayer, asking God to forgive Rosie and to give her an opportunity to share the goodness of the Lord with her.

Another nudge. Selma glanced at Rosie as she excitedly relayed the good news. "Guests are arriving every day this week. They will be here for Thanksgiving, and some are even staying through Christmas. Of course there will be others who arrive closer to Christmas. The rich, you know, who must not have to work to eat."

Rosie's speech was interrupted by Maggie. "Let us pray." Her voice sounded deep and coarse. "Thank You, Lord, for the food at our table. Bless those less fortunate. Amen."

Rosie gave Selma an I-told-you-so look as the chatter around the table continued during the meal.

Selma thought the food looked delicious. She inhaled the heady aromas. Her taste buds savored the bacon, eggs, and biscuits, which she slathered with homemade blackberry jam. She paid no attention to the talk around her as she ate. Her mind full of questions, her stomach quivered with every delectable bite.

A loud clap made her drop her fork. Maggie stood at the

end of the table, her face stern. "Let us advance to the hall."

Selma stayed close to Rosie, who took her hand and led her upstairs to the small servants' hall. Selma glanced around at the wooden rocking chairs and the bookcase lined with enticing volumes, wondering if there would be any time for such.

Rosie quietly asked, "Have you been given a tour of the house?"

"No. I was led straight to my room yesterday evening. Someone brought a tray of sandwiches as I settled in and gave me directions to the dining room for breakfast."

"You'll probably be given a small tour this morning. At least you'll see what they think you need to see. All of us on fourth floor attend to the upstairs bedrooms and halls. That includes the floors above the living hall and master and major guest rooms. We also clean the various bathrooms. We have indoor plumbing, you know." Rosie pulled at her apron. "Also, we get a two-hour break in the afternoons, but we are on call, so we have to sit in the servants' living hall so we can hear the call box. Oh yes, you'll probably have six bedrooms to clean. I'll be quiet. I'm talking too much."

"No, I need to know. Only six? And each has a bath?"

Rosie didn't get a chance to answer.

Maggie spoke, sending Rosie and the others to their duties. She turned to Selma. "You are Miss Bradford?"

"Yes, ma'am."

"I am Maggie McAllister. Come with me."

❉

Jacob Sinclair studied the guest room. His eyes glanced over the dark mahogany furniture, glad to see a writing desk on which to pen his correspondence. He peered longingly at the tall, handsome bed. The trip from New York had been long, and he yearned to rest. But he had been invited by his host to join him and other male guests in the gymnasium for a bit of exercise before a swim in the indoor pool to cool off. He then was to accompany them for a ride on the estate. He was thankful there were dressing rooms downstairs by the pool, so he would not have to return upstairs until after the ride. As he gathered what he would need from his trunk, the thought struck him that his friend William McAdams could have arrived, which pleased him.

As he was in the bathroom washing his hands, he thought he heard a knocking sound but dismissed it as noisy plumbing, remembering the sounds of the pipes on his previous visit. As he reentered his bedroom, the door flew open, and a lovely creature appeared, instantly putting her hand to her mouth as she breathed, "Oh my."

"Oh my, indeed. To what do I owe the privilege?" He grinned mischievously, knowing his dimples made for a dashing appearance. Slowly he pushed his black hair, damp from running his wet fingers through it, from his dark eyes.

"Oh sir. Forgive me, sir. I knocked. I did. Oh my goodness, I will probably lose my position."

"And who are you, and what position is that?" Jacob thought she might faint. He stepped closer, just in case.

She backed away.

"Please, I will not cause you to lose your job. Tell

me, who are you?"

"My name is Selma, sir. I'm a chambermaid. I was going to ensure your room was up to standard. I had no idea you were in here."

He saw the fear in the greenest eyes he had ever looked upon and damp curls straying from her cap. He stepped forward and gently placed his hand on her arm. "No harm done, miss. I was running water and didn't hear the knock. You are not at fault, so please don't worry." He removed his hand, as she was looking at it with concern.

She began retreating out the door, but her back hit the doorframe. She blushed and he thought she was the sweetest thing he had ever seen. He looked forward to seeing her again. He started toward her to see if she was hurt, but she turned and sped from his room. He laughed to himself. *What an enchanting young woman.*

❄

Selma entered the hall supply closet next to the gentleman's room and held up the end of her white apron to pat the perspiration from her forehead as it ran toward her eyes. Embarrassment coursed through her and seemed to take her very breath. She could not believe she had entered an occupied gentleman's quarters on her second day of employment.

They will surely let me go. Oh dear Lord, please handle this for me. I didn't intend for it to happen.

She counted seconds, but they didn't seem to go by. Finally she heard the gentleman's door open and close, the wooden floor creaking as he walked by, whistling, of all things. Obviously the incident hadn't bothered him.

As she quietly opened the door and backed out to gently close it, she felt something at her elbow.

Maggie stood in her path. "Problem, Miss Bradford?"

Heat rushed up and burned her ears. "Oh no, ma'am. I guess I haven't quite learned my way. I was looking for a duster." *Lord, forgive my little lie. I promise I will do better.*

Maggie forced her aside and entered the closet only to turn quickly around with a feather duster in hand. "You didn't look very well, it seems." She handed it to Selma and briskly walked away, mumbling to herself.

Selma's eyes followed the stately figure until she disappeared. She lifted her shoulders back, set her jaw, and walked to the now unoccupied bedroom to prepare it for the gentleman's return. She wished she could see her sisters right now and share what had happened. The thought of their giggling and teasing forced a smile to her lips. Pure joy filled her heart when she pictured her sisters and the love they'd shared growing up in the orphanage in Biltmore Village.

She was still smiling as she lifted the gray ashes from the edges of the fireplace, flicking a burning splint of wood toward the dying flames. She swept up the trail of soot that missed her bucket and left the room to dispose of the waste.

As she walked down the hall, she felt another joy that made her blush. Her stomach tingled as she thought of the handsome man she had just encountered. She shed the thought and forced her mind to return to her duties.

Chapter 2

Hands on hips, Selma looked around the messy guest bedroom. She already had cleaned the room of the gentleman she had walked in on yesterday, and it had not been near the catastrophe she faced now. What kind of person lived like this? She busied herself making the large four-poster bed, almost climbing on it to reach the middle, relieved she needed to change sheets only twice a week.

As she rounded the bedpost, she looked out at the beautiful fall day. Thanksgiving was only days away, and the trees were losing most of their colorful leaves. The mountains never looked more striking, though she had seen them all her life. How wonderful Christmas would be at Biltmore—a fairy tale come true.

She was about to tear her eyes from the glorious morning when she saw two people strolling arm in arm in the garden below. She moved closer to the window and peered at the handsome couple who turned and sat on one of the garden benches, giving Selma a full view of their faces. As the gentleman placed his arm around the lady's shoulders, her heart pounded.

It is him.

She scrutinized the beautiful lady, blond tendrils

escaping her bonnet, and knew she had to be his betrothed. Why else would he hold her so close?

She turned at the sound of a knock. "Rosie!"

"I was just passing by. Had to get supplies from the closet, so I thought I would say good morning. My, my, you look like an iron was taken to your face. Why are you so red?"

As Rosie walked into the room, Selma hurried from the window so her new friend wouldn't see what she had observed. Much to her chagrin, Rosie walked past her to the window and glanced down. "I see Mr. Sinclair is back and up to his shenanigans again."

"Who?"

"Jacob Sinclair. He's a regular guest. A friend of Mr. Vanderbilt's from school, I believe. The ladies adore him."

"Really? Where is he from?" Selma tried to appear nonchalant. She was somewhat relieved that maybe the lady was just one of his many acquaintances.

"New York. I believe he owns a shipping company." Rosie let out a deep sigh as she turned from the window. "If only we had their means and were in high society. I understand he has a home in Newport, Rhode Island, as well as elaborate quarters on Park Avenue."

Selma shuddered and wondered why she had even been a little bit attracted by the likes of Jacob Sinclair. "Rosie, God has brought us to this place and time for a reason. We are happy, are we not? Probably more so than those who have all this." She spread her arms to indicate the room. "We are rich in that we are assured of life eternal. You do trust in Jesus, do you not?"

Rosie's face showed a lack of understanding, but as she seemed about to speak, Maggie cleared her throat at the door.

"I assumed you both were given enough duties to keep you busy. Obviously, you were not. Do I need to add more?"

In unison Selma and Rosie exclaimed, "No, ma'am."

Rosie added, "We are sorry, Miss McAllister. I just happened to see her in here and spoke, her being new and all. It won't happen again."

"See that it does not."

❄

Jacob Sinclair caught sight of Selma at the window as he glanced up. He thought he saw remorse in her expression, but the distance and early morning sun distorted his vision. He gently removed his arm from around Betsy, an old friend from New York, but Selma had turned away. He didn't know why it mattered, except that for some reason, she had captured his attentions.

Betsy was speaking. "How's the shipping business, Jacob?"

"Doing quite well, Betsy. Thanks for asking."

"I haven't seen you in Newport lately. Did you not take up residence there this summer?"

"Actually, I spent only a week there. And you? Did your family spend the whole summer?"

"Yes of course. Daddy wouldn't have it any other way. But obviously, you didn't attend any functions that week."

"No, I didn't let anyone know I was coming. I just wanted time to rest."

"I missed you." She gave him a coquettish smile.

Jacob wouldn't lie to her. He did not even think of her except as an old friend. And since their paths crossed only during summers at Newport, he rarely thought of her at all. So he said nothing. He had sat by her at breakfast that morning, and she suggested a stroll in the gardens.

His heart told him that a woman with a servant's heart was better for him than one wearing a gown by Worth. He glanced up at the window to see if he could catch a glimpse of her again. He saw nothing. "Betsy, we better go in. You're getting cold." He stood and took her hand to assist her as she rose from the bench.

"What are your plans today, Jacob? I have to leave the day after Thanksgiving."

"You won't be here for Christmas? Biltmore won't be the same." He wanted to add something else nice, but he continued, "I think after lunch, I'll take a lone ride around the estate." He wanted to assure her he did not want company—any company. He gave her the smile that caused many a lady's heart to flutter. But his heart wasn't in it.

❈

Maggie had scheduled Selma an afternoon off. She thought she would walk the three miles to Biltmore Village to visit her younger sister, Melissa, at the orphanage. She wished she could see her older sisters, Charity and Peggy, who had left the orphanage before her.

Selma skipped lunch in order to prepare for her walk. She dressed in one of the two gowns she owned and put on her worn walking boots. Six miles was a bit of a distance, but she figured the trek would take close to an hour there and an hour back, so that would leave a couple of hours to spend with her sister. She would only need to check her out of class an hour early.

Bundled in her only coat, which she had received as a donation from the church in Biltmore Village years earlier, she walked hastily toward the orphanage. Her hair flowed around her shoulders, as she had left it loose to keep her ears warm.

After about a mile, her feet began to hurt, but she gritted her teeth and kept walking. It seemed the earth moved as a rumbling noise approached the road. She glanced around and saw nothing. The sound grew louder. Over the hill a horse appeared, galloping toward her. Her heart skipped a beat as she recognized the rider.

The man reined his horse to a stop, kicking dirt up on the skirt of Selma's gown. "This must be my lucky day."

Brushing it off, Selma glanced at him. "I can't imagine why."

"Because I have encountered my intruder again."

Selma blushed. "I really am sorry. I did knock, sir."

"Yes, you did. I thought it was the pipes. You couldn't have known I was there. Please don't think of it again."

"I imagine you will keep reminding me."

"Touché." He patted the horse's neck. "I promise I will not. Now where is the lovely Selma going today?"

She hesitated, not wanting him to know she was from the orphanage. Then she felt ashamed, because it was, after all, who she was. . .and God had placed her there for a reason.

"To the orphanage in the village. To see my sister."

"I should like to provide the transportation that takes you there."

"On that? With you?" She couldn't imagine sitting so close to a man.

"You have never ridden a horse?"

"A few times. But by myself."

"Hmmm, you've missed a lot." He laughed. "So now is the time. I can help you up, and you can ride in front. It will be a short trip. He's a very nice horse, and I'm a very nice man. What do you say?"

Selma thought of her aching feet. She considered the handsome gentleman offering her a quick ride. "I guess so. If it will be no trouble. . ."

"None at all." He flashed his charming grin as he eased down from the horse. He guided her foot into the stirrup, gave her a few instructions, and up she went, sitting side-saddle. He climbed up and seated himself behind her.

She felt his closeness and smelled the fragrant soap on his skin. Her stomach seemed to flip as he reached around her to take the reins. She hoped this would be a quick ride and that the wind would erase the heat she felt rising to her face.

Suddenly they were there, and Jacob was easing her off before dismounting.

"Thank you for the ride. It was a bit uncomfortable but saved me a great deal of time. And aching feet."

Jacob laughed. "You would get used to it. How long will you be visiting? I have some things I can do in the village, so

I can return for you afterward."

"Oh no, that won't be necessary. I can walk back." She couldn't imagine sitting that close to him again. It just wasn't proper.

"Nonsense. I can see those boots would blister your feet. Let me come for you. Say, two hours?"

Her lips hesitantly lifted into a shy smile. "I suppose that would be okay. You don't think I could get in trouble, do you?"

"Of course not. I am a guest, and you are on an afternoon off." He grinned. "Aren't you? You didn't sneak off from a day's work, did you?"

"Oh no, of course not," she responded seriously before realizing he was teasing. She laughed before thanking him again and turning to go inside.

❄

The visit with Melissa warmed Selma's heart, and all thoughts of the ride back disappeared until he returned. She became anxious thinking of sitting adjacent to him.

Her sister walked with her to greet him. "Hello, I am Melissa, Selma's sister. Thank you for giving her a ride."

"You are welcome, and I must say you are as pretty as your sister."

Selma saw the deep blush on Melissa's face and smiled. She knew the feeling.

Melissa managed, "Thank you, sir."

Selma couldn't believe the next remark from the dashing Jacob Sinclair. "Maybe you would like me to come and take you to visit Selma one day."

Melissa looked delighted. "Oh sir, that would be wonderful." She looked at Selma. "Wouldn't it?"

"I don't know if we can receive visitors. I'll see." Selma hugged her sister. "I need to go. I'll be back when I can. I'll try before Christmas."

Jacob helped Selma onto the horse before mounting. Both waved as they turned in the direction of the estate.

Minutes after they left, Jacob turned off the road onto a dirt path.

Selma shouted, "Hey!"

"This will only take a few minutes." He stopped at the French Broad River. After sliding from the saddle, he helped her down and led her to a small gray stone bridge. "Please sit a spell. Let's talk a bit."

"Really, I need to return. I didn't eat lunch, so I must be back for dinner."

"You will, I promise. I just want to talk to you."

"Concerning what?"

"You. Did you grow up at the orphanage?"

Selma gazed at the river. It appeared white and moved so fast it looked as if it were churning soap. "Yes, I did. Me and my three sisters."

"Was it hard?"

"Not really. It's all I knew, so how could I say for sure? We worked hard, did chores, and went to school. We can all read and write. We know history, and, believe it or not, we were taught some social graces."

"Why would I not believe you?"

She looked at his handsome face, his dark eyes glowing

with warmth. "I happened to glance out a window this morning. You were with a very attractive lady. You may not think I possess the grace she portrays."

"Oh but I do. And you are twice as pretty." He smiled.

"Are you patronizing me, sir?"

"No, Selma, I am not. I find you more beautiful and charming than most. It doesn't matter to me that you are from the orphanage, nor that you do not wear the latest fashions or try to flatter me with feminine wiles. I like your unpretentious approach to life."

Selma felt overwhelmed. She wanted to return to the estate, where she knew her position and where she was comfortable. "Please, sir, may we go?"

"Do I put you at unease?"

"Yes, I am afraid you do."

"I am sorry. I have no intention of doing that. We will go." He stood and took her hand to help her up. He pushed her long hair back and grinned broadly. "Next time we'll need to tie your hair to keep it from blinding me."

Selma blushed. "That would probably be a good idea."

His fingers lingered another second as he tucked a loose strand back in place. "But I would miss the sweet smell of it tickling my face."

As she was about to climb on, she paused and fixed her eyes on his handsome face. "Thank you for the ride. And thank you for being kind to me and my sister."

"You are most welcome, Selma. I have enjoyed your company today. I hope we encounter each other again soon."

She smiled. "Maybe we will pass in the hall."

Chapter 3

Selma ran her hand over the smooth ebony table. She lifted a small cup from the rose and white tea set, circling the rim with her finger. Carefully setting it down, she glanced at all the treasures in the room. Usually she was so busy cleaning and preparing the bedrooms that she didn't take the time to admire the furnishings or accessories. How could it be possible for someone to have so much wealth as to build this massive home and acquire all these belongings?

Selma had developed an interest in art and knew a little about paintings from books in the village library, so she knew the paintings by Renoir hanging throughout the house were very expensive. He was just one of the artists whose works were displayed.

"Are you in a trance, Miss Bradford?" Maggie's tone pierced Selma's thoughts.

"No, Miss McAllister. Actually, I was stopping a moment to admire the room. I never take time to appreciate what's around me."

"Because we don't have time for that, Miss Bradford."

"Oh, I am sorry. It was only a minute. I feel we overlook all the beauty God created."

"You think God created these things?" Maggie pointed

to the table holding the tea set.

"I think God inspired us to create by giving us the materials we use and the abilities to shape them."

"A righteous girl, aren't you?" Maggie lifted her head and sniffed.

"Made righteous only by the blood of Jesus, not myself. You see—"

"Get back to work, Miss Bradford." Maggie turned and hastily left the room. However, she quickly reentered. "You made me forget why I was looking for you. Please return Mr. Merriweather's books to the library downstairs. Do you remember where it is?"

"Yes, ma'am. You showed me my first day."

Maggie handed her the books and left without a word, leaving Selma to stare openmouthed after her.

I need to pray for her when I pray for Rosie. . . .

❄

Jacob settled into a wingback chair in a far corner of the library. *The New York Sun* and *The New York Times* had arrived, and he was anxious to catch up on the news in his home state, especially information about the possible merger of Brooklyn and New York City. It was about creating a larger metropolitan area. He wondered if that was a good thing.

It was President McKinley's first year in office and, of course, the newsmen were keeping up with his every move and decision. Jacob turned the pages and noticed an interesting article about one of his own ships loaded with Yukon gold, which that year had weighed anchor for Seattle.

Another section headlined women's suffrage.

Jacob leaned his head back and sighed. Change was in the air, along with Marxism, Impressionism, and other radical movements. He was afraid his country sometimes left God out of the picture. He knew, however, that He was always in control.

A thumping noise brought his head up, and he focused his attention across the room. He smiled. "Good morning."

Selma's head turned hesitantly toward him. "I dropped a book."

"I see that. Something you've been reading?" He loved an intelligent woman. He seldom encountered one in his world. It was about gowns and batting eyelashes.

"No, sir. I am returning books for a guest."

"Please come sit a moment."

"I shouldn't. I must get back to work."

"I fail to see why. After all, aren't you supposed to be nice to guests?"

"Actually, I am to care only for your rooms."

Her smile hit him in the heart. The lady possessed wit. He laid the paper down so he could concentrate on Selma.

"I think my friend and your employer would want you to appease me by joining me in conversation at my bidding." He could tell she didn't know what to do, so he added, "Please."

Selma glanced toward the door. "Well, only for a moment." She sat on the edge of a settee across from his chair. "You're reading a paper from New York?"

"You look as if you are about to jump and run away." He

grinned broadly. "Yes, dated days ago, but I love to know what's going on back home."

"I can understand that."

"Have you ever traveled, Selma?"

"No, never." She cast her gaze downward a brief moment.

"You would be intrigued with New York. It is a big city. It especially will be if it merges with Brooklyn."

"Yes, I heard that may happen. I am interested in what's going on outside Biltmore Village. I think I would like very much to travel."

"I predict someday you will. Honestly."

"That is my dream." Her eyes sparkled. "I want to see as much of God's world as I can."

Jacob nodded. "He certainly made a beautiful world. I am always amazed at His creation."

"As am I." Selma stood. "Thank you for allowing me to join you, but I really must go. Miss McAllister seems to keep a close check on me, always waiting around the corner with new orders. . . ."

"Why is it that I feel someday you will be the one doing the bidding?"

Selma shook her head. "That is not really important to me. I am very happy with my station in life. The Bible states that each of us should do our best at whatever position we have. I must go."

Jacob watched her walk out and close the door behind her. His voice was soft as he said, "You are very wise, Selma the chambermaid. I hope to learn many lessons from you."

❋

At dinner that evening Selma noticed Rosie was in a bad mood. She was mad at Maggie, who'd reprimanded her on the way she treated a guest, mad at the guest, and mad at herself for letting her feelings show.

She vented as she ate. "Selma, I don't know how you can be so sweet all the time. Especially to Maggie. She is the meanest woman I have ever known."

"Rosie, let me share with you something Mama Elsie taught us at the orphanage. First, we are all different, created by God to be that way. Second, we may have no idea what another person has gone through in life or how lonely that person may be. But know this. Most people respond to love. If you keep loving someone, usually you will be loved back. God gives us that love. In the New Testament, He tells us to love Him and love our neighbors unconditionally. Think about how you feel when you truly know someone loves you. That's what we all want."

"I've not been to church very often. But I think I understand what you're saying. Maybe we can talk more one evening after dinner. Not tonight. I am too upset."

"I would love to talk to you. And when we have a Sunday afternoon off together, we can catch a ride into the village and attend the three o'clock church service."

"I think I would like that." Rosie turned back to her food.

Selma pondered her conversation with Mr. Sinclair that morning. It pleased her that he spoke of God the way he did. He seemed to be a good man. As she continued thinking about the Christmas guest, Selma almost choked when she heard Rosie say his name. "What did you say?"

"I said, of all the gentlemen I have seen here, Jacob Sinclair is the most handsome. He is nice, too. I have encountered him in the hall several times, and he stops and inquires of my well-being. No one else does that."

At her words, Selma felt heat rush to her face, and she knew her cheeks must be glowing.

"You think he's handsome, too, don't you? Come on, tell me."

"Yes, I think he is. And he's nice. But we really shouldn't be talking about a guest that way."

Rosie laughed. "I can't help but notice someone that handsome."

"Rosie!"

"Well, he is a dashing sort. And you obviously agree. I see you turning red at the mention of his name."

"That's enough." Selma looked at those around her. "Please excuse me. I have to get up very early in the morning."

As she left the table, she heard Rosie say, "Sweet dreams."

She didn't look back, leaving Rosie and her irritating smile behind.

❄

Jacob awoke and stretched his long legs over the end of the bed. His mind wandered until he finally thought about it being the day before Thanksgiving. His mother had admonished him when he told her of his trip to the Biltmore estate for the holidays. Now he thought of his parents and how lonely they would be through Thanksgiving and Christmas without him. How could he have been so selfish? He felt ashamed. Yes, he worked, but he still leaned on his retired father to take the reins when he was out of town. Which, he admitted, was often. *What has gotten into me? Why am I thinking like this?*

Jacob took his Bible from the nightstand drawer and sat on the edge of the bed. His fingers rubbed the worn leather that carried his family name. It had been his father's, and the family tree page was faded. He thumbed through, stopping to read a verse here and there. Feeling more peaceful, he eased the Bible back into the drawer before dressing.

He was just about to leave for breakfast when he heard a knock. As he opened it, his breath caught in pleasant surprise. "Hello. By what good chance does the lovely Selma knock at my door?"

He noticed her stricken look as the words tumbled out. "Mr. Sinclair, I had nowhere else to turn. A message was sent by the orphanage that Melissa is very ill. The housekeeper has given me permission to go to her, but I have no means of transportation. I know I shouldn't—"

"Don't worry. I'll get my coat." Jacob noted she already wore hers. He placed his hand at the small of her back and led her downstairs, where he called for a carriage.

The ride was bumpy, as he drove with haste. He looked over at Selma only once, and her worried face saddened him.

When they arrived, Jacob helped her down. They found Miss Caps inside the front hall.

She led them to Melissa's room while explaining that the doctor was unavailable. "He is in the country delivering a baby. At times Melissa has been feverish to the point of being unresponsive. I have left my assistant with her."

Jacob heard Selma's cry as she ran to her sister's bed. He turned to Miss Caps. "Do you have any rubbing alcohol?"

"Yes. Should I get it?"

"Please. And a cloth and a pan of cool water, that is, if you don't mind. A nurse used this procedure when I was young."

"Of course not." Miss Caps left the room.

Jacob turned and approached Melissa's bed. His hand reached for Selma's shoulder and squeezed it.

She didn't seem to notice. She was talking softly to her sister.

When Miss Caps returned with the supplies, Jacob rubbed the alcohol on Melissa's arms, neck, and face, followed by cool water. He turned to Selma, whose eyes intently watched with hope. "Selma, I am going to leave the room. I want you and Miss Caps to undress Melissa and rub her whole body, just as I rubbed her arms. Use the alcohol, followed by the cool water."

"Of course," Selma whispered. "I understand."

Jacob left the bedroom and paced the front hall, praying for Melissa to get better. The assistant brought him tea, which soothed his stomach that was grumbling resentment at being unfed. However, he had no desire at the moment for food.

Hours later a door burst open, and Selma exclaimed, "Oh Mr. Sinclair, I think her fever has broken."

Jacob asked, "Is she dressed?"

"Partially, but I have her covered. Please come and see."

Jacob followed and, upon entering the room, headed straight for Melissa, who was coherent and talking to Miss Caps.

Melissa smiled at Jacob. "Thank you, Mr. Sinclair. I understand you were responsible for bringing my fever down."

"With help from these two lovely ladies. I am so glad you are better. We were worried about you."

Selma took his hand. "I, too, thank you. You were wonderful."

Jacob captured her tearstained face in a glance and then stared into her beautiful green eyes. "Thank you, Selma. I'm glad I could help and thankful that it was my door on which you knocked." He saw the slight blush on her cheeks and added, "I'm glad you consider me a friend." He watched the smile soften the tense expression on her face. "Shall we leave Melissa to some rest? I believe she will be fine now."

"Yes." Selma turned to Melissa's bed and knelt to cuddle her in her arms. "See you soon, sweetheart. Have a good Thanksgiving tomorrow."

Melissa's smile seemed to be that of an angel as she returned her sister's hug.

Jacob patted her on the head. "Get some rest. That is the most important thing now."

Jacob again placed his hand at the small of Selma's back as he led her out of the orphanage. He was reluctant to remove his hand when they approached the carriage. It felt so comfortable there.

❄

The ringing bell woke Selma from a deep sleep. Her neck was stiff and she wondered why. She felt the heat in her cheeks as she remembered her dream. Mr. Sinclair had asked for her hand in marriage in front of all the guests at Biltmore. She shook the remaining thoughts from her head, knowing such a thing could never be.

What wasteful dreams.

She determined not to spend her time entertaining such fanciful ideas. A man of means and notoriety having anything to do with a servant girl? And an orphan to boot. That would never happen.

Selma jumped out of bed and dressed. Chores had to be done early, for the day was Thanksgiving. She and the other upstairs servants would dine at two in the servants' dining room.

Before rushing to breakfast, Selma knelt by her bed to say a brief prayer of thanksgiving. She looked upward. "I promise, Lord, I'll thank You more later."

Breakfast consisted of scones and jelly and delicious-smelling cinnamon rolls that tasted a lot like her older sister's. Peggy had started making them with Mama when she was just tall enough to see over the kitchen counter. Thinking of her sister brought nostalgia that unsettled Selma's heart. She missed spending the days with her sisters.

After breakfast the servants went their own ways to fit a day's work in one morning. They had been told they could have the rest of the day off after their Thanksgiving meal.

When the time for the feast came, Selma was hungry.

She freshened up in her room, removing her maid's attire and donning one of her two gowns.

When she entered the dining room, all seats were filled but one Rosie had saved for her.

Maggie noisily cleared her throat.

Selma rushed to take her seat.

"Miss Bradford, would you please say the blessing?"

Astonished, Selma opened her mouth to speak, but Maggie interjected, "Please."

"Yes, ma'am, I would be glad to." She bowed her head. "Dear Father, we come to You today in thanksgiving for all the blessings You have bestowed on us. We especially thank You for Your love and grace and Your Son, Jesus. We thank You for His life here among us and for what He did for us on the cross. And for His resurrection and the assurance we have of everlasting life. Thank You, Lord, for the food we are about to eat. Bless it, please, so we will be healthy and strong and able to do service for You. Amen."

Selma looked toward Maggie, who stared at her with an expression of wonder. Then Maggie smiled, and Selma felt a sense of peace. Maybe her prayer had been used by God to open Maggie's heart.

Rosie took her hand and squeezed it. Selma saw a tear running down her friend's cheek. She felt honored that Maggie had asked her to pray, but honored more that she could exalt her Lord doing it.

❄

Purple salvia greeted Selma as she entered one of the many gardens that surrounded the house. She had been unable to rest, so she had donned her coat and tattered gloves and headed outside for her first stroll through the talked-about gardens.

She had heard that the famous Frederick Law Olmstead, designer of major parks in New York, Boston, and other large cities, was responsible for the landscaping project that turned two hundred fifty acres into a wonderland. The gardens near the house were based on Vaux le Vicomte near Paris. The librarian in the village had kept her abreast of all the news surrounding the building of the Biltmore estate. She had been hungry for details.

It amazed Selma so many flowers bloomed in the cool fall of the year. She recognized only a few, such as the salvia, goldenrod, and yellow mums, and wondered if any grew during the snowy winter.

Hearing footsteps, she turned around and bumped into Jacob Sinclair. The shock of touching him made her quickly withdraw. "I'm sorry. You were there before I knew it."

He removed his hat and bowed, teasing her with his eyes. "You didn't have to jump back so far. It was a mere brush."

She straightened. "I am not in the habit of brushing up to men." She felt that sounded foolish and added, "I mean, I wouldn't have purposefully touched you." She lowered her eyes. "I'm sorry. I can't seem to properly state what I mean."

"Oh Selma, we are friends. Remember? You don't have to do or say all the right things with me. I like you as you are. And, by the way, you are a delight in my eyes."

Selma looked into those dark eyes, eyes that sparkled. With what? What was it she saw? Was he being condescending, or did he truly like her? "I am not sure, sir, that delight is a thing I want to be in a man's eyes. It doesn't sound proper."

"Selma, you sure are stuck on the word 'proper.' I myself am not always aware of what is proper. I do not mean you any unkindness. I think you are a wonderful person. That's all."

Selma and Jacob both turned at the footsteps behind them. Selma thought she heard Jacob groan. But he said, "Betsy! What a nice surprise."

"Hello, Jacob." Betsy looked at Selma and grabbed Jacob by the arm as if to whisk him away. "I've been trying to find you, dear. I am leaving tomorrow. Remember? Let's see if we can arrange to sit together at dinner this evening. And guess what? Good news. I will return for Christmas."

As they strolled away, Jacob glanced over his shoulder and mouthed, "See you."

Selma felt dismay and uncertainty. He did say he would see her. But was he only being nice? She knew better than to encourage the feelings that struggled to occupy her heart.

She clenched her fist and looked down to see that her finger had just poked another hole in her worn glove. *Of course*, she thought. *This is where I am and who I am.* "And that's not a bad thing," she said aloud to anyone who could hear.

Chapter 4

Selma peered out a guest's window at the light gray clouds and wondered if it might snow. The Monday after Thanksgiving had brought a cold air mass to the mountain area. Everyone was abuzz about Christmas and the decorating that would begin later in the week. Memories of decorating with her sisters and Mama Elsie flooded her mind. Theirs was a simple Christmas but centered on Jesus' birth. This one would be extravagant, and she could only hope the true meaning would prevail. She shivered, since the fire in the room had died. Escaping her thoughts and letting the drape fall back, she turned to lay a new fire. She had yet to air out the bed. Her stomach tingled. The next room she would clean would be Mr. Sinclair's.

As she left the finished guest room, she glanced back to make sure it met the proper standards. Maggie had told her that Mrs. Emily King, the housekeeper, made rounds daily, and if the guest rooms were not up to par, she would be the one to suffer. What that meant was that Maggie would, in turn, make the chambermaids suffer.

Rosie had told her at breakfast that morning that Maggie thought she would get the housekeeper's job after the previous one left. But Mrs. King, who moved to North Carolina from England just this year, had been hired. Selma now felt sorry for Maggie.

When Selma reached Mr. Sinclair's door, she knocked hardily. Never again would she be so quick to enter a gentleman's room. However, she knew most of the guests left early for breakfast and spent much of the morning in the library or smoking room, reading or talking. Many times she had been told they lingered over the breakfast table with coffee and conversation.

When she made sure the room was vacant, she entered and began her chores. After emptying the ashes, laying the fire, and airing the bed, Selma dusted the furniture.

Finding a bookmark on top of the nightstand, she opened the drawer slightly to put it away. She saw the edge of a Bible and pulled the drawer out farther. Curiosity grabbed her, and she flipped the leather cover back. She quickly shut the drawer and looked around to make sure no one had entered and caught her. Her heart pounded with pride.

Mr. Sinclair's family Bible. I do believe he is a Christian.

❊

Since finding the Bible in his room the day before, Selma found Mr. Sinclair's room untouched. He had not slept there. Distressed, she wondered if he had gone. She walked to the nightstand and opened the drawer.

It's still here. Why would he leave it?

Maybe she labeled him too quickly. She would not think of leaving her Bible, even overnight. She was puzzled but put it behind her and continued her chores.

At lunch Rosie asked with that irritating grin, "Did you know Mr. Sinclair is gone for a few days?"

Selma looked at her friend with what she hoped was

a straight face. "I only know that his room was as I left it yesterday."

"I heard him tell Maggie Saturday he would be leaving Sunday morning. He didn't say where he would be going. It's funny. That Betsy woman is gone, too."

"I don't see any reason to connect the two. He probably has business to attend."

"Well, they seemed pretty close to me."

Selma didn't want to believe it, but she had no right to the feelings she harbored for the man. She changed the subject. "I hear we will be working our two hours off every afternoon to help decorate. What does that involve?"

Rosie's nose wrinkled. "The gardeners bring in fresh cedar and pine, and we decorate the mantels in every room. Many of the guest rooms will have their own Christmas trees. And there is the living hall. That tree is usually huge. Last year we even helped decorate the one in the entrance hall. I tell you, we will work ourselves to death. Most of the time we have to replace all the greenery before Christmas so it will be fresh."

"Sounds like fun to me. We only had one Christmas tree in the orphanage, and each of us hung only one special ornament."

"When it's added to all our other work and the number of guests here, it becomes very tiring."

Selma thought about that. "Yes, I suppose it would."

"And I am so sad this season. I know I won't enjoy a minute of it."

Selma saw the moisture in her friend's eyes. "What's the matter?"

"My mother. I have received word she is not doing well. My sister wrote and said she is very ill and may not recover. She lives in Virginia, so I won't be able to go to her." Rosie looked questioningly at Selma. "Do you think she will go to heaven?"

Selma's heart sank. How to answer? "Rosie, do you know if she believes in Jesus?"

"Like I told you, we didn't go to church very often." Rosie hesitated. "But she did sing a few church songs to me. I truly want her to go to heaven. I want to go, too, and be with her."

"Rosie, it is very simple. The Bible says if you believe in the Lord Jesus Christ and confess your sins, you will be saved. Do you believe that Jesus is God's Son and that He died for your sins?"

"I don't believe otherwise, so I guess I do."

"Pray to Him, Rosie. Ask Him into your heart. When you retire tonight, talk to Him. He loves to hear from us." Selma looked around the table and noticed others were listening. She smiled and nodded, hoping that anyone who heard and didn't believe would receive the message. After standing to leave, she hugged Rosie and whispered in her ear, "I will pray for your mother. And you."

❆

"When Scrooge awoke, it was so dark, that looking out of bed, he could scarcely distinguish the transparent window from the opaque walls of his chamber. He was endeavoring to pierce the darkness with his ferret eyes, when the chimes of a neighboring church struck the four quarters. So he listened for the hour—"

121

The shrill bell made Selma jump and drop the Charles Dickens novel. Having found *A Christmas Carol* in the servants' hall bookcase, she had devoured it daily during her afternoon break, losing all sense of reality. But when the bell sounded, so did duty. She picked up the book and shelved it quickly as she hurried to the call box.

Mr. Sinclair's room. He must have returned.

Selma adjusted her cap, sticking the rebellious curls under it, and smoothed her apron. Her heart beat rapidly as she hurried to his room downstairs. She knocked and disappointment overtook her when she heard Maggie's voice.

"Come in."

Selma opened the door and faced her superior. "Yes, ma'am?"

We just received word that Mr. Sinclair is on his way back. I think you need to air his bed and lay a fire."

"Yes, ma'am."

"And do it quickly. The message may have been slow."

"Yes, ma'am."

Maggie left and Selma began by arranging the kindling. Because the fire had not been built for a few days, the room was cold. She shivered and hoped it would heat before his arrival.

As the fire popped and crackled from the fresh wood, Selma set about airing the bed and dusting the furniture. She was bent over wiping the bottom of the nightstand when the door opened. She stood and turned, finding Jacob Sinclair smiling mischievously.

"Do all the guests have the opportunity to catch the

charming Selma at work? Or am I just lucky?"

Selma felt her cheeks burn. "Sir, I am so sorry. I never meant it to happen again. Miss McAllister just rang me from this room a short time ago to ready it for you. We didn't really know when you would return."

As he walked toward her, she stepped back and bumped into the nightstand.

"There you go again, injuring yourself to get away from me. I won't hurt you. I promise."

Selma looked down. "I know that, sir. It was just a reaction." She glanced up and her heart flipped as he took another step toward her.

"Selma, you and I are friends. What is it that causes you such alarm?"

"Sir, it is just not proper for us to be friends."

"There you go with the 'proper' word again. Tell me, why is it so wrong?"

Selma looked into his eyes and saw nothing but warmth. "I think the two of us are so very different. In our stations in life, in our experiences, and, I guess, in everything. I do not know your world, nor do you know mine."

"I see." He stepped closer. "So you think as God's children, we are so different? That I don't have the same feelings, the same desires as you? That I'm not human?"

"I truly do not know. I guess so. Jesus was a servant. He loved everyone. So I am sure it's possible."

"That I am human?" He laughed.

Selma smiled. "Yes, I believe you are a good man. You helped me when my sister was ill. You have been nothing but kind."

"So, sweet Selma, what's the problem?"

I could never tell you that. "I suppose there is no problem."

He reached for her hand and pulled it to his lips. "To friendship. You are more a lady than any woman I've met. Don't forget it." He looked around. "The room is perfect, Selma. If you wish, you may go."

Selma brushed past him, her pulse racing as their arms touched when she left the room.

❄

Selma awoke to a cold room. . .but a warm heart. The decorating would begin that day, and she looked forward to it. She remembered how the evergreen smelled when it was delivered to the orphanage. The tree and branches of cedar were donated by Mr. Vanderbilt himself. She couldn't begin to imagine the aromas that would fill his large home. She jumped up, made her bed, and quickly dressed for breakfast.

Rosie was seated when she arrived.

Selma patted her shoulder as she sat by her friend. "Good morning."

The returned salutation rang dull. "Good morning."

"Dear me." Selma grinned. "What is wrong with Rosie today?"

"I just can't get excited about an afternoon of decorating." Rosie's lips pouted as she looked at Selma. "I was so tired last night. I'm still exhausted."

"May I suggest as soon as you return upstairs you do some stretching and toe-touching?" Selma was serious but kept the laugh inward as she thought of her friend's possible response.

"You're joking."

"No, Rosie, not a bit. You can work it in with your chores."

"Selma, dear, I do quite a bit of bending and stretching just doing my chores. As do you."

"But it is different when you really stretch and use all your muscles. Please try it." Selma paused. "We all feel better when we get excited about Christmas, too."

"And how will you manage to get me excited about all the decorating?"

"Rosie, think of Jesus. His birth and lying in a manger. He is our Savior. Think of the bright star and the shepherds. We celebrate Him, Rosie. Every mantel you decorate, every tree you adorn, every gift you give. . .think of how we are celebrating our Lord."

"It does give me gooseflesh now. I did pray, Selma. I asked Jesus to come into my heart."

"Then see." Selma felt her eyes water. "This is reason to celebrate. It is all about Him."

"You're right. But there is something else. You mentioned gifts. We have so little money to buy them for everyone we love. What are you going to do?"

"I plan to find a ride into the village my next afternoon off and look around. I would like to buy my sisters a small present. And Mama Elsie. I also want to buy you something."

Rosie's smile revealed such happiness that Selma hugged her friend. "You see, we are going to have a wonderful Christmas."

They discovered their duties coincided that afternoon, as

they both were to decorate the entrance hall. Rosie told her it always came first. They decided to meet and walk down together. But first the chores had to be done.

Selma found all the rooms empty. Except one. Mr. McAdams answered the door when she knocked. She begged his pardon and said she would return.

He grinned broadly. "What is your hurry, young lady? If you can wait a minute, I am about to leave."

"I'll come back."

"You can't tell me George works you that hard. I'll have a word with him."

She ignored his teasing smile. "Oh no, please, sir. It's just that I'm trying to finish so I can help decorate the entrance hall. He is certainly not to blame." Selma cringed at the thought of being mentioned to Mr. Vanderbilt.

"Very well, then. I won't say anything. You have a good day, miss, and enjoy the Christmas merriment. By the way, could I have your name?"

Selma was aghast. She thought he would surely say something to Mr. Vanderbilt. "It is Selma, sir. But you won't reveal my name?"

"Of course not. I just wanted to know for myself. Please continue, Selma." He eased his door shut.

Selma backed away and hurried to the next room. Unease gripped her as she considered their conversation, in spite of his promise.

❄

Jacob joined a small gathering in the library. As he began reading the latest newspapers that had arrived from New

York, William McAdams walked in.

Jacob spoke softly as his friend approached. "Good morning, William. Join me?"

"Certainly." William sat as close to Jacob as the chairs would allow. Jacob knew that he, too, was thinking of keeping the noise level low so they wouldn't disturb others.

They talked quietly about current events, the weather, and the coming Christmas season. Jacob sensed his friend wanted to talk about something more but others were present.

Gradually the room emptied until they were the only two remaining. Jacob looked soberly at his friend. "Something on your mind, William?"

"Uh no, not really. But I just encountered one of the loveliest women I've ever seen. She had the most beautiful green eyes."

"Really? And who might that be, as I think I must have missed her."

"She is an upstairs maid who cleans our rooms. She said her name is Selma."

Jacob dropped his paper. "Selma?"

"That's what she said."

"How did you come to know her name?"

"She came by to clean, and I was still there. We talked a second, and I asked her name."

Jacob rubbed his face, trying to decide what to say. He turned to watch the fire roaring beneath the carved walnut overmantel. Looking back at his friend of ten years, he finally spoke. "William, I think I am in love with her."

"What?" William sat up on the edge of the chair. "How

could that be possible?"

"I have encountered her several times. I took her to the orphanage to see her sister who was ill. I don't know what to tell you. It just happened."

"My goodness, Jacob. What are your intentions?"

"I don't know. I can't even imagine. She, of course, would be terrified if I suggested anything. She thinks our stations in life are so far apart. It's hard for her to even admit we are friends."

"Jacob, has marriage entered your mind?"

"Yes, I think about it. I just don't know if it would work. She has been sheltered. What I mean is her world is so small. She longs for travel, but she seems content with life as it is."

Jacob looked up at the sound of someone walking into the room. "Let's drop the subject. We'll talk later." He picked his paper up and began to read, realizing his revelation shocked his friend.

Chapter 5

J acob rested in his room, considering the conversation with William in the library. He groaned when the knock on the door sounded until he realized it could be Selma. Instead, he found Miss McAllister, who handed him a note. He thanked the severe-looking woman and closed the door, thinking she needed something to cheer her. He unfolded the piece of paper.

> Dear Mr. Sinclair,
>   I am in the stable courtyard, my carriage just arriving. Please hurry down and escort me inside.
>
>   All my love,
>   Betsy

Jacob crumpled the paper and threw it into the fire. He watched the edges of the paper turn black before being consumed. It struck him that it mimicked just how he felt. He grabbed his hat and coat and headed for the stables, leaving the fire spitting from the burned note.

❄

Selma wished she were more like Melissa. Her younger sister was such a tomboy and wouldn't have minded plopping down in the middle of the floor to dig through the large containers of Christmas ornaments. Selma clenched her hands and decided to do the same.

She searched through a box. So many beautiful ornaments. She especially liked the hand-painted ones with red birds and candy canes. She pulled out one with a manger scene and hugged it to her chest. She dug deeper and exclaimed, "Look at this, Rosie! It is a little boy on a sled in the snow. Flakes are falling all around him. The painter made it look so real."

She started when a male voice responded. "Ah, let me see. I think I had one similar as a boy."

Selma, embarrassed to be found in such a position, turned to see Jacob, his arm clutched by the pretty, blond Betsy. She turned her face away so they wouldn't see it reddened by the heat she felt. She stayed quiet as she handed the ornament to Rosie to hang on the tree.

As she reached for the next bulb, Jacob walked over to Rosie to inspect the one Selma had given her. "I do believe it is like one at home. Beautiful, isn't it?"

When Selma didn't respond, Rosie chimed in, "Yes, it is. But there are so many more. I wonder if Selma will dawdle looking at them. We have so much to do." She laughed in a teasing but nervous manner.

Jacob responded, "Then let us not keep you." He ushered a yawning Betsy up the grand staircase.

Rosie looked at Selma when they were gone. "You ninny! You were so rude. He was speaking to you."

"Oh, he was? I thought he spoke generally."

"You should've seen how he looked at you. I honestly

think you hurt his feelings."

"Well I'm sure Miss Betsy will restore them."

"You're jealous!"

Selma remained quiet.

"You *are* in love with him, aren't you?"

Selma saw others coming to join them, so she didn't reply.

Rosie bent closer and looked down at her. "We will talk about this later."

✽

Selma dressed for breakfast and thought how glad she was her friend didn't have a chance to speak about Mr. Sinclair again. It had taken until the time to check the guest rooms that evening to decorate the enormous tree that towered past the second-floor balcony. So many servants had joined in that it was impossible to talk privately. But now, as she walked down the stairs to the dining room, she silently prayed Rosie wouldn't bring up the subject.

Thankfully, everyone sat at the table when she arrived, and Rosie was deep in conversation concerning the decorating of the living hall that afternoon. Selma remained quiet until Maggie entered and said the blessing.

When they began to eat, Rosie spoke softly to Selma. "We never finished our conversation."

"And what conversation was that?"

Rosie's eyes rolled at Selma. "You know of what and whom I'm speaking. And I know you can't tell me about it now, but you must, Selma. You can't keep something like that locked in your heart. You need to talk to a friend. And that would, of course, be me." She flashed an impish smile.

"Very well, if we have a few minutes alone this afternoon, we'll talk. But I imagine there will be a crowd, and the living hall is much smaller than the entrance hall." She heard her friend sigh. "But we'll hurry and try to get away early."

"Good. I will meet you at the top of the stairs, and we'll walk down together the same time as yesterday."

"Fine."

❄

Jacob arrived as early as possible at the breakfast table. He wanted to eat hurriedly and reach the stables before encountering Betsy. He didn't exactly know how he was going to handle the situation, but it appeared Betsy had intentions to pursue him during the holidays. He liked Betsy, but he didn't have any desire to spend his visit with her arm hooked through his.

He reached the stables before anyone else. Having his first choice of the riding horses, he picked a tall, stately black mare and searched for a stable hand to assist him. He was able to saddle the horse, but his host preferred his staff do it.

A stable hand named Robert, whom he had previously met and liked, walked up. Jacob shook his hand and showed him the black mare he wished to ride. All the male servants lived above the stable, and riding early was no problem. He wondered sometimes when the servants slept. They attended the guests until late at night and were available at the break of day.

After Robert handed him the reins, he rode to the village. He needed his hair trimmed and wanted to visit the mercantile for supplies. He also wanted to stay away from the estate for a while and give Betsy time to maybe find another suitor. Jacob smiled at the idea. He didn't want to hurt Betsy, but if she continued her attempts to dominate his time at Biltmore, he feared he must.

After his trim and shave, Jacob browsed the shops in the village, always amazed that George Vanderbilt had most of them and the beautiful cottages built to support the estate. The vendors and customers purchased and consumed the products raised on the thousands of acres surrounding the Biltmore home. He admitted the scheme was truly brilliant.

He wandered into the bakery, drawn by the sweet and spicy aroma. He purchased an apple tart and coffee before settling in the corner of the shop, where he watched an awakening village.

After relishing the tasty treats, Jacob strolled to the mercantile and bought his supplies. The storekeeper bundled them in brown paper, so he carried them with him on his walk.

The local library was opening, so he entered and selected an Asheville newspaper, set his package on a table, and pulled up his chair to read.

When lunchtime arrived, he ate chicken and dumplings at a small restaurant filled with villagers who seemed friendly and willing to share their tales. From there he returned to where his horse was tied at the barbershop, fastened his supplies to the saddle, and made a slow trek back to Biltmore.

Leaving the stables, Jacob entered the main house through the gentlemen's quarters and unobtrusively returned to his room. After disbursing his supplies to their proper places, he strolled down to the living hall, hoping Betsy was settled in her room for the afternoon.

Upon entering, the chatter gave him a sense of excitement. He found servants decorating a tree, the mantel, and every available space in the room. He spotted Selma, whose back was turned as she stretched cedar across the mantel. He walked softly toward her. "May I be of assistance?"

The cedar hit the floor as a surprised Selma turned and struck him with her elbow. "Oh sir, I am so sorry."

"Well at least you are injuring *me* now rather than yourself." He laughed with joy at the sight of her.

Her smile, which was much too brief, melted his heart. It was as if she remembered who they were, and her countenance stiffened. "I think, sir, I would rather injure myself."

He glanced down at her hands and, seeing a small drop of blood, drew them closer. "I think you have. You need to wear gloves to protect your delicate hands from the sticky cedar." He saw her blush. He didn't want to embarrass her or cause her concern and directed his attention to the circle of women who had stopped to stare. "I am missing the opportunity to decorate this year. I would love to help you ladies, if I wouldn't be imposing. Would you mind very much if I assisted you?"

They chimed together. "Oh no, sir."

"Good. Then give me my instructions."

Obviously bold, in spite of her size, Rosie came forward. "If you could hang ornaments where we can't reach, sir?"

"I would be delighted." Jacob turned toward Selma.

"First, let me help this young lady place the cedar on the mantel. I am afraid I must have scared it out of her hands."

The servants laughed as he kneeled and picked up the cedar. When he stood, he was pleased to see Selma smile again.

❄

Selma was surprised she felt comfortable with Jacob assisting them. She laughed with the others at his humorous remarks and clumsy way of handling the ornaments, amazed that none broke. An hour passed by all too quickly.

Her smile faded when Betsy walked into the room, elegant as always, her dark-green brocade skirt swishing and her head in the air as she headed straight for Jacob. Selma saw her shake her head as she looked up and admonished him. "What are you doing?"

Selma's glance caught Jacob's face. She thought his teeth clenched before answering, "What does it look like?"

Betsy motioned toward the other side of the room. "I do believe you are helping the servants do their job. I wouldn't suppose that would be acceptable to George. Would you?"

Jacob frowned. "To George, or to you?"

Selma had to stifle a grin at the look on Betsy's face.

Betsy put her hands on her hips. "To any of us, Jacob. None of us appreciates your consorting"—she looked around—"with these people."

Selma gasped. What nerve!

She watched as Jacob slowly climbed down the ladder and faced Betsy, but was disappointed when he spoke. "Let us take our leave." He escorted her out.

When the immediate shock of the lady's brashness faded, the servants gathered around, talking and raving. Selma heard Rosie stomp her foot as she exclaimed, "What a snobby woman!"

Selma felt her heart breaking but stiffened as she remembered the differences between people with means and those without. It was just to be.

※

Jacob led Betsy to the tapestry gallery and chose a sitting area near one of the limestone fireplaces. The room was large, and the divided sections provided guests a place for quiet conversation. Three tapestries personifying prudence, faith, and charity adorned the wall. Jacob noticed other guests had gathered at the far end of the room.

He settled Betsy on a love seat and faced her. "Betsy, you and I do not share the same beliefs. I personally cannot conceive that God made different classes of people, some better than others. Jesus Himself was a humble servant. Can you deny that?"

"Why no, but He was, after all, a carpenter's son." Sarcasm dripped from her words.

"Betsy, He was and is Lord of all. You cannot diminish who He is. He is King of Kings. He is our Savior. If you do not believe that, then you should read your Bible. I cannot fault you. I can only pray for you."

"But Jacob, look at what and who we are."

"*What* we are is lost without our Lord. *Who* would be sinners. If you haven't found Him, I pray you will. I seriously doubt anyone with faith would stoop to condescending remarks such as you made upstairs."

Jacob wiped his brow. "I enjoyed working with those ladies. And to be honest, Betsy, I really don't enjoy being with you right now. I like you and wish the best for you. But you need to search your soul, and if you don't find the Holy Spirit there, I'll be glad to read the scriptures with you and talk to you. But please set aside any ideas about the two of us having any other kind of relationship."

Betsy stood, her face red. "Then so be it, Jacob Sinclair. There are other men here who seek my attention."

Jacob stood and faced her. "Then please, let them have it." He turned and walked from the room.

❄

Retiring early, Jacob lay watching the fire as he recalled the events of the day. He knew he had been stern with Betsy and regretted part of his behavior. But he didn't know any other way to clarify his position. He felt pity for her if she truly didn't believe in a Jesus who was humble and not self-serving.

But he felt anger, too, and he prayed about it, even as he remembered Jesus' reaction to the moneychangers at the temple. Scripture indicated instances when anger was okay. He tried to justify his belief that this was one of those times.

Jacob also knew his feelings for Selma grew deeper each time he was around her. He pulled the covers tighter and drifted off to sleep, wondering what he could do to persuade her to give him a chance to prove the simplicity of his love—an emotion felt by a man for a woman, regardless of class or money.

Chapter 6

Selma couldn't believe three days had passed since she had seen Jacob. She had tried to stay busy, suppressing thoughts of him when they surfaced. She determined, however, to make this a good day, as she had the afternoon off. She had arranged to ride into the village with the housekeeper, Mrs. King, for an afternoon of Christmas shopping. All her savings were pocketed in the little cloth bag Mama Elsie gave her as a gift when she left the orphanage. Enough for all her presents. She smiled at the thought as she hurried to the stable courtyard to catch her ride.

Arriving in the village, Selma promised to return to the carriage at four before setting out toward the cluster of shops. She couldn't pass the bakery without wandering in and looking at the delicacies displayed under glass. She promised herself if she had any money left, she would buy a pastry. She gazed at the one with lemon filling. She closed her eyes momentarily as she inhaled the aroma of baked goods then reluctantly left.

She entered the mercantile located next door where she had been employed before going to Biltmore. Searching for the perfect gifts was harder than she thought. She picked up a pair of gloves, and as she assessed them, she heard an unmistakable voice.

"Those are nice and warm. They must be a gift for Melissa."

Selma did an about-face. "How did you know?"

"They are lovely but sensible. As you are."

Selma was never around Jacob that she didn't feel heat rising to her face. "Thank you. I am considering them for Melissa."

"I believe you've made a perfect choice. But if you want to look further, I would like to join you."

Selma looked around. "Are you alone?"

"Of course. Why would you think otherwise?" His lips eased into a smile as he teased her.

She knew he assumed she was thinking of Betsy. She was not going to admit it, however. "I didn't think it. I just asked."

"I see. But you didn't respond to my request."

"Yes, you may join me."

"Thank you." He gave a small bow. "After you, my lady."

Selma was conscious of his presence as she looked at handkerchiefs, scarves, and other small articles, making modest purchases along the way. She wondered if he thought her like Ebenezer Scrooge for looking at cheap items. She sought a gift of love, and the cost didn't matter.

She stopped at a counter to look at a jewelry display, eyeing a gold heart-shaped locket through the glass case. She wanted to look more closely but knew it was too expensive.

"Let's have a better look." Jacob's voice was gentle to her ears.

"I could never afford it."

He ignored her as he pointed through the glass and asked the salesclerk, "Would you mind removing this locket for us to see?"

The lady handed it to Jacob. It looked dainty in his large hand as he held it up. "Beautiful, isn't it?"

Selma looked up at him. "Yes, it is."

Jacob turned to the salesclerk. "We would like to purchase this, please."

"Oh my." Selma almost dropped her packages. "Please put it back."

"Selma, this locket is made for you. Let me buy it as a Christmas gift."

"Oh dear me. No, sir. That wouldn't be proper. You shouldn't even think such a thing."

"You've been very kind to me, Selma. I imagine I wouldn't be the first guest at Biltmore to show appreciation."

Selma felt her face fall. The words crushed her. She felt belittled and cheapened, like a tavern waitress. "I'm paid for my job, sir. I don't need gratuity."

Jacob looked surprised. "Why Selma, I didn't mean that at all."

"It sounded like it to me. But surely you know I couldn't take a gift like that under any circumstance. Now if you will excuse me, I will continue my shopping. Alone."

She heard Jacob apologizing behind her as she walked off, head high, shoulders rigid. She quickly paid for her last selection and determinedly left the store. As she passed the bakery she grimaced, as her taste for pastry had dissolved with her respect for Jacob. She couldn't get away fast enough.

❄

Jacob held his mare to a trot as he returned to Biltmore. His heart was heavy as he explored his actions. He realized what he had done to offend Selma and regretted it deeply.

As he thought of potential ways to mend the situation, he allowed the horse to ease down the short bank by the gray stone bridge to drink from the river. He patted her neck as she noisily drank the water. The simplicity of the animal's needs softened his heart.

If only ours were not so complicated.

He thought of Betsy and women like her who seemed so shallow. Not in his lifetime had he met anyone like Selma. Even his mother, whom he genuinely admired, loved her aristocratic life.

The mare's head jerked up at the screech of a crow flying low over the river. Jacob patted her as he gently pulled the reins to the side and nudged her back to the road.

Jacob was in no hurry as he took in the scenery. Rounding a curve he stopped the horse to look at the large home ahead. What would entice a man to build such a mansion?

In George's case he knew the reason. His host had become enthralled with the castles he visited in Europe. Paintings of similar estates hung in various rooms throughout the house. Too, George was fond of his friends, and being hospitable, he wanted plenty of rooms for guests. Jacob knew he added amenities for their pleasure, as well as for his own. He was sure George would marry and raise a family. He seemed serious about an American lady he was courting in Paris.

The house with its turrets and towers appeared larger as he rode on. Jacob thought of his home in New York. It was spacious and certainly beautifully furnished, as was his home in Newport. But they didn't seem to matter anymore. Because they wouldn't matter to Selma.

❄

Selma was glad Mrs. King remained quiet on the way back to Biltmore. The ride seemed as bumpy as her heart felt as it fluttered with each thought of Jacob's insulting words. For once she didn't notice the rolling landscape, which attracted so many cardinals and squirrels this time of year. She closed her eyes to hold back the hot tears trying to escape, knowing the cold wind would send them running across her cheeks. The thought of Mrs. King seeing her cry was unbearable. What would she tell her?

As soon as the carriage arrived in the stable courtyard, Selma lowered her head as she thanked Mrs. King for the ride. Then she scurried to the entrance of the house, trying to disappear before the housekeeper entered.

She held her packages close as she ran upstairs to her room on the fourth floor. Setting the presents on the dresser, Selma threw herself on the bed and cried until supper.

When she awoke she wanted to wash her face. She found the pitcher on the dresser empty. She took it and softly opened her door as she headed for the bathroom at the end of the hall. She hoped she wouldn't see anyone.

Too late. Rosie was approaching her door. "Selma, what's wrong? You've been crying."

"Really, I'm fine."

"No you're not. What's the matter?" Rosie pushed Selma back through the door, which she shut once they were in the room. She took the pitcher from her hands and set it back on the dresser. "Tell me."

Selma perched on the edge of her bed and watched Rosie as she joined her. "Actually, I probably would feel better if I talked about it. You told me I needed to confide in a friend."

"I am that friend. Now talk."

"Rosie, you've guessed how I feel about Mr. Sinclair. I get these tingles in my stomach when he's around. He's been so nice to me." She paused and looked down, her fingers fiddling with her skirt. Finally she looked Rosie square in the face. "I was foolish enough at times to think he felt the same. Oh friend, I was wrong. He doesn't think of me that way at all." A sob burst forth with the last word.

"I think you are wrong, Selma. It appears to me he does feel that way. I have seen how he looks at you. His eyes absolutely shine."

Selma shook her head the whole time Rosie spoke. "You don't know. He made it clear today."

"How?"

"He offered to buy me a locket."

"Oh Selma, how nice."

"No, it was not. I ran into him at the mercantile while shopping. I saw this beautiful necklace." Selma felt her eyebrows rise as her eyes widened. "It was so expensive, Rosie!"

"And?"

"He told me in so many words it was for my services rendered as an employee here."

"No! He couldn't have. What did you tell him?"

"I said I make a salary. That I don't need his tip."

"I can't believe he treated you like that. You can't be blamed for being upset. Even if your feelings weren't involved, that was an insult."

Selma wiped fresh tears away. "I can't believe I allowed myself to think of him as I did. I truly hope our paths never cross again."

"Oh Selma, I'm sorry, but as Christmas is several days away still, you're sure to see him."

"Then I will treat him like any other guest."

"Good." She rose and grabbed the pitcher. "Now let me fetch your water so you can wash your face, and we'll go to supper together."

"Thanks, Rosie. For everything."

❄

When Sunday arrived, Jacob longed to attend services at the village church. Robert was holding his horse steady when he arrived in the courtyard. Jacob thanked him as he placed his foot in the stirrup and heaved himself up. A quick turn-around to point the horse toward Approach Road, and he was on his way.

Jacob inhaled the cold, brisk air before breathing out, watching the white vapor blow away as the horse galloped toward the village. He was later than he intended, so he urged the horse to go faster by gently nudging the mare's sides. He used one hand to pull his hat down tighter.

When he arrived the church was full, and he was lucky to find a seat in the back. He saw Selma sitting toward the front. Jacob had been on the lookout for her so he could apologize for his cruel words. How fitting that he would see her at church, where forgiveness was often preached.

He watched her as they sang "What a Friend We Have in Jesus," occasionally viewing her beautiful profile. His heart felt heavy at the thought of her possibly not forgiving him.

At the end of the service, Jacob hurried out of the church and stood near Rev. Martin Thomas, who was shaking hands with members of his congregation.

When Selma came out, she was talking to Rosie. As she turned to take the pastor's hand, she saw Jacob. He heard her short intake of breath, but she returned her eyes to the pastor, smiled sweetly, and thanked him for a moving sermon.

He caught her arm as she passed. "Selma, a word, please." When she hesitated he tightened his hold. "Please."

Selma looked to Rosie. "I will be only a moment. Please ask Mrs. King to wait for me." She turned back to Jacob. "Only a second. I can't keep the carriage waiting."

The dirt path that led to the side of the church was deserted. Jacob coaxed her in that direction, arriving at an old wooden bench, long settled under a bare oak. "Please sit down, Selma."

"I really don't have time. Please say what you need to quickly."

"I want to apologize for what I said at the mercantile. I didn't mean it the way it obviously came out. I was just looking for a reason for you to accept the locket. I know you are proud, and nothing else came to mind. The truth is, Selma, I really wanted you to have it because I like you so much."

He saw tears gather in her eyes, making them greener. He wanted to sink into their lovely depths.

Her words were soft, her voice shaky. "I accept your apology, Mr. Sinclair. I do. But you realize, of course, it would have been impossible for me to accept the locket under any circumstances. I must go now. I can't keep Mrs. King waiting."

As he lifted his hand to her cheek, she moved away. He had wanted just one brief touch, but she was gone. He watched her walk to her carriage, her proud shoulders high, and he despaired.

What has gotten into you, Jacob Sinclair?

Chapter 7

Perspiration beaded on Selma's forehead as she knelt on her hands and knees to push the red embers back into the fireplace before they caught the house on fire. She had gone to a guest bedroom to throw a log on the fire, causing the complete collapse of the crumbling wood under it. After ensuring the danger was gone, she clumsily sat on the floor to clean up the ashes and dust encircling her. Using her sleeve, she wiped the sweat mixed with tears from her face. She cringed when she heard the door open.

Mr. McAdams walked in. At first he laughed at the sight of Selma sprawled on the dirty floor. Then she supposed he saw the tears, because his face changed immediately. He walked toward her, his eyes tender, as he helped her up. "Selma, what happened?"

She allowed him to ease her to a standing position, tears still streaming. "I am so sorry. I laid another log on the fire, and it all fell out. I pushed the burning embers back in, but I was so afraid I would burn the house down. I know I am going to lose my position." She looked to him for comfort.

"You will not lose your job, my dear. No one has to know. Let me help you clean this mess, and you can be on your way. Do we have any rags to dampen? If you will sweep, I'll follow with a wet cloth."

"Oh sir, that wouldn't be proper. I couldn't allow it."

"Fiddlesticks. I helped my father on a farm as a boy. I can do anything."

Selma searched his face. "Really?"

He smiled. "Really. You must have a picture in your head of wealthy folk being served from their birth. Not true. Take Jacob Sinclair, for example. His family is in shipping. I've seen him and his father roll up their sleeves and help load the boats. Actually, his father began by laboring at the docks and worked his way up."

Selma felt heat rising to her face and lowered her eyes. "I didn't realize. It's just that I haven't gotten the impression—"

Shock gripped her as she felt his finger under her chin lifting her face.

"I'm sorry, Selma. I meant no harm. Surely I didn't want to embarrass you. I see you, too, have feelings for Jacob."

She steadied herself. "What do you mean when you say, 'You, too'?"

"I probably spoke out of turn. It's just that Jacob cares for you, and I think you must have affection for him. Enough on that thought. I didn't mean to bring it up. I can certainly see why he feels that way."

Now her face was burning. "Please, let's clean this mess. I have so much to do today. Miss McAllister wants all the greenery changed on the mantels. The other is wilting, and it's only a few days before Christmas. I need to hurry."

"Of course. I'll fetch a wet cloth."

Selma watched him enter the bathroom. *Thank You, Lord, for sending this nice man my way. And, Lord, have I misjudged Mr. Sinclair and his intentions?*

❄

Jacob looked up when his friend William entered the library. He was thankful no one else was around so he could speak openly. He motioned him over and put his newspaper on the side table. "Hello, William. I'm glad to see you. I didn't get to talk to you at breakfast."

"Yes, I'm sorry. I was cornered by our host." He smiled as he leaned toward Jacob and spoke quietly. "He is in love, you know."

"So I gathered. He's beginning to speak of her often."

"Um-hmm." He sat in the chair next to Jacob. "Speaking of love, I just had an encounter with your beautiful Selma."

"Really? How so?"

"She was sitting in the middle of the floor among ashes and dust when I entered my room. A log fell and knocked burning embers and ashes out of the grate. She was fearful I would tell, and she would lose her position."

Jacob laughed. "She was fearful of that the day I met her. She is something, is she not?"

"Yes, she is that. She blushed when I spoke your name."

"Why did you mention me?"

"She acted as if I was not supposed to help her. It's as if she thinks we do not ever work. I explained that we enjoy what we do and told her about you and your father laboring hard at times. She blushed. I told her you have feelings for her and that I gathered she returns the affection. She turned a bright scarlet then." William laughed.

Jacob didn't. "You probably scared her to death. She is

always talking about being proper."

"Tell me, Jacob, what are you going to do?"

"I haven't figured it out yet. I would love to talk to her at length. I had a short conversation with her after church Sunday, but she was in a hurry to catch her carriage."

"I happen to know she will be helping to change the greenery on the mantels today. Why don't we retire to the living hall, in case she comes in?"

Jacob picked up his newspaper. "I feel like a young man talking to a girl for the first time. I don't even know how to act around her. It's not like I haven't escorted lovely women to various events for years. It's just that she's so different."

"Well, you are not getting any younger, Jacob. I say we take advantage of this opportunity." William laughed as he stood.

Jacob rose from the chair. "I'd remind you, friend, you are but a year behind me. And so far, very behind in the race. At least I have feelings." He slapped William on the back as they left the room.

❄

Selma watched as the pinecone loosened from the wilting swag she was removing from the mantel. Her fingers shook as she listened to familiar voices nearing the living hall. She continued to gaze at the cone as it rolled from the mantel, hit the floor, and bounced over to the tip of a finely shined shoe.

Slowly she brought her gaze to the owner and faced an amused Mr. McAdams. "Oh my. I am so sorry." Selma spoke to Mr. McAdams, but Mr. Sinclair standing next to him held her attention. She only hoped neither gentleman heard the sound of her heart beating.

Mr. McAdams was the first to speak as he stooped to pick up the pinecone and hand it to her. "Whatever for? This is not the first pinecone to fall from its branches."

Selma noticed that Mr. Sinclair remained quiet, only a slight smile on his handsome face. She brought her attention back to Mr. McAdams as she tried to restore sensibility to the situation. After all, she did not want to give the impression she was always distraught. "You are quite right, Mr. McAdams. I appreciate your retrieving the cone for me."

Selma returned to her work. She sensed their presence, however, as they walked farther into the living hall and took seats on a nearby settee. She felt gooseflesh on her arms, as she didn't want them observing her working. Soon, though, they seemed deep in conversation and her nerves quieted.

As Selma stepped off the stool, she watched as the two men rose from their seat and faced the door by her. She turned to see Betsy flouncing in, wearing a huge smile and holding up her skirt and petticoats so high Selma could actually see her ankles.

Frowning, Selma whisked up an armful of greenery and stalked past the two men to the opposite side of the room. She greeted several other servants and assisted them as they hung swags of pine and cedar over the main entrance to the hall.

Intentionally not looking toward Mr. Sinclair and Mr. McAdams, Selma chatted and laughed as she worked. However, she could not help but catch bits of conversation

151

between them and Betsy.

Jacob's voice grated on her as he spoke. "Why, Betsy dear. Why don't you join us for dinner this evening? It's been a while since we've had a chance to chat."

"Jacob, you and I are bound by our similar thoughts. It would be a pleasure." Betsy held her hand for a kiss, which both gentlemen granted.

Selma let the greenery fall to the floor and hurried from the room. She had to get away from the two-faced man who had spoken of caring for her while, she could tell, he was mesmerized by someone else.

❄

Jacob watched her go. He assumed she had heard the invitation to Betsy. Little did she know he had invited Betsy because of William. They were not well acquainted, and he thought his friend might find Betsy charming.

He made his excuses to his friends and left them to fend for themselves. Determined to find Selma, he strode across the room and made his exit through the same door as she.

Not seeing her, Jacob hurried down the stairs and through the entrance hall, the conservatory, and the billiards room. He finally found her in the breakfast room. She was alone, struggling with a box of pine and cedar as she pulled it toward the mantel.

He rushed to help her. "Selma, my dear, I need to explain something."

Her look was cool. "And what, sir, would that be?"

"I wonder if you might have gotten the wrong idea when I asked Betsy to dinner. You see, I was asking for

William. Mr. McAdams. He seems to like her, shallow or not. However, I do think she has tried to change a little."

"And why should that be any of my business?"

"You know why. You know how I feel about you."

"I do? And I suppose you know how I feel about you?"

"I'm pretty sure I do." He smiled.

Selma lowered her eyes for a second. When she looked at him, her face showed concern. "But even if I have feelings, what good can it do? I've said we are from different worlds. We share nothing in common. Don't you see that? And can't you see how you respond so lightheartedly to Betsy. You are her kind."

"You can forget Betsy. She is nothing like me. What I see is that you and I appreciate humor. We can laugh. We both have similar attitudes about life. I am not a pretentious man. Surely you know that. We both believe in a God who created us and loves us. Who gave His Son for us. These are the important things, are they not?"

"I do believe you are a man of faith, Mr. Sinclair. But I am only a simple girl with a simple life. You have traveled and acquired a taste for things I know not. You can't really believe it won't make a difference."

"Selma, for the last time, my name is Jacob. All I know is that I love you. And, rest assured, you are knowledgeable about many things I am not. My main desire is to take you to those places. To marry you and take you home to New York and raise a family. I don't know how all this happened in so short a time. I have not even courted you. But I know it is real. And you do, too."

A noise in the room interrupted their conversation.

Mrs. King, the housekeeper, walked in, and the scorn in her face caused even Jacob to bristle. "Miss Bradford?"

"Yes, ma'am."

"Are you quite through here?"

"Not really, ma'am. I have the greenery to place on the mantel."

Jacob stepped forward and addressed Mrs. King. "I am sorry that I have caused Miss Bradford any lost time. I was having a brief conversation with her, but I am about to leave. Pardon me if I have stepped outside of my boundaries." He gave the housekeeper the dimpled smile, which he'd been told melted hearts.

He noticed that it wasn't lost on Mrs. King, who blushed and waved his apology away. "Nonsense. You haven't intruded at all, Mr. Sinclair. I am quite sure Miss Bradford enjoyed the respite."

But when Mrs. King stood her ground and didn't leave, Jacob gave a slight bow and left the room, a bit vexed at the unresolved conversation with Selma.

❋

Speechless, Selma stood by the breakfast room mantel. *He loves me?*

First came the clearing of the housekeeper's throat. Then the patting of the foot.

Selma's stomach quivered with each gesture, waiting for the much-feared dismissal.

Surprising Selma, Mrs. King smiled.

Selma stood still, bewildered.

Finally when Mrs. King's smile faded, she said to Selma, "Miss Bradford, is this where you are supposed to be?"

Her smile returned, so Selma was unsure what to expect. "No, ma'am."

"Then why are you here?"

Selma didn't know what to say.

Mrs. King seemed to be stifling laughter. It was almost as if it was about to overflow any minute.

"I was working in the living hall. I became a little flustered, so I came down here, thinking it wouldn't be so crowded."

"Uh-huh." Mrs. King's eyes glittered. "Could it have been that you were meeting a certain guest down here?"

"Oh no. I had no idea he would come to the breakfast room." Selma was happy to tell the truth.

"Well, Miss Bradford, the gentleman seemed smitten with you. I could see it in his eyes, in his very countenance. This happens. I saw it in England many times before coming here—love between two classes of people. And usually it is a servant or a governess a gentleman takes to. Would you like to know why?"

Selma felt the heat in her face. This was not quite what she expected. She just wanted the dismissal done with so she could abandon this situation. But she straightened to her full height, squared her shoulders, and looked Mrs. King straight in the eye, sure her supervisor would belittle her. "Why, ma'am?"

"Because people like us are sincere. We know what life is really about. And since we have so much less than them, we can appreciate everything, the small and the large. So Miss Bradford, don't ruin your chance in life if this gentleman is taken with you. If he is a fine, upstanding Christian man, then good luck to you. But let this be between you and me. And please, Miss Bradford, no matter what the circumstance in life, we do our work, when and where needed. Understood?" She turned, not waiting for a response, her long skirt brushing against a chair as she left the room, chuckling softly.

An amused wonder relaxed Selma's stiffened body, one limb at a time. She was, to say the least, flabbergasted. Jacob declared his love. And Mrs. King encouraged it.

❅

Jacob asked William for a private word after dinner. They strolled to the bachelors' wing, bypassing the smoking room, as Jacob didn't like the stifling air. They settled in the gun room, closing the door behind them.

William looked at his friend. "What's on your mind?"

"I have reached a decision, and I need your help."

"Certainly. What have you decided, and what can I do?"

"I am going to marry Selma. I just need you to help me devise a plan how to do that. And help me carry it out."

"You sure have faith in me, my friend. But I will do what I can. But how to do it? Just ask her."

"You know it's not that simple. Somehow I have to create a situation where she finds it difficult to refuse. Where her mind can't so easily be changed. Listen. What if I have it all prearranged for Christmas Eve at the ball? You know, someone can fetch her and bring her down so I can propose marriage."

"Jacob, I know better than to ask this, but are you demented?"

Jacob winced. "No, of course not. But what do you think?"

"Just how do you propose pulling this off?" William leaned forward. "By the way, you want my help, but you seem to have it all planned."

"I want you to tell me it'll work. But I really need your help to carry this off."

"I see. So where will she get a dress?"

"I'm working on that."

"And the ring?"

"I have something else in mind for now. I think that is handled."

"And a willing lady?"

"Yes. That, too. How can she refuse when she sees the trouble I've gone to?"

"Do you know how preposterous this sounds?"

"Perhaps. But it is the only thing I think will work. Selma is so adamant about our different stations in life. I have to provide the conditions whereby she might not refuse me."

"And have you run this by George? It is, after all, his party."

"He is keen on the idea. He's in love, too, so this is so fitting."

"It's a risk, friend. But I'll do whatever I can. Count me in."

"Thanks. Oh, and you can keep Betsy busy. She is one of the problems, I think."

"Jacob, I'd be glad to do that." He winked.

Chapter 8

Jacob had devised a plan, but he admitted to himself he would need a woman's help buying the dress. He knew Selma was friends with Rosie, a chambermaid he had encountered on several occasions. He had enlisted Mrs. King in arranging a meeting with Rosie and now was on his way to the tapestry room.

He saw the petite redhead immediately when he walked in. Anticipation was predominant in her expression. He thought she would be a good cohort.

Rosie stood nervously by the window when he took her hand and raised it to his lips for a light kiss. Her blush brought a smile as he greeted her. "Rosie, I'm so glad you could meet with me. Please have a seat."

"Yes, sir." Rosie almost fell into the chair as he sat across from her on a settee, her eyes round, questioning.

He bypassed the small talk and went straight to the matter he wanted to discuss. "Rosie, I need help. I have arranged with Mrs. King for you to take an afternoon off and help me find a dress for Selma to wear to the Christmas Eve ball."

She looked stunned. "The ball? Selma?"

He had not wanted to give all the details but decided he must take her into his trust. "I plan to propose that evening. I must ask you to keep this to yourself. No one is to know. This has to be a surprise."

"I don't know what to say." Rosie clapped her hands together. "Of course I will be glad to assist you. I do know Selma is in love with you. Convincing her is another matter."

"I know it is out of the ordinary, but Rosie, you seem to know Selma believes we are two worlds apart. I have tried to convince her we are not. We are just two people who fell in love. If I don't surprise her with this plan, then I'm afraid I will lose her. I'll be leaving after Christmas and may never get another chance."

"I see your point. When are we to go?"

"Tomorrow. I have other business in the village first, so I will pick you up at one at the stable yard. Everything is arranged, so don't worry. Please don't let Selma know what you are doing. Do we have an agreement?"

"Certainly. I will see you then."

Jacob stood and took her hand to help her rise. "Thank you, Rosie. Selma and I will always remember your friendship and assistance."

❋

Jacob's first stop was the mercantile in Biltmore Village to see if they still had the locket Selma loved. He was delighted to find the keepsake and had it wrapped in their finest paper. He then went by the orphanage before traveling back to Biltmore to pick Rosie up for their excursion to Asheville to procure Selma's dress. He hoped he and Rosie could find something perfect. His mind was constantly running through the plan.

The knock on the door was answered by Miss Caps. "Good morning, Mr. Sinclair." Then she frowned. "Is anything wrong?"

"Oh no. I'm sorry if I startled you. I would like a few words with you."

"Certainly, please come in. Would you like some tea?"

"No thank you. I only have a moment."

Miss Caps led Jacob into the small parlor and sat in a chair, offering him the faded red settee opposite her. "You're doing well?"

"Yes, very well. Which is what I need to discuss with you." Jacob paused, thinking of Selma. He smiled at Miss Caps. "To be blunt, I am about to propose to Selma on Christmas Eve, and I would love for you and Melissa to attend the ball. Of course I would send a carriage for you. And I still need to contact Selma's sister, Peggy, at Reynolds House. She would also share the carriage with you." Jacob paused a second as another thought struck him. "With your permission, of course. Will you give us your blessing?"

Miss Caps brought her hand to her chest. "I honestly feel this is too sudden. But I have seen how you look at each other. I really believe God has a hand in this. So yes, Mr. Sinclair, I will give you my blessing and pray all goes according to God's plan." She scanned his face. "What about your family?"

Jacob really needed to be on his way. "As far as my family is concerned, I have penned them. However, the deed will be done by the time they receive the message. I can't wait for them to meet Selma. My father will be supportive, my mother skeptical for a time, but they will love her. I have been praying about it."

"Mr. Sinclair, this is a very romantic story, but I don't

think my high-minded Selma will take to this scheme so easily. I hope you do not find yourself embarrassed. I do think Peggy may have gone with the Reynolds family to see relatives for the holidays. But I can assure you, Melissa and I will be there to support Selma. I wish you the best."

Jacob stood and bent to take Miss Caps's hand. He kissed it lightly. "Good. I will have the carriage here at seven. Give Melissa my regards. I am sure she is in school?"

"Yes, and when she returns, I will tell her everything."

Jacob nodded. "Please don't get up. I can see myself out." He hurried. There was more to be done.

❅

Rosie stuck her head between the door and the frame. "Selma? Are you okay? I missed you at breakfast and didn't see you during early morning chores."

Selma raised her head so that the quilt lowered to show her puffy eyes. "Sorry."

Rosie inched her way in, softly closing the door behind her. She sat on the side of Selma's bed. "Want to tell your best friend?"

"No."

"Okay. I'll just sit here and keep you company until you do."

Selma sat up. "No. Please, go away."

"It can't be that bad. And how are you getting away with this? Have you seen Maggie?"

"She came looking for me. I told her I felt ill. And, Rosie, I do."

"You don't look ill to me, Selma Bradford. You've been crying is all. What is the matter?"

Selma fell back onto the bed. "It's a mess. Everything. I'm going to try to find a position somewhere in Asheville."

"What's a mess? Is this about Mr. Sinclair?"

"He says he loves me."

"And that is something to cry about?" Rosie pointed her hands toward her chest. "I'd be shouting with joy."

Selma sat up again. "Really? You wouldn't be scared?"

"Of what?"

"That you'd be so different—a servant—when he is so wealthy and has been everywhere? When he is used to large homes and grand ladies?"

"No, I can't see why it matters if he loves you. And, Selma, I can really tell he does."

"Or maybe I'm just something he can't have. He's so used to getting everything he wants, I'm sure. But then I think what a fine Christian man I believe him to be. I'm so confused. But I appreciate your words. And you are right. I am not really ill. I need to get up and dress now, Rosie. I have work to do."

"Good for you. I'll see you at lunch. I know you have to be hungry."

As Selma rushed to dress for the day, she realized she had no appetite. Her churning thoughts of Jacob had taken it completely away.

❄

A saleslady approached Jacob and Rosie at one of the finer clothing stores in Asheville. "Hello, I'm Mrs. Hanks. How may I assist you?"

"What would you carry that someone would wear to a

Christmas Eve affair—a banquet and ball?"

Mrs. Hanks looked at Rosie. "For you?"

"No, ma'am. I'm just helping with the size and all."

Mrs. Hanks gave a knowing nod. "Please, dear, come with me."

Jacob was offended by the look on the saleslady's face. He felt she was thinking in error. So he told a brief account of what was taking place.

Mrs. Hanks laughed. "Well, this is my first time to encounter this dilemma." She smiled at Jacob. "Sit and I'll fix you some tea, sir. You can rest while we look."

Jacob settled in a comfortable chair in a room adjacent to the shopping area and selected a local newspaper to read while he drank his tea. He had not finished reading when Mrs. Hanks and Rosie brought in the perfect dress and shoes to match.

❄

It had been a long, tiring Christmas Eve workday. Selma plopped onto her bed to rest. All the guest rooms on her floor were filled now, and each servant was assigned extra rooms to attend.

At four the servants' party had been held in the grand entrance hall. They'd enjoyed an assortment of pastries and punch. Mr. Vanderbilt reached under the large and heavily adorned Christmas tree and gave each a present. All the ladies received elegant hand mirrors. Selma lovingly placed hers on the dresser when she returned to her room.

Selma knew the servants in the three kitchens were busy preparing the Christmas Eve dinner to be served in the banquet hall. She was glad her chores were finished, except to check the rooms later in the evening to ensure there was plenty of wood on the fires. She drifted off to sleep, wondering what it might be like to be a part of the festivities that would take place that evening.

A loud knock awoke her. She ambled to the door in a half daze to face Maggie holding, hopefully, something besides clothes for her to darn or clean. It looked like a guest's dress.

"Yes, ma'am?"

"You are to put these on and immediately go to the banquet hall." She handed her a dress and a pair of shoes.

Selma looked at the items and back at Maggie. "Why?"

Maggie's face showed no answers. "I don't know. Just do it." Maggie handed her the clothes and shut the door.

Selma laid them across the bed and stared a long time before running to get Rosie.

After following Selma to her room, Rosie, too, glanced at the clothes. "Why, Selma?"

"I don't know. But if I don't do what they say, I may lose my position. So help me dress."

"I'll put your hair up, too." They searched in Selma's little box, ragged with age, and found a perfect comb to hold her hair in place.

Selma stood back and looked in the mirror of her dresser. "Oh my." She took in the ivory gown, with its small covered buttons. She held up her arm to look at the soft lace covering the ends of her sleeves. Tendrils of hair fell on her slender neck, exposed by the soft scoop of her bodice. She needed some pearls or something to adorn her neck but had nothing appropriate.

Rosie pinched Selma's cheeks for color and told her she was beautiful.

After sliding her feet into her shoes and fastening the few buttons over her toes, she was ready. She hugged Rosie, who was smiling mischievously. At what, she did not know. She was glad, at least, Rosie found it amusing. Then she was gone.

❄

Jacob watched from the corner of the banquet hall as Selma gracefully entered and was greeted by William. As they talked, Jacob slipped out and went to the winter garden. He was so proud of her and thought she looked beautiful. Mrs. Hanks and Rosie had picked the perfect dress. He waited on the bench and watched for her arrival.

William walked her to the inside garden's door and indicated Jacob's presence before leaving.

As she drew near, Jacob stood and held out his hand. She took it, hesitancy combining with a soft smile on her face.

Jacob smiled back. "Selma, dear, you are so beautiful this evening. Please have a seat."

Gingerly holding her dress, she lowered herself onto the stone bench. She never took her eyes from him.

He sat beside her as he pulled a box from his jacket pocket. He looked into her eyes, made greener by the contrast of the ivory dress. "Selma, I brought you a Christmas present. Would you please open it and accept it as a gift of love?"

She took the package and slowly removed the wrapping. When she lifted the lid off the small box, she gasped. She raised her face and looked at him wonderingly. It was the locket she had admired at the mercantile.

"Please take it out."

She removed the heart-shaped locket and held it in her hand.

Jacob saw a tear running down her cheek. "Here, let me." He took the locket, stood, and placed it around her neck. As he worked with the small chain, he talked to her, his voice low. "Selma, I love you. I want to marry you." He sat after clasping the chain. "Miss Caps and Melissa are here. They have given their blessing, along with Rosie, who helped me purchase your dress."

He edged off the bench and dropped to his knees. "Would you do me the honor of being my wife?"

Large tears escaped Selma's eyes. She took the offered handkerchief. "Oh Jacob. I have been so wrong. Last night I read Jeremiah 29:11. God does have a plan for each of us, and He has presented me with the opportunity to marry someone I love. How could I fight that? Of course I will be your wife. I'll try hard to make you a good one."

Jacob stood and took her hand, coaxing her to her feet. He gently kissed her cheek. "Selma, I can only ask that you remain true to yourself. After all, you are the woman with whom I fell in love. Let's join the others for a celebration of our Lord and a celebration of our love."

"Yes. I'm afraid, Jacob, but I will follow your lead."

"You are the most beautiful lady here. And the kindest.

Hold your head high, for you, Selma, are made perfect in the Lord." He led her to the dining table, just in time for the blessing.

After the annual Christmas feast, George Vanderbilt gave a short speech to his friends before asking Jacob and Selma to join him at the end of the banquet table for an announcement.

Jacob took Selma's hand and faced her. "Selma, I love you with all my heart, and I'm sure God has placed you in my life for a reason." He turned toward the guests. "I have proposed marriage to this wonderful lady, and she has accepted." Jacob glanced around the room and chuckled. "I know some of you wonder why she would."

Laughter and a few remarks reiterated his statement. Jacob saw Betsy departing in a huff, but he continued. "We have not planned our wedding, but whether it is here or in New York, we hope you will attend. More importantly, keep us in your prayers.

Deafening applause broke out in the banquet hall as people congratulated them. Jacob turned to see if Selma realized her acceptance among his peers. Her joyful countenance told him she understood. He took her in his arms and kissed her before everyone.

The applause resumed even louder. Some were leaving their seats. The first ones to offer hugs were Mama Elsie and Melissa. Jacob was overwhelmed at the joy he saw on their faces.

As the celebration continued, Jacob escorted Selma around the room and introduced her to his friends. At one point they stood by the door, and he glanced toward the banister circling the second floor. "Selma, look up there. Rosie is trying to get your attention." He hugged Selma to him as she waved at Rosie.

"Jacob, Rosie's smile is one of the best presents we could receive." She touched his cheek. "But she also has received a wonderful present this Christmas. . .the gift of salvation through the Lord of all—the baby in the manger, Jesus."

Jacob tilted Selma's head toward his and kissed her again, tightening his embrace. "And so have we."

Sylvia Barnes thought after retiring early as a manager for BellSouth (now AT&T), she would sit on a swing and drink coffee. However, she opened a gift shop/tea room for three years, served as a part-time court clerk/deputy city clerk, and worked in her county's after school enrichment program before finding a yellow pad on which she penned her first novel. Sylvia teaches a ladies' Sunday school class and is active in many church activities. She and her husband, J. W., live in the country outside of Pelahatchie, Mississippi, with numerous dogs, cats, armadillos, and moles. They have two grown daughters and three grandchildren.

A HONEY OF A CHRISTMAS

Rhonda Gibson

Dedication

To Atalyse Baron. I love you, Honey Bee.

Chapter 1

PEGGY'S CINNAMON ROLLS

Fall 1898

"M iss Bradford. I see you are late returning," the head cook reprimanded. He moved on without a backward glance.

Peggy Bradford hurried to her station. She glanced down at the recipe she'd laid out earlier, along with the proper ingredients, and then began mixing dough for her specialty, cinnamon rolls.

She didn't make an excuse, simply continued to work. Later Peggy would explain that she'd been stopped by a guest who had stumbled into the wrong hallway, looking for additional towels for his morning dip in the pool. She'd leave out the part where he'd invited her to join him. Heat filled her cheeks at the thought.

She took the dough that she'd just prepared and rolled it out into a twelve-by-nine-inch rectangle. Next Peggy spread a mixture of butter and sugar over the dough. While her hands worked, her gaze moved about the busy kitchen. Kitchen cooks and assistants rushed about, preparing breakfast for the guests of Mr. Vanderbilt. Tantalizing scents of warm yeast and baking bread filled the air, bringing her comfort and a sense of deep pleasure in what she did.

During the short time she'd worked here, Peggy had come to marvel at the activity around her. Men and women worked side by side to create wonderful breads and sweets for the Vanderbilt family. She couldn't contain the happy feeling that traveled up her tummy and into her face as she realized she was now a part of the Biltmore house.

Peggy felt deep gratitude that Mrs. Reynolds had talked her into working for Mrs. Vanderbilt. The pastry kitchen had tiled floors and walls for easy maintenance and was stocked with the latest in culinary equipment. Her work-table top was marble, which helped keep her dough from sticking to the surface.

Her hands worked of their own accord as she rolled the dough up and pinched the seam to seal. She'd made these cinnamon rolls most of her life. At Reynolds House, she made them every day, only not in the amounts needed at Biltmore.

Peggy cut the prepared dough into rolls and placed the cut side up in a lightly greased pan. Automatically her hand reached for the ingredients to create another batch of dough. As far as Peggy was concerned, Biltmore proved by far the grandest place she'd ever seen or worked in.

"Miss Bradford, please join me."

Peggy looked up at the chef who had called her name. He was an older gentleman with a slight limp. A veined hand waved in the air as he motioned for Peggy to step into the hallway. Had the head chef given Chef McConnell the job of reprimanding her for her tardiness?

She stood before him with her hands clasped in front of her fresh red-checkered pinafore. Her eyes met his. Of all the chefs in the kitchen, he was her favorite. Chef McConnell always had a kind word, and he enjoyed showing her how to prepare the dishes he worked on. It was a pleasure to set up his worktable in the mornings. But no matter how kind and likable he was, Peggy dreaded the scolding she felt sure he'd been assigned to administer. Peggy's hands trembled. She clasped them tighter to conceal any movement.

Chef McConnell cleared his throat before speaking in a quiet voice. "Miss Bradford, I realize this is your afternoon off, but would you be so kind as to make a trip to the gardens?"

Relief washed over her as she realized he had no intention of scolding her. "Of course." She fought to keep her lips from smiling.

For a brief moment, pleasure softened his features. Just as quickly, the stern set of his jaw tightened. "The honey wasn't delivered this morning, and we do not have enough for the evening meal. If you leave shortly after lunch, you should be able to ask the head gardener for the missing honey, and they'll bring it here in time for the last meal of the day."

Peggy nodded. The honey wagon normally arrived at the estate early in the morning. What could have happened to it today? She'd heard a new man had taken over the apiary; maybe he'd lost track of time.

The chef allowed a small smile to touch his lips and eyes before composing his face once more. "Good. I knew I could count on you." He walked back into the kitchen.

Then it dawned on her what he'd asked. She'd have to give up her afternoon trip home. She might even have to go near an apiary. Her hands began to shake once more. The clearing of a throat drew her attention back to the pastry kitchen.

The head chef caught her eye, frowned at her, and indicated with the motion of his head that she should return to work.

No longer did the smell of yeast and rising bread fill her with joy. Would she have to go close to an apiary? The thought of being near honeybees filled her with dread. One sting and Peggy knew she would probably die.

Peggy continued to make cinnamon rolls, but her heart wasn't in it anymore. The plans she'd made to go to the village to see her sister and Mama Elsie would have to wait, and she'd have to figure out a way to stay far from the actual apiary. *Lord, please keep me safe as I do my job this afternoon.*

"Miss Bradford! Where are those rolls?"

The question shook her from her thoughts, and she hurried to the oven to pull out several sheets of cinnamon sweetness. Peggy knew that she'd had a bad morning. The head chef would have no problem releasing her from duty if she didn't focus on the job at hand. She pushed all thoughts of bees, honey, and her lost trip home from her mind.

Later Peggy looked at the clock and sighed. Where had the morning gone? She cleaned up her worktable and waited for Chef McConnell to inspect it before allowing her to leave.

At his quick nod of approval, she hurried from the room.

Outside the door she questioned whether she should change clothes to inquire about the honey or wear her uniform. Officially she was off for the afternoon, so she could change into a simple day dress. But she'd also been asked to go to the gardens for the honey. A quick look over her shoulder told her Chef McConnell already had begun working on another pastry and that she shouldn't bother him.

Making the decision to go to her room and change into a day dress, she hurried down the hall.

❄

Mark Ludman enjoyed the cool afternoon breeze. He'd spent his morning at the apiary and the new orchard, and now he fixed the wheel on the wagon he used to deliver honey to the big house.

He thought himself lucky to have landed such a nice job at the Biltmore estate. Thankfully his main job, the care of the apiary, didn't take as much time now as it did in the spring and summer. The bees were preparing for winter, giving him time to help bring in the harvest.

The sound of humming caught his attention, and he looked up from the repaired wheel. A young woman wearing a light-blue dress with a matching bonnet walked toward him. He leaned against the wagon and waited for her to draw closer. She lifted her head and allowed the cool breeze to blow the ribbons of her bonnet about her face.

Unaware of his presence, she plucked a dandelion and blew the white cap off, a smile teasing her lips as it floated on the light breeze.

"Good afternoon," he called to her.

She startled and dropped the stem, looking his direction. "Hello."

He knew that the jagged scar down the right side of his face, which he'd acquired as a child while playing in the barn, gave him a haggard look that frightened most women. Mark offered a smile as he asked, "Can I help you find someone?" He pushed away from the wagon and came to stand beside her on the road.

She folded her hands within the skirt of her dress, took a deep breath, and answered. "I need to see the head gardener about delivering honey to the kitchens. It seems that we don't have enough for this evening's meal."

Mark extended his hand. "I'm Mark Ludman. I think I can help you with the honey situation."

Her warm palm felt small and soft within his hand.

"I'm Miss Bradford. How can you help me, Mr. Ludman? Are you the gardener I need to see?" She pulled her fingers from his and tucked them back into the folds of her dress.

"Not exactly. I'm more of an assistant to the gardener."

She lifted her chin. "I see. Then how can you help me?"

He admired the way she handled the situation. In his experience with women, most would have been startled by his sudden appearance, and some would have even been fearful. If this young woman were either, she didn't show it. "I can drive the honey wagon up to the main house and since it's loaded with honey, that should take care of your problem."

Miss Bradford's light-blue eyes twinkled in the sunlight. "Thank you. That would be most helpful."

Mark walked back to the wagon. He pulled himself up onto the seat, removed the brake, and clicked his tongue to get the mares moving forward. When he came even with her, Mark stopped. "May I offer you a ride?" He waited for her to decide what she wanted to do. For a brief moment, he thought she might decline his offer. Silently he prayed she wouldn't.

She looked up at him. "That would be most kind, Mr. Ludman."

"Call me Mark." He set the brake and jumped down to assist her into the wagon.

When she was seated and he'd climbed back onto the wagon, she replied, "Thank you, Mr. Ludman, but it would be most improper of me to address you by your given name."

Warm laughter burst from his lips. Mark watched a light blush travel up her neck and into her cheeks. Strong, yet modest. Was it possible he'd met the woman of his dreams on the Biltmore estate?

Peggy's Cinnamon Rolls

Ingredients:

  1 pint flour
  1 tablespoon sugar
  ½ teaspoon salt
  2 teaspoons baking powder
  2 tablespoons butter
  Milk, enough to soften dough
  Powdered cinnamon, to taste

Instructions:

Sift together flour, sugar, salt, and baking powder. Rub in butter; mix with milk to soften dough. Roll out ½ inch thick, spread with soft butter, granulated sugar, and powdered cinnamon. Roll up like jelly roll, cut in 1-inch slices, lay close together in buttered greased pan; bake.

Chapter 2

OATMEAL COOKIES

Peggy enjoyed the sound of Mark Ludman's laughter. She sensed deep down that he wasn't laughing at her, but that he simply appreciated her straightforwardness. At least she hoped that was the case.

From the corner of her eye, she admired the way his muscles worked as he guided the horses up to the big house. His dark brown hair and eyes seemed to sparkle in the afternoon sunshine. Laugh lines had formed around his mouth and face, giving him the appearance of an easy-natured man. Of course Peggy couldn't be sure her thoughts were true, but she did enjoy entertaining them just the same. The scar that ran from his right temple to his jaw marred his otherwise handsome face.

"What do you do at the big house?"

Peggy realized she'd been staring and ducked her head to hide her embarrassment at being caught. "I'm one of the pastry cook's assistants."

"Ah, that would explain the sweet scents of vanilla and cinnamon." He inhaled as if smelling her.

Peggy felt warmth fill her cheeks. "Yes, I suppose I might

carry the scents of baking."

He laughed. "You smell like cinnamon and spice and everything nice."

She joined in his laughter. "Well, that's what little girls are made of." Once more she realized he'd put her at ease. Men normally made her feel awkward and skittish.

"Might I ask another question?"

Peggy felt her lips twitch. "And what might that be?"

"How long have you worked at the Biltmore estate?" He clicked his tongue to prod the animals to move a little faster.

She adjusted her bonnet. "Not long."

He quirked an eyebrow in a silent question.

Peggy felt she needed to explain. "Mrs. Vanderbilt visited Reynolds House on a day that I'd made cinnamon rolls. At Mrs. Vanderbilt's request, I'm working at Biltmore during the holidays. After that I shall return to my normal position at Reynolds House. How long have you been here, Mr. Ludman?"

"I'm new here as well. Since you work in the kitchen, I assume you have long hours?"

She squirmed on her seat. "I work a split day, so the hours aren't too tiring."

"A split day?"

"Yes, I work from four to ten in the morning and then again from four to eight in the evening." She looked at her hands. Her hours were different from the other kitchen staff, but that was the schedule Mrs. Reynolds and Mrs. Vanderbilt agreed upon. Peggy knew Mrs. Reynolds requested the split so she'd have rest in the middle of the day. She didn't bother telling the man beside her that she also got every Sunday off to visit her family.

Mark pulled the team up to the delivery door and jumped from the wagon. He helped her down and smiled into her eyes. His hands rested on her waist a tad too long. She stepped away. "I hope we meet again, Miss Bradford."

She nodded her agreement. "Thank you for the ride, Mr. Ludman." Peggy turned to walk inside.

Just as she would have slipped into the door, she heard him say in a soft, deep voice, "Sugar and spice and everything nice, that's what Miss Bradford is made of."

❋

Peggy hurried to her room to savor her meeting with Mark Ludman. He seemed like a nice enough man, but men could be deceiving, at least that's what Mama Elsie always said. Elsie Caps wasn't really her mama, but since she'd raised her and her sisters, they'd taken to calling her Mama Elsie at an early age.

Peggy dropped into the chair in her room and sighed. He wasn't the handsomest man in the state of North Carolina, but he wasn't exactly ugly, either. She found him handsome in his own charming way. She felt drawn by his warm eyes; they reminded her of brown sugar. And he had such an easy smile. The scar didn't bother her; she felt it added character to his attractive features. She pulled her thoughts from the flaw. It didn't matter how he acquired it. In her eyes he was still good looking.

What would Selma and Charity think of Mark Ludman? Both of her sisters were now married, and they'd met their husbands on the Biltmore estate. Was she following in their footsteps? The thought brought a grin to her face. She was the oldest, and they'd always followed her around. Now was it her turn to do as they'd done?

"Don't be a silly girl, Peggy. You aren't going to be here long enough to fall in love at Biltmore." The chair rocked gently as she pushed out of it and looked to the alarm clock beside her bed. It was too late now to go into the village. Disappointment settled deep within her chest. She'd been looking forward to seeing Mama Elsie and Melissa, her youngest sister.

Peggy picked up the novel she'd been reading and walked out the door once more. If she couldn't go home, she'd do the next best thing and head to her favorite spot along the river to read. But first she'd stop by the pantry and find a snack to take with her.

Later, settled with her book under the shade of a bald cypress tree, she leaned against the firm trunk and sighed. Peggy held her face up to the warming sun. She so enjoyed early fall days and the scent of autumn in the air.

This wasn't as nice as going home, but she loved being in nature, enjoying the splendor of God's creations. The front of the Biltmore estate still showed signs of its construction, but here by the river, everything looked the same. Woods, river, and the sounds of nature surrounded her.

She settled the small bag that held an apple, chunk of cheese, and a couple of oatmeal cookies beside her. A flock of geese flew overhead. Their honks and squawks filled the afternoon breeze and gave her a sense of peace.

After several long moments, she opened her book and began to read. A soft *plunk* drew her attention. Peggy lifted her head and listened. After several more seconds, she went back to reading. Again she heard the sound. Laying the book to the side, Peggy stood and looked about.

A young boy fished a little ways down the riverbank. He pulled back his pole, and she watched as the cork flew through the air and landed on the water's surface with a *plunk*. He waited a few moments and then pulled his line from the water. It was obvious to her that he was impatient and wasn't allowing enough time for the fish to notice the worm that wiggled on the end of his hook.

Selma had been the same way when she was a little girl. Peggy walked the short distance to the boy. "Hello."

He looked up. Light-blue eyes studied her for a moment before he cast his line into the water again. "Hi," the young boy answered, not taking his gaze off the cork.

Sandy red hair shone in the sun. He really needed a hat. Peggy couldn't help the motherly feeling that washed over her. She'd been mothering all her life so wasn't surprised by the emotion. "How's the fishing?"

He grunted. "Not so good. I don't think they are biting today." The line whipped out of the water once more.

"Maybe you aren't leaving your line in long enough," she suggested, offering a smile.

A frown marred his freckled face. "Maybe."

"I used to fish with my sisters." When he didn't comment, she offered, "I'm Peggy."

She watched as he sighed, laid his pole down, and

walked over to her. He extended his hand. "I'm Joshua, but everyone calls me Josh."

As soon as she released his small hand, he returned to the fishing pole.

As he picked it up, his eyes cut toward her. Peggy couldn't control the smile that crossed her face. She knew he wanted to jerk the line out again but refrained from doing so.

Instead, he asked, "What are you doing out here?"

It was a fair and blunt question. "It's my afternoon off. I was reading a book when I heard you."

"Oh. I'm sorry I disturbed you."

She grinned at him. "You didn't disturb me. My curiosity got the better of me, and I just had to see how the fishing was going."

He pulled the line out and began to gather his things.

Peggy frowned. "What are you doing?"

"I'm leaving so you can read in peace. Papa says that days off should be enjoyed, and that I shouldn't bother any of the adults." Josh picked up his pole.

She hated that she'd ruined his fishing. "Wait! I don't want you to go."

Josh faced her. "You don't?" The disbelief and distrust on his face caused those motherly instincts to kick in again.

"No. We can share the riverbank. I would enjoy having someone to talk to."

He studied her face. Josh seemed like the type of boy who'd made a habit of studying faces. Something in hers must have agreed with him, because he nodded. "Then I'll stay."

"Good, I'll go get my book." Peggy hurried to the tree where she'd left the hardback and her bag. She scooped them up and hurried back. A quick glance around the area revealed a tree not far from the boy, and she settled on the ground beside it.

Josh returned to his place at the water's edge, rebaited his hook, and began casting.

She noted he now left the line in the water a little longer. Her gaze moved up to the sky. It wasn't that late in the afternoon. Why wasn't he in school?

"May I ask you a question, Josh?"

"I don't see why not."

"Good. How old are you?"

"Ten. How old are you?"

Another fair question. "I'm almost twenty-four." *An old maid.*

Peggy decided to push that thought down. She'd not met the right man, and even those she had met and considered for marriage had wanted to leave the area. Until her sisters were all settled, Peggy had no intentions of moving anywhere.

Josh seemed satisfied with her answer and continued fishing. His gaze returned to her several times, but he didn't start a new conversation.

Peggy picked up her book and tried to read, but too many questions ran through her mind. Why wasn't he in school? Had he skipped to go fishing? What made him seem so leery of her?

She dug into the small bag and pulled out a Buncombe

apple. It crunched as she bit into the tender skin. Joshua turned in her direction. Peggy grinned. "Are you hungry? I have oatmeal cookies and some cheese I can share."

"No thanks." He returned to staring at the cork that bobbed in the water. His young shoulders slumped, and he seemed deep in thought.

"Josh, why aren't you in school?" Peggy asked, aware that it was none of her business. The boy had been pretty direct with her so far, so she hoped he'd answer her question.

Time passed slowly as the geese continued honking and flying overhead. Peggy glanced up at them and waited. They formed a lopsided vee shape. Soon the birds were only a black speck in the sky, and she turned her attention back to the boy.

She couldn't see his face and wondered if he was simply going to ignore her question, or was he struggling with how to answer her? Peggy picked up her book and tried to focus on the words once more.

"I didn't go. I should have, but. . ." He stopped speaking and cast his line. A frown marred his young face, making him appear older.

Peggy moved to the bank, where she sat beside where he stood. She kept her voice soft and prayed it didn't sound too much like an adult's. "Why didn't you go?"

He sat, too. "I've never told another soul but. . ."

She hesitated, afraid to push him.

His gaze moved to the book in her hand. "But maybe you can help me. If you have the time, that is." His blue eyes met hers and held them.

"I'll help if I can," she promised, making sure not to break eye contact with him.

He looked away. "That's just it, you might not can. The other boys say I'm too dumb."

Children could be so harsh to one another. Her heart ached at the look of sorrow and hurt she had seen in his eyes. Peggy reached out and took his hand. "Why don't you tell me how I can help, and we'll prove those other boys wrong." She gave it a reassuring squeeze.

He pulled his hand out from under hers and whispered, "I can't read."

She looked down at the cover of her book. In bold letters she read *A Christmas Carol* by Charles Dickens. She'd read the Christmas story twice now and loved it. Reading was her favorite pastime. The words within books took her to other places and let her experience life through other people's eyes. She couldn't imagine a life without reading.

Peggy's gaze lifted to the stream. "I'll help you," she promised. But how? Would she be able to come to the stream every day? And when it grew colder, would he be able to come to her or her to him? She needed more information.

"Have you told your parents?"

He watched the cork bob in the water. "No, my mother died when I was three, and Papa is just too busy."

Peggy was no stranger to the heartache of losing one's mother at an early age. She wanted to reach out and hug him. "When you say your father is too busy, do you mean you've asked for his help, and he's been too busy for you?"

"No, Papa doesn't know. He would help, but it would

take him away from his work, and that wouldn't be good. Grandpapa says I should leave Papa be, that he has much too much to do. He says reading's not that important, anyway." He pulled the line out of the water and set the pole beside them. "I need to go get another worm. Seems mine has jumped off the hook."

Peggy watched him go in search of a place to dig up a worm. She walked back to her spot under the tree and picked up the book and bag. What kind of man told his grandchild not to bother his parent? And that reading wasn't important? She shook her head. Her anger grew as she thought about the boy's father. How could he not know his son couldn't read? Didn't he help Josh with his homework? Read to him at night?

Her hand caressed the front of the book in her lap. Reading was her form of escape; it took her to places she'd never visit in real life and gave her many hours of pleasure. Reading recipe books and copying them helped her do her job. How could someone say that wasn't important? Or not be aware that his child couldn't read?

Josh returned and threaded the worm onto his hook. "Will you still help me, Miss Peggy?" His eyes held hope and desperation.

"Only on one condition." She rejoined him on the bank.

He cast his line and then met her gaze. "What's that?"

She held out the small bag. "You have to try my new oatmeal cookie recipe."

Oatmeal Cookies

Ingredients:
  1 egg
  ¼ cup sugar
  ¼ cup thin cream
  ¼ cup milk
  ½ cup fine oatmeal
  2 cups flour
  2 teaspoons baking powder
  1 teaspoon salt

Instructions:
Beat egg until light; add sugar, cream, and milk; then add oatmeal, flour, baking powder, and salt, mixed and sifted. Toss on a floured board, roll, cut in shape, and bake in a moderate oven.

Chapter 3

YUMMY APPLE CAKE

Mark followed the trail that led to the stream where he knew Joshua would be fishing. His teacher, Miss Hart, had stopped by the apiary to inform him the boy hadn't returned after lunch. Much to his amazement, he'd discovered Joshua had a habit of not returning after lunch.

He heard laughter and splashing and followed the sound. "If that boy is with a girl, I'm going to tan his hide," he muttered, pushing aside a tree limb.

And then he stopped. His son stood on the bank with Miss Bradford. For the first time in a long time, Joshua was laughing and having a good time. He watched as his son held up a wiggling fish for Miss Bradford's inspection.

"I think this is the biggest one yet, Miss Peggy."

Her name whispered across his tongue. "Peggy." It tasted almost as sweet as it sounded. Mark shook his head. What man stands in the shadows and thinks about a woman's name like that? He stepped into the clearing.

Joshua turned. "Papa." His smile faded.

Peggy looked at him, too. Her smile faded as well. "Hello, Mr. Ludman."

Mark walked to them. When had he become the bad guy? "Son, your teacher came calling this afternoon."

"Uh-oh." Joshua's head went down, and he gathered his fishing pole and the string of fish he'd caught.

Mark shook his head. "We'll talk about her visit later tonight." Then he turned his attention to Peggy. "How are you this afternoon, Miss Bradford?"

She, too, was gathering her things to leave. "I'm well, Mr. Ludman."

The stiffness in her voice alerted him that something had displeased her. "Have I done something to offend you?"

She spun around to face him. Her gaze moved to Josh, who was shaking his head ever so slightly in a silent plea. "I'm sorry. I need to get back to the kitchen. It's my night to bake."

"Would you like me to walk you back?"

Her frosty voice chilled the pleasant afternoon. "No thanks. Maybe you should walk your son home and let him talk to you. And, this time, listen to him." Peggy clutched her book close to her chest and headed down the path he'd just traveled.

Mark turned to Joshua. "What was that about?"

The ten-year-old boy shrugged. "I don't know."

He stared at his son. His chin hung so low it almost touched his chest, and he refused to make eye contact. "Now why don't I believe you?"

❄

Peggy stomped back to the Biltmore house. Anger at Mark Ludman surged through her whole being. She'd had no idea

193

he was Josh's father. The man she'd met earlier today seemed so considerate of others. But he obviously didn't pay enough attention to his own child.

Halfway back she stopped and slapped herself on the forehead. *How can I be so stupid?* She'd forgotten to arrange a time and place to meet Joshua for his first reading lesson. Peggy sighed. "That's what comes from allowing your temper to overtake you."

The rest of the afternoon seemed to fly by as Peggy created spice cakes for the evening meal. She loved her job and felt blessed to be spending the holidays at Biltmore. Mrs. Vanderbilt was going all out with decorations and gifts for the residents of Asheville and the people who worked on the estate.

Chef McConnell smiled as he inspected her worktable before allowing her to leave. "Thank you for going for the honey wagon today, Miss Bradford. I've spoken with the head chef, and he suggested we give you a couple of extra hours off tomorrow to make up for today."

"That is very kind of you. Thank you." Peggy hid her hands in her apron. Her mind worked as she thought of what she could do with the extra two hours off. Would she be able to find Joshua?

"You are free to go." Chef McConnell dismissed her with a grin.

Peggy nodded and then returned to her room. She sank into a chair and studied the small room. It was airy and comfortable with a chestnut dresser and matching wardrobe. She longed to fall into the comfortable iron bed and sleep, but her mind remained on Joshua Ludman and the fact that she didn't know how to contact him.

She dressed for bed, crawled between the fresh sheets, and picked up her book. Maybe if she read for a while, her mind would relax and allow her to sleep. Four o'clock in the morning would arrive sooner than she cared to think about. Peggy yawned.

Around eight the next morning, one of the kitchen maids came to her station. "There is a young boy at the service door asking for you."

Peggy looked to Chef McConnell and, when she had his attention, indicated she needed to step out of the kitchen for a moment. At his nod, she hurried to the back door.

Joshua stood on the step. "I'm sorry to bother you, Miss Peggy, but I was wondering if we can start my classes today?"

She nodded. "Yes. Meet me by the stream after school today. I'll only have about thirty minutes, but I think that will give me enough time to figure out where you are."

His lips lifted in a grin. "I'll be there." He turned to go.

"And don't skip school this afternoon," she called after him.

His young voice floated back to her. "I won't. Promise. See you later." Then he was gone.

Peggy hurried inside, washed her hands, and went back to her station. Chef McConnell walked over to her. "Is everything all right, Miss Bradford?"

She picked up the dough and began to knead it. "Everything is fine, sir. I am teaching one of the local boys to read, and he had a question."

"That's very honorable of you." He leaned against her worktable. "Are you qualified to teach?"

His voice sounded soft and warm. Peggy looked up into his face. Kind eyes greeted her. He didn't mean the question to sound condemning, and for that she was thankful.

"I'm not sure. But he needs a teacher and has asked me to help him." Peggy pounded the dough.

His big hand patted her shoulder. "I like your determination. Just don't let it interfere with your duties."

Peggy grinned at him. "I won't."

❄

Mark introduced a small puff of smoke through the entrance door of the hive. The smoke caused the bees to remain calm and kept him from getting stung. He waited a minute or two to make sure the smoke had the desired effect, and then he removed the outer cover from the top of the hive. The smoke caused the bees to be drowsy and prevented them from flying away as he set the top to the side and began examining the hive.

Cleaning the colony and making sure everything was in order took him about fifteen minutes per hive. After an hour Mark stood and stretched his back muscles. His gaze moved over the sea of frames that contained beehives. He knew more would need his attention out in the fields, meadows, and mountains that surrounded the Biltmore estate.

This was one of those days when he'd rather be in the field with the head gardener. The bees hummed around him. The sweet smell of honey filled his nostrils. He knew he should be content, but he wasn't. He enjoyed bees, the smell of honey, and the outdoors but thought there was more to life. He closed his eyes and could see the bountiful fall harvest of orange pumpkins, fat potatoes, and green kale in the gardens. He grinned. Those were true fruits of labor.

Mark moved on to the next box and repeated the same procedure. Last evening it had taken a couple of hours to get out of Joshua what had been bothering him. He felt sure his son's problem provided an inclination as to why Peggy had been angry with him, too. What kind of parent was he that he hadn't realized Joshua's problems at school stemmed from his not knowing how to read?

"Hey Mark, need a couple of extra hands?"

Mark looked up to see his friend John crossing the orchard. John was an assistant gardener who often came by to chat during his afternoons off.

"Sure. How about I take a little break and chew something over with you." Mark put the hive back together and joined John under a nearby apple tree. He pulled an old crate up and sat on it.

John leaned against the trunk of the tree. His eyes sparkled as he teased, "Woman troubles?"

Mark really didn't have woman problems, other than the fact Peggy Bradford seemed miffed at him. That did bother him somewhat. He shook his head to clear it of all thoughts of Peggy.

"Well that's good to know. So what's the problem?"

"My boy isn't doing too well in school."

John pushed away from the tree and picked up a stick. "That's too bad. What's the problem?"

"Reading."

"Not a strong point of mine either."

Mark studied his friend. "You can't read?"

"No, I can read, it just isn't easy. My letters get turned around, so I have to really focus on them. Is that your boy's problem?"

Now there was a thought. Were Joshua's letters turned around? Mark rubbed his chin. "I don't know. Miss Bradford is going to work with him some in hopes of finding out what the problem is."

"Hmm, then it would seem your problem is solved. So what are you stewing over?" John took out his pocketknife and began whittling the stick.

Now that they'd come this far, Mark didn't really feel like telling his friend the full extent of the situation. Especially after discovering John had reading troubles, too. He stood. "Never mind, it's not important."

John didn't move, didn't look up. He simply said, "It is important, if you are blaming yourself for not knowing Joshua had a problem."

Mark stared hard at him. "How could I not know?"

"Did Joshua ever ask you for help with his homework?" Mark shook his head.

"Did he ever ask you to read something for him?" Again the answer was no.

John slid the knife along the wood and then asked, "Did you ever see him with a book, and it looked like he was reading it?"

Mark thought back to the many evenings he, his dad

Martin, and Joshua had sat in the living area of their cabin. Often Joshua held a schoolbook or a newspaper. It had appeared he was reading. "I suppose so."

"The boy hid it from you. You can't be blamed for that. If he is anything like I was at his age, he didn't want you to know." John grinned at him over the piece of wood. "How did you find out?"

Mark groaned, knowing his answer would bring on more questions. "Joshua told Miss Bradford, and when I found them together down by the fishing hole, she was a little miffed at me. I asked Joshua why, and after much talk on my part, he finally told me what he'd told her."

"She blames you?"

Mark moved to the next hive and began blowing smoke into it. "I'm not sure, but I think so."

John had followed his line of reckoning but didn't comment further.

After several long seconds, Mark looked up at him. The other man studied his face. Mark waited for more questions and felt his neck grow warm as another grin spread across John's face.

"And it bothers you that she thinks you are a neglectful father?"

Mark inspected each frame of the hive before answering. He wanted to be truthful in all things. He'd started this conversation and knew he'd have to continue on with it, or John would assume more than the truth.

"Well?"

"Yes, it bothers me. But only because we've just met." *I*

199

don't want her to think ill of me.

As if John could read his mind he said, "And you don't want her to think that you are a bad father."

Mark clamped the lid back onto the box and moved to the next. He motioned for John to go to the opposite box. He blew smoke into his hive and then handed the smoke can to his friend.

"That's perfectly understandable." John smiled, revealing crooked white teeth. "No man wants the woman he's interested in to think he's a bad father." Then he laughed.

Mark wasn't sure if his expression brought on the laughter, or if John just thought himself funny, but either way, Mark wasn't amused.

He decided to ignore his friend and focus his thoughts on the woman who had recently entered his life. Did he see Peggy as a future mother to his unborn children? Mark thought of her auburn hair, soft blue eyes, and full, pouty lips. Maybe he wouldn't mind exploring a future with her.

Yummy Apple Cake

Ingredients:
   1 pound apples
   1 pound sugar
   ¼ pint water
   1 lemon
   Orange, to taste

Instructions:
The apples cut and cored, the sugar put to the water, so as to clarify the sugar, with the juice and peel of the lemon and a little orange. Boil it till it is quite stiff; put it in a mold. When cold it will turn out. You may put it into a little warm water to keep it from breaking when taken out.

Chapter 4

CREAM CRULLERS

Joshua popped another cream cruller into his mouth. "These are great, Miss Peggy!" he said around a mouthful of pastry.

Joy pure and simple caused Peggy to smile. "You'd think you've never had doughnuts before."

He swallowed and then answered. "I haven't had them but a couple of times in my whole life." Josh reached for another doughnut.

She pulled them out of his reach and shook her head. "No more until we read a little."

"Aw, do I have to?" His eyes followed the sack she tucked away.

Peggy pulled the Bible out of her larger bag and opened it to Genesis, chapter one. "Let's start here." She pointed to the first scripture.

Joshua read, "In the. . ." and paused.

Together they worked through the thirty-one verses. Peggy realized that Josh could read some words but seemed embarrassed when he stumbled over the larger words or the ones he didn't know on sight. She cautioned him to slow down and take his time.

As they gathered up their belongings, Josh said. "Thanks for helping me, Miss Peggy."

"Just remember to slow down and sound out the words you aren't sure of." She put the Bible back into her bag and pulled out the sack of cream crullers. Peggy handed them to him. "I'll make up cards to help you learn other words, and we'll continue to practice your reading."

"Papa said he'd talk to my teacher about getting some other books that I can read." Joshua pulled a doughnut from the sack.

Peggy swung her bag onto her shoulder. "So you talked to your father about your reading problem?"

"Yes. He felt really bad that he didn't know." Joshua followed her back to the road.

"I'm glad you talked to him. You should never hide things like this from your parent." She stopped and looked at him.

Joshua rubbed the toe of his boot into the dirt. "I know."

"Good. I best get going. Chef McConnell gave me a little extra time off today, but that time is almost over." She turned to go back to the Biltmore house.

"Wait!" Joshua ran up beside her. "Are we going to meet tomorrow, too?"

A light breeze swept around Peggy. Chills covered her arms and legs. "Yes, but we really need to find a better place to meet. The days are growing colder."

"We could meet at my house." Joshua offered, talking around a glob of pastry.

Peggy thought for a moment. She'd like to spend more time with both Mark and Joshua but didn't think it respectable for her to go to their home unsupervised. "No, but maybe I can ask the housekeeper if we can use a sitting room." She studied the boy. His head bent over the sack, and his attention focused on the sweet treats, not her words.

He looked up. "What?"

She smiled. "We'll meet here tomorrow, and I'll see what I can do about a new meeting place."

"All right." He turned to go.

Peggy stopped him, "Hey Joshua, why don't you save the rest of those until after dinner. I'd hate for your father to think I spoiled your meal."

He looked longingly into the bag and then rolled the top down. "All right." Disappointment laced his young voice.

She watched as he trudged off in the opposite direction. Peggy smiled. Joshua seemed to be a very well-behaved boy. Mark Ludman's son would be a fine young man someday, just like his father. What was it about Mark that intrigued her? Peggy decided to put that thought behind her and focus on something else.

Thoughts of the schoolteacher came to mind. Was she young? Interesting? Interested in Mark? After all, she'd made a special visit to his home to tell him Joshua had been skipping school. Maybe she should check with the schoolteacher. She might have suggestions on how to help Joshua.

❄

Mark saw her coming up the path toward the house. He'd finished his chores early and wanted to see Peggy. Had her meeting with Joshua gone well? He leaned against a tree and watched her approach. She seemed deep in thought. Her teeth worried her bottom lip as if she were working through a problem. Had Joshua misbehaved?

"Good afternoon, Miss Bradford." He enjoyed the emotions that crossed her face. First, startled, and then she relaxed. Mark thanked the Lord above that Peggy didn't shy away from him, like so many others had done.

"Hello, Mr. Ludman." She continued walking.

"Mind if I join you?" he asked, falling into step beside her.

Peggy brushed a wayward curl from her face. "Not at all. I was just thinking about you."

He allowed a touch of amusement to enter his voice. "Good thoughts, I hope."

A soft pink filled her cheeks. "I mean, I was just thinking about your visit with the schoolteacher. Were you able to acquire the needed reading books?" The wayward curl fell to the side of her face once more.

"No, I was too busy to go today. I'm thinking a quick trip in the morning is needed. I'm sure Miss Hart won't mind a quick visit. Once my day starts, I tend to lose track of time." Mark fought the urge to stop her and slip the curl behind her ear as she'd done a few moments before. But he didn't think she would appreciate such forwardness.

"I understand. Once I am in the kitchen I am inclined to do the same." Crispness laced her voice that he hadn't detected before. She stepped around a mud hole in the dirt path.

He moved with her. "How did it go with Joshua today?"

She stopped and turned to face him. The bag that hung from her shoulder swayed with her. "About Joshua." Her hands tangled in her apron. "I need to apologize. I over-reacted yesterday and behaved rudely." Her gaze moved to the ground.

Mark found he didn't like this subservient stance, not on Peggy. He gently lifted her chin and tucked the silky softness of her hair behind the shell-shaped ear. "You have nothing to be sorry for. I should have known, and I didn't."

"But—"

Mark stopped her by gently laying his finger across her lips. "It's done. Let's forget it." His gaze moved to her lips. He couldn't stop his finger from gently feeling the softness of her mouth.

Peggy stepped backward. She nodded and then resumed walking. "It went well. He can read but gets nervous and falters when he can't pronounce a word. With a little practice, I'm sure he will do much better in school."

Her cheeks were aflame. He wanted to kick himself. He'd caused her embarrassment with his unwarranted advance. Not sure how to fix the stiffness between them, he simply said, "Good."

They walked on toward the house in silence. Mark was sure she wouldn't want to talk to him again. He had been too bold in touching her. He cleared his throat and offered, "I'm sorry I was forward back there and promise it won't happen again."

Her silence didn't make him feel any better. She continued to walk onward, her gaze focused straight ahead.

Just before they reached the servants' entrance, Peggy stopped. "If it is all right with you, I'd like to continue working with Joshua. I'm going to ask permission to have him come to the servants' sitting room."

"Are you sure it won't be too much of a bother?" he asked, amazed she still wanted to be around his family.

"Yes, but I don't get off work until eight in the evening, and I know that is too late for a young boy to be out alone. Would it be too much to ask you to attend his lessons?" She twisted her hands in her dress but continued looking him in the eye.

Mark grinned. "I would be honored."

She nodded and turned to leave. He wondered if she would sneak a peek back at him. As she entered the door, Peggy glanced over her shoulder. His grin turned into a full smile as something in his chest jumped with joy.

CREAM CRULLERS

Ingredients:

    1½ cups sugar
    1 cup milk
    2 eggs
    Butter the size of an egg
    2 teaspoonfuls baking powder
    3 cups Flour

Instructions:

Mix all ingredients except flour in bowl. Then mix in enough flour to roll out soft. Twist dough off into balls, and then fry in hot lard.

Chapter 5

CHRISTMAS CUT-OUT SUGAR COOKIES

Peggy pulled the horse and buggy to a stop, set the brake, and climbed down. Miss Hart's house sat against a small grove of trees. She reached down to pick up her basket of sugar cookies. The sweet smell drifted toward her and brought forth happy thoughts of the day she would be making them for Christmas at Biltmore.

Dread filled her as she looked toward the house. "You are doing this for Joshua," she whispered to herself. Then she took a deep breath to meet the schoolteacher. "It has nothing to do with Mark and the fact that he thinks highly of the woman," she added. Peggy straightened her hat, smoothed invisible wrinkles from her dress, and knocked on the door.

A crisp breeze blew across the porch. Peggy pulled her jacket tighter around her waist and leaned closer to the house. The slight scent of baked ham and pinto beans wafted from the doorway. Peggy closed her eyes, enjoying the scent of comfort food. Warmth filled the doorway, and the air became even heavier with the aroma.

"Good morning. May I help you?" a cool authoritative voice asked.

Peggy's eyes popped open. Embarrassment burned her cheeks. How could she have been caught standing on the woman's porch with her eyes shut? "Oh, I am sorry. I was just enjoying the heavenly scent of your ham and beans." The words tumbled from her lips.

The woman before her stood tall and willowy, her gray hair piled into a simple style on top of her head. She wore a faded dress with an apron covering the front. At that moment she looked more like a baker than Peggy did. "I see. How may I help you?"

"I'm Miss Peggy Bradford. May I please speak to Miss Hart?" She shivered as another gust of wind sailed across the porch.

"Come inside." The older woman shut the door behind Peggy.

Peggy's gaze swept the clean room. Quilts and blankets decorated the backs of chairs that sat around a small table. A bookshelf filled with books of all sizes rested beside the fireplace, and a colorful rug covered the spotless wood floor.

"What can I do for you, Miss Bradford?" A small, amused smile touched the woman's light-blue eyes, softening her face.

Peggy realized she was facing Miss Hart. "I came to discuss Joshua Ludman." She raised her chin ever so slightly to look the other woman in the eyes.

Miss Hart moved to the couch. "Please be seated." She indicated a soft-looking chair to Peggy's right.

Once Peggy sat, the schoolteacher asked another question. "So Miss Bradford, did Mr. Ludman send you to me for assistance?"

She felt like squirming under the knowing gaze that rested upon her. "No, ma'am. Joshua asked me to help him and since I'm not a teacher, I came to you for help."

"I see." Those soft blue eyes searched Peggy's.

Peggy wondered how much the other woman could read from her face. Did Miss Hart know that jealousy had been eating at her ever since the day she'd learned of the other woman's visit to Mark's home? Did she see the relief that Peggy felt knowing she was an older woman and probably would have no interest in the Ludman family, other than education?

"How exactly are you going to help Joshua, Miss Bradford?" Miss Hart folded her hands in her lap.

"Please call me Peggy." At the other woman's nod, she continued. "I'm not sure. He asked for help with his reading, and I've gone over scripture with him a couple of times. He's not that bad of a reader."

Miss Hart nodded again. "He's not a bad reader. As I told Mr. Ludman yesterday, the boy has confidence issues, not reading issues."

"What would cause that?" Peggy placed her basket between them on the table. "Would you like a cookie, Miss Hart?"

She stood. "I'd love one, but you must call me Emilia, if I'm to call you Peggy." Her eyes sparkled as she waited.

Peggy smiled. "Emilia it is, then."

"Good. Let's move to the kitchen, where I can make us both a cup of coffee to go with those cookies." Emilia led the way to the back of the house.

As Peggy followed, she enjoyed the comfortable, homey feel of the house. It reminded her of the orphanage, warm with Mama Elsie's special touch. "I love your home," she offered as they entered the kitchen. Thoughts of Christmas entered her mind again. Would the schoolteacher decorate it in greens? Would it smell of Christmas treats and pine like Mama Elsie's did?

Heat and the scent of ham-filled beans clung to the women.

"Thank you, Peggy. Go ahead and sit at the table." Emilia moved to the woodstove and began making coffee.

Peggy stopped in the center of the room at the drop-leaf table. She set the basket in the center and removed the cover. Then she took her coat off, hung it over the chair back, and sat.

Her gaze moved about the kitchen. It looked much like all the other kitchens in the area, but she did notice three fruit-and-vegetable prints hung on one wall. She pointed to the pictures. "Those are very pretty."

Emilia looked over her shoulder. "Those were painted by one of my past students. He worked on those for three years and then gave them to me for Christmas his last year of school." She carried two steaming mugs to the table.

Peggy joined her. She found that she liked the schoolteacher more than she'd planned. Perhaps together, they could help Joshua.

❊

Mark and Joshua drove up to the servants' entrance. "You be on your best behavior, Joshua. It's not often the outdoor staff gets to mingle with the house staff."

"I will. Miss Peggy said she'll meet us here at eight thirty."

True to her word, Peggy stepped out of the door. She wore a blue calico dress. Her eyes sparkled as she looked at them.

Joshua jumped from the wagon and hurried to her side. "Hi, Miss Peggy."

"Good evening, Joshua. Did you bring your books?" She folded her hands in front of her dress.

"Sure did. They're in the wagon. I'll be right back."

Mark watched his son race back to the wagon. He grinned at Peggy. "Are you sure this will be all right?"

She returned his smile, revealing even white teeth. "I'm sure. We have permission from the head housekeeper."

"Here they are!" Joshua held up the books.

Mark climbed down and handed the reins to the stable hand, who stood beside the wagon.

"This way then." Peggy entered the house. She led them into a hallway. At the first door, Peggy turned and showed them into the servants' sitting room.

"Wow!" Joshua exclaimed in a loud voice as they entered the room.

"Joshua." Mark growled the boy's name. He, too, was a little awestruck by the beauty of the room.

"Sorry. That came out a little too loud." Joshua continued to follow Peggy into the room. She sat at a small table and motioned for Joshua to join her.

"You may sit in that chair, Mr. Ludman." Peggy indicated

a rocking chair off to the side.

He made his way to the chair and sat. Two other women occupied the small room. They were sewing and chatting in low voices. It was a nice space, clean and furnished to allow the occupants' comfort and activity. He noted a board game on a small table in one corner. A secretary graced another wall.

His gaze moved over his son and Peggy. Their heads were together as they looked down at the book Peggy had chosen to read. Josh's young voice stumbled, Peggy's joined his, and Mark caught the smile she aimed at Josh.

Her encouragement was just what the boy needed. He continued reading in a steady voice. Peggy's head was at such an angle that her neck was exposed; soft curls rested against her creamy skin. His fingers twitched at the thought of touching her hair again.

A giggle from the other side of the room drew his attention. The women looked down at their sewing, easily hiding their faces from his view. Had he been staring? Mark leaned his head against the chair's back and closed his eyes.

What was it about Peggy Bradford? She was pretty to look at. Her interest in his son was endearing. And her sweet voice sent a shiver down his spine.

His thoughts turned to the feelings he'd experienced when he'd courted Joshua's mother more than a decade ago. Molly had been the daughter of their next-door neighbor. They'd been friends since childhood, and it had been expected that they should marry. He loved her in a different way than he loved Peggy.

Mark's eyes popped wide open. Who said anything about loving Peggy?

CHRISTMAS CUT-OUT
SUGAR COOKIES

Ingredients:
 ⅔ cup sugar
 ⅔ cup lard
 2 slightly beaten eggs
 2 cups flour
 ½ teaspoon salt
 1½ teaspoons baking powder

Instructions:
Mix all ingredients together until mixture forms a ball. Place dough in covered bowl. Refrigerate four hours or overnight. Next day, on floured board, roll out to about ¼-inch thickness. Cut out shapes with cookie cutters of your choice. Bake until edges just start to brown.

Chapter 6

MOLASSES CANDY

Peggy pulled her prettiest churchgoing dress over her head and quickly buttoned up the front. Mark would be there any moment to take her into Asheville. She couldn't believe it had been two weeks since she'd started her lessons with Josh in the sitting room. The brush flashed through her hair. Excitement crackled within her body much like the static electricity between the brush and hair.

Mark and Josh had become a big part of her life at Biltmore. Every day Joshua gained more confidence in his ability to read, and she had made a friend for life in the young boy. Her heart skipped as she thought of Mark. He'd been a constant companion with his son each evening. His dark-brown eyes warmed to sweet chocolate every time she caught him gazing at her. The ready smile on his lips brought joy to her life. Thoughts of spending a lifetime with the two of them had entered her mind more than once during the last two weeks.

A soft knock at the door pulled her from her musings. She quickly slipped the last pin into her hair. Peggy pulled her sweater on as she walked across the room.

A kitchen maid smiled at her when she opened the door. "Mr. Ludman is waiting for you at the back entrance, Peggy."

"Thank you, Sylvia." She took her pocketbook down from the nearby hook and closed the door behind her. "We're going into Asheville this afternoon. Can I get anything for you?" She expected her chocolate-loving friend to ask for a box of chocolates.

"No thanks. I'm going tomorrow." Sylvia walked with her toward the kitchens. "Chef McConnell said not to forget the boxes of molasses candy. He's excited that you made some for his mother, too."

"I was happy to make it for him. Chef McConnell really is a good man, and his mother is a friend of Mama Elsie's, so I'll leave them with Mama Elsie, and she'll get them to his mother." Peggy knew she chattered unnecessarily but felt nervous.

"That's nice. Have a good time." Sylvia waved and continued on to the main kitchen.

Peggy headed for the housekeeper's pantry, where she'd left the candy. She lifted the top box off and left it for the housekeeper with a note thanking her for allowing her to teach Josh in the servants' sitting room. Peggy hurried to the door. Just before exiting, she stopped, took a deep breath, and straightened the lightweight jacket she wore over her best dress. She stepped across the threshold and offered what she hoped was her best smile.

"You look lovely," Mark said as he took the candy. He placed it in a wooden box under the seat and then helped her up into the wagon.

"Thank you, Mr. Ludman." She sat and smoothed her skirt. "Are we picking Joshua up on our way to town?"

Mark pulled himself up onto the seat. The wagon swayed. "No. I hope you don't mind, but he and my father-in-law had some extra things they wanted to do today. So it will just be the two of us. And since no one else is around, can you please call me Mark?"

She felt the flush fill her face. A full day with Mark. Alone. "I don't mind, and I suppose I can."

As the wagon rolled along, Peggy searched for something to say. She'd counted on Joshua to make things light and merry. A cool breeze tugged at her hair.

"While you visit with your family, I need to do a little Christmas shopping. I know it's early, but I may not make it back into Asheville and want to get Joshua at least one store-bought gift." Mark smiled in her direction. "I can't believe there are only ten more days until Thanksgiving."

Peggy surprised herself by saying. "I know what you mean. Mark, if you don't mind my coming along, I'd like to do a little Christmas shopping myself." She'd planned to go, anyway. "The kitchen staff has been talking and planning for the holidays, and my understanding is that the closer they get, the less amount of time we'll have to ourselves." Peggy tucked her hands in her skirt.

"Good. I could use some help, if you have the time." Mark held the reins in his hand with ease.

"I'll try. What kind of help do you need?" She turned sideways on the seat to face him.

"Help with Christmas. I've never been very good at it.

Molly always took care of those things, but since her death, I'm afraid I haven't done a very good job of it." He glanced over at her once more before turning his attention on the horses.

"Molly was your wife?"

The muscle in his scarred jaw tightened. "Yes, she was."

Maybe she shouldn't have asked. "I'm sorry."

"No, I brought her up. Molly's been gone five years. You have nothing to be sorry for. We were best friends since childhood. I loved her very much."

Something in the way he said Molly's name brought out an emotion that Peggy had never felt before. She looked down at her hands. Was she jealous of his wife? Heat filled her cheeks. Maybe it was too soon to be on a first-name basis with Mark, after all. He still loved his wife. Even though Peggy knew she'd fallen in love with him, she'd not be second to any woman. Dead or alive.

"Enough about that. Can you think of something Joshua would like for Christmas?" His brown gaze drifted across her face before returning to the road.

❄

They ate lunch at a small diner, Mark's treat to Peggy for helping him shop for Joshua. Thanks to her, Christmas morning Josh would find a small tin toy, a boy on a sled. When Josh turned the key, it would roll across the floor. The perfect gift for a ten-year-old. He also had marbles and a slingshot to add to his small mountain of gifts.

Peggy had done some shopping, too. Her bags were a little heavier than his, but he didn't mind carrying them as she looked inside the windows and oohed and aahed over the many items on display. Since he'd talked about his wife, she'd been a little less friendly, but he had only himself to blame for that. Five years of marriage had taught him a few things, like how to read the signs of a woman trying to keep her distance.

While she'd visited with her family, he'd done a little shopping on his own. His mind had worked on how he felt about Peggy. He'd have to assure her that his love for Molly would never die, but that there was room in his life for a new wife. They'd only known each other a few weeks, but Mark knew he loved her very much. And he planned on telling her so, when the time was right.

He arrived to pick her up and watched as she waved good-bye to Mama Elsie and her youngest sister Melissa. "I had a great day, Mr. Ludman. This has been fun."

There it was again. She'd started calling him Mr. Ludman again. Why had he mentioned Molly today? *Lord, help me to find a way to explain to her that my love for Molly is different than this new love I have for her.* "For me as well."

He pulled the wagon to a stop in front of St. Luke's Episcopal Church. He felt Peggy's curious gaze upon him as he studied the triangular windows of the church. "Have you ever seen this church?" Mark asked, knowing she probably had.

"Yes, I have. Why do you ask?"

"I just wondered." He continued to study the building as he tried to figure out how to say what he wanted to. "Do you know if it replaced another church in this spot?"

From the corner of his eye he saw her study the church. "No, I don't believe it did." A smile graced her beautiful features. "I love the stained glass windows. They are simple and beautiful."

He looked fully at her. Like the church, Peggy was simple and yet very beautiful. "Me, too."

She twisted the fabric of her dress and began speaking fast. "They consecrated the church on July ninth of this year. I didn't attend the service, but I understand it was wonderful. Did you attend?"

Mark took her hands within his own. Her wide eyes stared at him as a soft pink filled her wind-kissed cheeks. "No, that was a few months before I met you. We'd just moved here."

"Oh I see." She looked down at their clasped hands.

He looked at them also. Hers were small within his. Mark rubbed his thumb across the back of her hand. It felt soft. Then he turned them over and looked at her palms. "You know, I think there are people who attend this church who went to another at a different time. What do you think?" He raised his eyes and saw her quick nod.

"I really don't understand this conversation, Mr. Ludman." Peggy tugged at her hands.

Mark smiled and released her hands. He scooted closer to her on the seat. "I'm not sure how to explain it, so I'm using the church as a reference."

"Explain what?" Peggy's light-blue eyes looked up into his.

His heart rate picked up. "That I think I'm falling in love with you."

She scooted away. "That can't be possible. Just this morning you were telling me you loved your wife."

This was it, the moment of truth. He had to make her understand. "I did, very much. But Molly has moved on to heaven, and I'm still here. She would want me to go on with my life, find a new love. A different love." Mark reached out and touched a soft curl that had escaped the confines of the style she'd placed it in earlier in the day.

"Mark, I can't be second to Molly."

He released the curl and slid his palm along her soft jaw. "I'm not asking you to, Peggy." He felt her cheek press into his hand ever so slightly. "Molly and I had a different kind of love than what I'm feeling for you."

"I don't understand." She pulled her face away.

Mark looked back to the church. *Lord, please help me.* "This church is new, much like our relationship." He turned back to her, and she nodded that she understood. "The people who attend it now attended another church at another time. This church is new, different, and they love it. They might still miss their old church but know that they can't or won't return to it."

Her gaze now rested on the new building. "So now they are dedicated to this church? Is that what you are trying to tell me? That you loved Molly, but you can't go back to her, and so you are looking for a new relationship?" Confusion and understanding battled within her voice.

"Yes, you are the first woman I have met in five years who makes me want to dedicate my life to her." His voice came out a whisper. His heart beat in his chest like the wings of a bee. *God, please let her understand what I'm trying to say.*

Peggy looked back at him. "I need time to think about this, Mark."

He picked up the reins and turned the horses toward the Biltmore mansion. "I will give you the time you need, Peggy. Because I believe God has brought us together." Mark looked up to the sky that reflected the blue in Peggy's eyes and prayed it was so.

Molasses Candy

Ingredients:

1 quart molasses, maple is best
1 teaspoon soda
Buttered pans
Roasted corn, optional
Peanuts, optional
Walnuts, optional
Almonds, optional
Hazelnuts, optional

Instructions:

Take one quart of molasses; boil until crisp when put in water; then stir in one teaspoonful of soda dissolved in a little warm water; stir until well mixed. Pour into buttered pans. Pull part until white and make into sticks. In the remainder put roasted corn, peanuts, walnuts, almonds, or hazelnuts.

Chapter 7

GINGERBREAD

Mark hauled a bale of hay into the cow's pen and cut the straw binding that held it together. He sighed. Two days had passed since he and Peggy had returned from town. Had he scared her off with his talk of falling in love?

He inhaled the sweet fragrance of hay and feed. Maybe he should have waited? Mark stomped to the barn and sat on the bench beside the open doorway. Why couldn't he have just kept his mouth shut?

"Hi, Papa. What are you doing out here?" Joshua sat beside him on the bench.

Mark grinned at his son. "Taking a break."

"Break from what?"

He laughed. "Work, son. I am working."

Joshua shook his head. "I know you are working, but what are you working on?"

He dropped an arm around his son's shoulders. "Feeding cows at the moment. Want to help?"

A look entered Joshua's eyes, and a smile spread across his face. "Sure." He jumped to his feet. "What do I need to do?"

It dawned on Mark that he didn't involve Joshua enough in his everyday life. "First, we'll find you a pair of gloves. Then I'll show you where to get the hay and which cow pens we still need to do. Still want to help?"

"Yep."

Mark stood and stretched. If Peggy didn't come around, he'd still have Joshua and his father-in-law. He almost laughed. A far cry from a woman and companion for life, but still nice to know he had loved ones he cared about and who cared about him.

As they loaded the hay wagon, Mark and Joshua talked. Mark learned Joshua was doing much better in school now, and he knew it had to do with Peggy and her encouragement. His son talked about books. He had found a *Farmers' Almanac* and told his father he'd like to try his hand at farming. Mark had to admit that he felt the same. Maybe they'd look into buying a small piece of land in the spring.

"Papa, what do you think of Miss Peggy?" Joshua cut the line on the bale of hay Mark had just dropped into the pen.

"She's nice enough." He studied his son's face.

Joshua laughed. "I like her a lot." He stood. "You know, I wouldn't mind if you liked her enough to marry her."

Now where had that come from? Were his feelings that apparent?

"I mean, she's nice, she can cook, and I think she likes you, too." Joshua pressed on as they walked back to the wagon for another bale of hay.

Mark pulled the bale from the wagon. "When looking for a wife, Joshua, you need to look at the whole picture, not just if she's nice and can cook." He grunted and dropped the hay close to a couple of cows.

"Like what?" Joshua cut the string and spread the hay.

"Like is she a God-fearing woman?"

Joshua pulled the twine and rolled it into a ball. "She goes to church every Sunday, and I know she reads her Bible."

That was true. Mark had seen no evidence that Peggy didn't love the Lord. During the few times they'd shared a meal, she waited for prayer before eating. Many times, when she was doing lessons with Joshua, she'd been reading her Bible when they'd arrived in the servants' sitting room.

"And she needs to be someone you can trust."

Joshua studied his father's face. "You trust Peggy. If you didn't, you wouldn't have let her teach me."

Mark nodded.

"What else?"

"She'd have to be someone you'd want to spend time with because you enjoy her company, not because you have to." Mark continued with his work. He knew he enjoyed being with Peggy and the more time he spent with her, the more he wanted to be with her.

"Is that why you take Peggy to town? Take her extra honey? And started goin' to her church on Sundays?"

Mark saw the knowing grin on his son's face as he pulled himself into the wagon. "Okay, you've made your point."

"So are you going to ask her to marry you?"

He climbed back into the wagon. "It's a little more complicated than that. First, I have to find out how she feels about me, and then we'll talk marriage."

Joshua twisted around on the seat beside him. "So you are going to ask her to marry you?"

Was he? He looked into his son's questioning eyes. "If she'll have me, I'll ask."

Joshua slapped his gloves against his thighs and gave a whoop. The cows bellowed in response and Mark groaned. "A new mother for Christmas, that will be great!"

"Now son, don't go telling anybody about our conversation. I'd like to talk to Peggy before news gets out how I feel." Mark slapped the reins over the horses' backs and headed to the barn.

"Aw, Papa, I won't say a word."

"Good." Mark knew from the grin on Joshua's face that the boy was going to have a hard time not sharing this secret. He really needed to visit Peggy and see how she felt about him.

❄

The smell of gingerbread spices filled her senses to the point of overpowering her. She loved the fragrance, but today it smelled too strong for her liking. Thanks to a mishap in the kitchen this morning, gingerbread dough coated both Peggy and the kitchen aide Sylvia from head to toe. Poor Sylvia still had another hour to work before she could wash it off.

Peggy took a quick bath. It amazed her how fast one could bathe at Biltmore. Hot running water still thrilled her. She'd miss it when she returned to Reynolds House.

She dressed and picked up the basket of gingerbread that Mrs. Vanderbilt had requested be delivered to the Wilsons.

Peggy loved the way the lady of the house sent treats to several of the larger families on the estate. Chef McConnell learned early that Peggy enjoyed making the deliveries, so until Christmas she'd be the delivery girl.

When she stepped outside, a young man met her at the back door. "Chef McConnell asked me to bring the wagon to get you, Miss Bradford."

"That was thoughtful of him. Thank you...?" She waited for him to give his name.

"Malcolm James, ma'am."

"Thank you, Mr. James." She watched a smile glitter in his eyes. Peggy wondered how old Malcolm James was; he obviously wasn't used to being called Mr. James.

He nodded and then moved forward to help her into the wagon. Peggy thought him a nice young man and knew he worked hard to keep his position at Biltmore. His workday was full, and she knew he didn't have time to drive her across the estate.

Once she was seated, he moved to climb aboard the wagon.

"Would it be all right with you if I go alone today?" She picked up the reins and smiled at him.

Malcolm looked over his shoulder as if looking for assistance from someone. "Um, I don't know." His brows drew together.

"I've gone alone many times before and will be perfectly safe."

Another wagon weighed down with produce pulled up to the service entrance. He studied it, knowing the others would need him to help unload it. His gaze moved back to her. "If you're sure."

The approach of Christmas was creating more work for all of them. She knew Malcolm didn't want to get into trouble, but that he also didn't want to leave her alone. Peggy grinned at him. "I'm sure."

He nodded and handed the gingerbread up to her. She watched as he sprinted to the wagon and pitched in. *In a few years that could be Joshua*, she thought, taking up the reins and setting the horses into motion.

Cold air whipped around the wagon as she traveled. Every day it grew colder, and she longed for the warmth of the kitchens. The sound of horse's hooves behind the wagon alerted her she was no longer alone on the road. Peggy pulled to the side to allow the other traveler to pass.

"Good afternoon, Peggy. This is a nice surprise." Mark walked the horse beside her wagon.

That familiar flickering of her heart created a sweet sensation in her chest. She smiled up at him. "Good afternoon, Mark." For two days she'd thought of him, and now she didn't know what to say.

"And where are you off to?"

She lifted the basket of gingerbread. "I'm making a delivery for Mrs. Vanderbilt. What about you?"

"I'm headed out to the orchard." He leaned on the saddle horn and smiled down on her. "If you have time, would you like to join me at the river where you fished with Joshua, when you are done with your delivery?

Peggy thought of the peaceful spot and spending time

with Mark. Both appealed to her senses. "I'd love to, but I may be awhile. I'm headed to the Wilsons'. Mrs. Wilson likes to visit for an hour at least."

"That's perfect. When I get done with my work, I'll wait for you there."

She nodded. Peggy wished she had time to return to the kitchens for a snack for them but knew she didn't.

"I'll see you then." Mark waved good-bye and turned his horse off the road.

Peggy watched him disappear into the woods. Her breath caught in her throat as she realized she and Mark would have a few minutes alone. Totally alone.

Gingerbread

Ingredients:

⅓ cup butter
⅔ cup boiling water
1 cup molasses
1 egg
3 cups flour
1½ teaspoons soda
½ teaspoon salt
1 teaspoon cinnamon
1 teaspoon ginger
¼ teaspoon cloves

Instructions:

Melt butter in water. Add molasses; egg, well beaten; and dry ingredients, mixed and sifted. Bake in buttered shallow pan.

Chapter 8

SWEET SANDWICHES

Peggy's heart beat rapidly as she made her way to the river. Since Mark's declaration of falling in love with her, all she'd done was dwell on her own emotions. She'd known for several weeks she was falling for him as well. Now they could discuss their feelings and decide where to go from here.

She pressed through the woods on foot. The closer she came to the sound of the running water, the more her breath caught in her throat. Never in her life had she felt this way about a man. To take her mind off her raging emotions, she focused on what she might say if he asked her to marry him. She wouldn't want to move away from her family. Melissa was still home with Mama Elsie, and she wanted to be able to help Mama Elsie with her younger sister, if need be. A new thought came to her. What if Mark decided to move away from Asheville? Hadn't he said they'd recently moved here? What were his plans for the future?

Peggy laughed aloud at her silly thoughts. No mention of marriage had been made, and the truth be told, she and Mark needed to get to know one another better.

Splashing filled her ears as she came into the clearing. Mark knelt beside the river's edge running his arm through the water as if washing it. His sleeves were rolled up, and his arm had red welts on it.

"What happened?" She knelt beside him.

"Bee stings."

Her heart leaped with fear. "Bees?"

"It's my own fault. In my rush to hurry, I forgot to smoke the hive."

Peggy sat back on her heels. "Smoke the hives?" Even she heard the confusion in her voice.

Mark nodded. "Yes, we smoke the hive to calm the bees."

"I didn't realize that gardener's assistants worked with bees." Her heart did a sharp twist as she realized that Mark worked with bees. Why else would he want to calm them?

"They don't."

She frowned at him. "But when we met you said you were a gardener's assistant."

Mark picked up a towel and gently patted his arm dry. "I guess I should explain. I am the beekeeper, and I also help out the gardeners and gardeners' assistants. But my primary job is beekeeping."

Peggy stood. "I see." *Lord, how can this be possible? How can I love a man whose occupation can take my life? Why have You allowed this to happen?* Even as she silently cried out to the Lord, Peggy felt her heart breaking. It wasn't fair!

Mark stood, too. "I don't understand why you are so upset." His words were soft as he moved to her side. He reached out to touch her shoulder.

Peggy flinched and moved away. What if he had a bee clinging to his clothes? Fear welled up and almost suffocated her. He frowned and then dropped his hand.

"I'm sorry, Mark. But we can't see each other anymore."

Shock, then hurt flashed across his rugged features. "Why? I thought you cared about me."

"I do, but. . ." She couldn't finish. Her words would seem foolish to him. He wouldn't understand. "I have to go." Her voice sounded strained in her ears.

Confusion laced his voice. "But why?"

Peggy wanted to scream that she was allergic to bees and just being near him could be fatal for her. She wanted to explain that all her life she'd avoided the small insects and being near him she could come into contact with them, but she didn't. Instead, she picked up her skirts and ran to the edge of the woods. "I'm sorry, Mr. Ludman. I just do."

She felt his eyes upon her but didn't turn back. Peggy ran to the wagon and climbed aboard. Tears flowed down her face as she realized the only man she'd ever loved would never be hers.

The trip back to the Biltmore house didn't seem to take long. She handed the reins to the young man who'd first given them to her.

"Miss Bradford? Are you all right?" Malcolm asked.

Peggy tried to offer a smile and felt it wobble out of control. "I'm fine. Thank you." Then she hurried inside.

Her room offered quiet but no comfort. She fell across the bed and cried until no tears were left. Still her chest ached from the pain she knew wouldn't go away for a very long time.

Hours later she awoke to the sound of a bell ringing in her room. She looked to the box and watched the arrow point to the pastry kitchen. Her gaze moved to the clock and realized she was late for work. Jerking upright, Peggy hurried into her uniform, combed her hair, and walked as fast as she could to the kitchen.

Chef McConnell waited for her beside the door. "Are you all right, Miss Bradford?"

She tucked her hands into the fold of her apron and answered. "Yes, sir. I'm sorry. I fell asleep."

He studied her face. "Are you well?"

Peggy nodded. She knew her eyes were swollen and her cheeks flushed. *Lord, please don't let him ask for an explanation. Please.* Her silent prayer was quickly answered.

"I see." He rocked on his feet and continued to study her. Then after several long moments, he said, "Please go make your sweet sandwiches and afterward, I'd like to speak further with you on this matter. If you get to feeling worse, let me know."

He didn't believe her. Peggy nodded and hurried to her station. She must look horrible for him to think her sick.

Sylvia carried a large cake pan to her station. "Are you all right?" Her green eyes reflected concern.

Peggy really wished people would stop asking her that. "I'm fine. Thank you." She took the pan and turned her back to the room. Could this day get any worse?

❉

Mark thought about chasing after her but knew that until she was ready to talk, all he'd do was frighten her more. He'd

236

seen the fear in her eyes and heard it in her voice. What had he done to cause such fear?

While he fixed a dinner of beef stew and corn bread, Joshua set the table, and his father-in-law sat in the far corner reading a paper. It would have been nice having Peggy prepare the meal. He'd help, of course, but having her in his kitchen would brighten the whole household. The chances of that happening now seemed little to none. He might as well wish for the moon.

"That stew sure smells good, Papa." Joshua joined him at the stove.

The thought that he'd have to tell Joshua that Peggy wasn't going to be a part of their lives any longer tore at his heart. "I hope it tastes good, too, son." He stirred the contents of the big old pot. It had belonged to Molly. Mark tried to picture her standing at the stove cooking. He could see her smile when she looked over her shoulder at him. He'd loved her very much but knew he needed to move on. He wasn't going to give up on Peggy. Not yet.

Mark carried the stew to the table, and Joshua grabbed the pan of corn bread. They placed them on the table. "Dinner's ready, Frank."

Molly's father pushed himself from his chair. "Good, I'm as hungry as a bear." He dropped into his place at the table.

Mark waited until Joshua was ready and then said the blessing. After he said, "Amen," he silently added his own prayer request: *Lord, please help me find out what I did that scared Peggy today.*

Sweet Sandwiches

Ingredients:

Their weight in pounded sugar, butter and flour
4 eggs, whisked
¼ teaspoon salt
Jam or marmalade
2 square cake pans

Instructions:

Beat butter to a cream; dredge in flour and sugar; stir these ingredients together well and add eggs, which should be thoroughly whisked. When the mixture has been well beaten for about 10 minutes, butter the cake pans, pour half the batter in each pan, and bake at 350 degrees for 15 minutes. Test cake to see if done. If not, bake for a few more minutes.

Let cool, then spread one cake with layer of jam or marmalade. Place other cake over it, press pieces slightly together, and then cut into long finger pieces; pile in cross-bars on a glass dish and serve. Sufficient for 5 or 6 servings.

(Peggy used one large cake pan and spread the jam on one side of the cooked cake and then folded the second half over the first.)

Chapter 9

APPLE BLACK CAPS

Peggy felt horrible. She'd prayed about what happened between her and Mark the day before. Tossing and turning all night, she came to the conclusion she should have been honest with him and told Mark about her allergy to bees.

Thankfully her lessons with Joshua were over. Otherwise, she would have to face both of them, and right now she didn't think she could do that. What had Mark told Josh? Her heart broke again at the thought.

A glance at the clock confirmed that it was ten, time for her first shift to be over. She cleaned her station and then walked over to Chef McConnell. They'd talked the night before. She'd confided that her heart had been broken when she'd learned Mark Ludman was the beekeeper and not a true gardener's assistant. He'd advised her to pray for the Lord's will, and now she wanted to tell him her decision and ask a favor.

He glanced up from the three-layer cake he was decorating and smiled. "What can I do for you, Miss Bradford?" His gaze moved back to the cake.

"I don't know if you noticed, sir, but I baked an extra dish of apple black caps?"

A quick nod verified that he had noticed. She pressed on. "I was hoping I could have the dish to take to the beekeeper and his family for dinner."

He wiped his hands on the big white apron he wore. "You'll have to pay for the ingredients and bring the dish back." His eyes bore into hers.

Peggy nodded. "I will."

"Good. I'll ask the housekeeper the price and will give you the bill this afternoon." He returned to his cake and waved his hand in dismissal.

Sylvia handed her the dish with a grin and whispered, "I'm glad he's letting you do this."

"Me, too." Peggy took the dish and hurried back to her room, where she changed into a blue dress and matching bonnet. Her heart hammered in her chest as she stepped outside.

The young man who had helped her before hurried up to her. "Can I help you with something, Miss Bradford?"

"I need a wagon for this afternoon, Mr. James."

"I'm sorry, Miss Bradford. No one told me you needed a wagon. I'll go see if we have one available." He rushed off.

Cold air swept around the building, tugging at Peggy's bonnet. She looked in the direction the young man had gone. It would take him a few moments to return. She decided to go back inside and get her coat.

A few minutes later she returned, just as he brought the wagon to the door. "Here you are, Miss Bradford." Malcolm jumped down and took the baking dish from her hands.

Peggy climbed onto the seat. She held out her hands for the baking dish. Her gaze moved about the back door. Several young men stood off to the side, talking beside the wall.

He handed her the dish. "Do you want to go alone again today?"

Her gaze returned to his. Malcolm looked as if he'd like to go. Since they didn't look too busy, she decided she'd like for him to come with her. "Do you know where the bee-keeper lives?"

"Yes, ma'am." He nodded.

"Then would you mind driving me to his house?" She told herself she asked him to accompany her because she needed a chaperone.

"Not at all. Let me tell the others where I'm going."

Peggy nodded and waited while he ran to the group of young men. The truth was if he attended, she'd have an excuse to leave quickly. After all, when she explained her reaction to bees and that they could never be together, Mark wouldn't want her around, anyway.

Malcolm jogged back and pulled himself into the seat beside her. On the way he whistled under his breath, and she thought about how she'd tell Mark there was no future for them. Her eyes burned with unshed tears.

They pulled up in front of a small house with wooden shutters and a porch. An older man came around the cabin with an armload of firewood. He stopped and looked toward them.

Malcolm set the brake and called out, "Good morning, Mr. Mathers. We're looking for Mark this morning. Is he still around?"

The old man looked from Peggy to Malcolm. "Not this morning. He's moving the hives closer in today. Can I help you?"

Both men looked to Peggy. She stood to get out of the wagon. From the corner of her eye, she saw the old man looking around for a place to lay the wood. Waving her hand at him, she set the covered dish on the seat. "No need to stop your work, Mr. Mathers. I'll bring the apple black caps to you, sir."

Malcolm jumped from the wagon and hurried to her side to help her down. Once her feet were on the ground, the young man handed the dish to her.

She turned to face Mr. Mathers. Her thoughts went to Joshua. He'd mentioned early on that his grandfather had told him not to disturb Mark about his reading. She felt an instant dislike for the old man; still, she needed to get the dessert into Mark's hands.

He nodded and then led the way up the porch. Opening the screen door with his foot, he shoved through it and indicated for Peggy to follow. Once inside the door, Peggy waited for him to drop the load into the wood box and then extended the apple dish. "Would you please see that Mr. Ludman and his son get this?"

He cocked his head to the side. "You're Peggy Bradford, aren't you?"

"Yes, sir." She continued to hold out the dessert.

The screen door shut behind Malcolm as he followed them into the house.

Mr. Mathers rubbed his chin. "Then I think you and I should have a chat, young lady."

Peggy looked to Malcolm. He shrugged.

Mr. Mathers indicated one of the two rockers that rested on each side of a wood burning stove. "I'm harmless, Miss Bradford."

He might think he was harmless, but she'd seen firsthand how his words could harm. Hadn't his words injured Joshua and Mark's relationship? Joshua had almost gone through life thinking he couldn't read, all because this old man had told him not to bother his father with his problems. The boy had thought he couldn't confide in his own father. Yes, words could hurt.

"Malcolm, why don't you go water that horse out back? Our talk will be done by the time you return." The old man dismissed the boy, turning his back on him and sitting down in the other rocker.

Once Malcolm shut the door behind him, Mr. Mathers turned his attention on Peggy. He indicated the dessert dish that she still held in her lap. "Why did you bring that here, Miss Bradford?"

Peggy glanced down at the dish. Her respect for elders kept her from telling him it was none of his business. "I. . ." She stopped. Why did she bring the dish? Hadn't she realized Mark and Joshua wouldn't be home at this time of day? *Yes.*

She'd planned on leaving the dish and her apologies and

heading back to the Biltmore house. It was the coward's way, and she'd taken it. Not only because she feared getting stung by a wayward bee, but also because she feared her love for Mark would show on her face. Saying good-bye to him and Joshua would have been too hard.

"That's what I thought," he said in a soft voice.

Peggy looked up and found he'd leaned forward to search her face.

"Don't look so shocked. I can see you love Mark. You have to." His brown eyes looked deeply into hers.

"I have to?" she asked. "And why is that, Mr. Mathers?"

He leaned back in his chair and rubbed his chin again. "Mark hasn't looked at another woman since my Molly died. Both he and Joshua talk about you with respect and a sense of devotion. And there is no denying the heart, Miss Bradford. Yours has fallen in love with my son-in-law."

Peggy's heart expanded then broke. Mr. Mathers had told her what deep down she already knew, that Mark cared for her. "Thanks for letting me know he cares for me, but what makes you think I feel the same way about him?"

Mr. Mathers nodded. "It's in your eyes, child."

She shook her head in denial. The last thing Peggy wanted was for Mark to know that she loved him and his son very much.

He leaned toward her and said gently, "What I don't understand is why you won't admit it?"

Peggy scooted away from him and tried to ignore his knowing look. She couldn't lie and outright say she didn't care about Mark.

"Why, Miss Bradford? He's a good man. He works hard, loves his son, and would make a wonderful husband. So why?" With each word he'd leaned even closer to her.

In desperation Peggy heard the words squeeze from her tight throat. "Because he's a beekeeper."

Mr. Mathers looked as if she'd slapped him. He moved back into his own seat and admitted, "I don't understand."

A lone tear slipped down her cheeks. Peggy sighed. What would it hurt to tell the old man? "I'm allergic to bees, Mr. Mathers. One sting and I could die."

"I see." He rocked back in his chair.

Malcolm knocked on the door and then entered the house. "I refilled your horse's water troughs, Mr. Mathers. Is there anything else I can do for you?"

Peggy swiped at her wet cheeks. She hadn't realized the tears had flowed from her eyes. She took a deep breath and stood to go.

"No, Malcolm. Thanks for taking care of the animals for me."

"Anytime. Miss Bradford, are you ready to go?"

At her nod, Malcolm turned to leave. She followed him back to the horse and wagon.

On the porch Peggy realized she still held the apple black caps. She turned back to the old man, who had followed them outside, and handed the baking dish to him. "Would you give this to Mr. Ludman and ask him to return the dish to the Biltmore house when he's finished with it?"

She hesitated and then pressed on. "Please tell him I don't want to see him anymore."

Mr. Mathers took the dessert and nodded.

"Thank you." Peggy hurried down the steps and allowed Malcolm to help her onto the wagon.

❋

Mark sighed as he turned from the servants' entrance. This was the third time in two weeks he'd tried to talk to Peggy. Each time he was told she was not available. Mark had no reason to doubt she was busy. Everyone was preparing for Christmas. He walked back to the wagon, where Frank waited.

As he took the reins and headed home, his father-in-law said, "So you're going to let her get away, aren't you?"

He took a deep breath. "I can't make her see me, Frank."

"No?"

"No." Mark slapped the reins a little too hard across the horse's back. The little black mare glanced over her shoulder and snorted. "Sorry, old girl."

He glanced sideways at his father-in-law.

"Seems to me if you love her, you'll figure out a way."

Mark ignored him. He stared straight ahead. Soft snow-flakes began drifting to the ground. He tugged his collar up and ducked his head deeper inside the warmth of his coat. Christmas would soon be here, and what was he going to do?

"I heard Mr. Lark is selling his farm on the other side of Asheville."

That caught his attention. Mark looked to the old man. He'd sunk deeper into his coat, too. Frank gazed off in the distance as if he'd just been sharing some local gossip.

Joshua had been talking for weeks about farming, growing crops, and setting up a vegetable-and-fruit stand in the fall. Would they be able to buy the Lark land? "Did you happen to hear how much he wants for the place?"

"Nope, but I was thinking maybe we could go and check this afternoon, if this snow doesn't get too deep."

Mark nodded. Maybe this was the chance he needed, but then there was his father-in-law to think about. Frank loved the beekeeping business. Mark chewed the inside of his jaw.

"You know, if we bought the place, I could have a couple of small hives and still harvest honey while you and the boy bring in the fruits and vegetables. Of course someone would need to take care of the cow, chickens, and maybe a couple of pigs." Frank rubbed his chin as if deep in thought.

"You wouldn't mind only having a few hives to take care of?" Mark asked. After all, it was because of his father-in-law that he'd taken the job at Biltmore. Frank had insisted he could help take care of the insects, but the truth of the matter had been that he couldn't. His mind wanted to, but his body just couldn't keep up with the amount of work required. Mark had ended up doing the job alone.

"Of course, I'm getting old, Mark. A couple of hives is about all I can handle. I've lived my life the way I wanted to. It's only fair that you and Josh be able to do the same." He reached out and patted Mark on the shoulder.

For the first time in years, Mark felt as if he was no longer being held down by the past. He grinned. "Thank you."

Josh would be thrilled with a farm for Christmas. He'd

been disappointed when Mark had told him that it didn't look as if he and Peggy would be married by Christmas. This might make him smile again.

A smile tugged at his lips. Then again if he could get Peggy to agree, they could marry shortly after Christmas and have a farm. A real farm. Doubts entered his mind. Would Peggy enjoy taking care of a cow, chickens, and a couple of pigs? Or was she content to forever cook for others? In a fancy kitchen?

Apple Black Caps

Ingredients:
    1 quart nice apples
    Sugar
    Cloves
    Yellow rind of lemon or orange

Instructions:
Pare apples, core without breaking; set side by side in baking dish that will just hold them. Fill centers with sugar, and place two cloves in the top of each one; grate over them the yellow rind of lemon or orange, and put into moderate oven only until tender. Do not let them break apart. As soon as they are tender, turn broiler on and broil until black. Serve either hot or cold.

A porcelain-lined baking dish, or a gratin pan, is the best dish for cooking the black caps, because either can be set on a clean plate and sent to the table. If the apples have to be removed from the dish in which they were baked, they may be broken, and then the appearance of the dish will be spoiled. The flavor of the dish may be changed by varying the spice.

Chapter 10

Peggy's Christmas Fruitcake

Peggy pulled the fruitcakes from the oven. The fragrant smells of candied fruit filled the kitchen. She placed them on a counter and looked about the busy kitchen.

In a few days, it would be Christmas, and she'd be heading home again. Mama Elsie expected Charity, Selma, and herself. Melissa was already there, helping Mama Elsie bake and decorate. Would Mama Elsie be disappointed that she hadn't found love at Biltmore like her younger sisters?

Only she had found love. For days she'd been avoiding Mark. She couldn't ask him to give up beekeeping for her, and she couldn't be around bees. So she'd resigned herself to avoid him. Then after Christmas she'd return to the Reynolds family, and life would go on. *An empty life.*

She swiped at the tears that came unbidden.

"Miss Bradford."

Peggy's spine straightened. Chef McConnell stood behind her. She wiped her eyes and then turned to face him. "Yes, sir?"

"A word, please." He spun on his heel and headed down the hallway.

She followed, expecting the worst. Would he dismiss her? Why couldn't the tears only come in the privacy of her room? He led Peggy into the servants' sitting room. Her gaze moved about the empty room. Thankfully no one would witness her reprimand. He indicated a chair and after she sat, he took the other one across from her.

"Normally I wouldn't get involved, but this time I feel I need to. Christmas, Jesus' birth, should be a time of joy, yet I can see you are hurting and full of grief," he said.

Peggy opened her mouth to tell him she was fine, but he raised a hand to stop her.

"I know it's none of my business and that we're not family, but I care about you like a father cares for his daughter, and right now I think you might need some fatherly advice."

Fresh tears filled her eyes and spilled over. Her own father had died when she was young. She knew her heavenly Father loved her, but the love of an earthly father had been absent from her life for so long. She felt her throat close with yearning. All she could do was nod her acknowledgment of his words.

"Mr. Ludman has been coming around frequently during the last few weeks. He seems quite smitten with you, and from the look on your face, I'd say you feel the same way. Am I correct?" He rested his arms on the white apron across his knees.

Peggy wanted to answer, but her throat was too tight, and her eyes wouldn't stop tearing up. Again she nodded.

"What is stopping you from loving him? Is it the Biltmore rules? Are you afraid you'll be fired?" He leaned back and pulled a large white handkerchief from his pocket, offering it to her.

She accepted it, blew her nose, wiped her face, and cleared her throat. "No, sir. I can't be with him because he's the beekeeper." His frown told her he needed further explanation. "I'm allergic to bee stings. Mama Elsie says I'll die if I get stung again."

Understanding showed on his features. "I see."

Peggy wiped her face once more and twisted the kerchief in her hands. "So we can't be together."

"Yes you can."

Didn't he understand? She could die. "How?"

"If you were to marry this young man, would you be working with the bees?"

"No." Peggy really didn't think he understood. "But when he comes home, he might have one on him, on his clothes. I could be stung." Fresh tears spilled down her face as she voiced her fears.

"Peggy, if you truly love him, you will trust him to not bring the bees inside. He could change his clothes in the barn and come in, wearing fresh clothes or something like that."

As she blew her nose, her thoughts went to what he'd just said. Was that possible? Could Mark protect her?

Chef McConnell said, "Peggy, I know you are a church-going woman. Don't you trust God to protect you?"

Her head snapped up, and she looked into his eyes. Hadn't she read the scripture this morning that said to trust in the Lord with all her heart and lean not on her own understanding? She knew she had. It might not have been written just like that, but it was what she'd read. "Of course I do."

"Then trust in Him."

Peggy offered him back his handkerchief, but he waved it aside. "You can return it to me later." He patted her shoulder. "Why don't you take a few minutes and compose yourself? Then you can return to the kitchen."

She nodded. "Thank you, Chef McConnell. I'll think and pray on all you've said."

❄

Satisfaction radiated from Mark's being. He'd just signed the papers on the Lark farm and as hard as he tried, he couldn't stop the smile that insisted on spreading his lips. Joshua bounced on the seat beside him. He talked nonstop of the crops they'd grow and the livestock they'd buy. Thankfully the cow and chickens had come with the farm.

The thought of the barnyard animals and the small herb garden outside the kitchen door brought visions of Peggy working and living on the farm. He looked down at the honey pot at his feet. He'd attached a card and planned on dropping it off at the kitchens for her.

Two more weeks had passed, and she still hadn't spoken to him. He knew the kitchens were busy preparing for Christmas, and that he'd probably not be allowed to see her again today, but that didn't stop him from pointing the wagon toward the Biltmore house. Mark wanted to share everything with her and prayed that this time would be different.

"Papa, would you drop me off here? I'd like to go tell Benjamin about our new farm," Joshua asked.

Mark pulled the horses to a stop. "Be home by dinner," he called after the boy who'd already leaped from the wagon, headed toward his friend's home.

"I will." Joshua waved and continued on.

Mark clucked his tongue and gently flicked the reins. The closer he came to the mansion, the more his stomach fluttered. Would she see him? What would she say? They hadn't talked in so long. Could Frank be wrong? Was it more than the fear of bees that kept her away? He shook his head and demanded the questions to stop.

"Mark, you've prayed about this. May He give you the desire of your heart and make all your plans succeed. God has given you the strength to see this through. If she still doesn't want to talk to you, you'll have to abide by her decision." Reciting scripture and talking to himself did nothing to settle the butterflies in his stomach.

In the distance, a woman walked toward him. He didn't recognize her, but something in the way she walked, with her face tilted toward the sky, made him think of Peggy. Mark guided the horses to the side of the road so that when she got even with him, she could pass. He stopped and set the brake.

The closer she came, the more he felt sure the woman was Peggy. In a low voice he said, "Thank You, Lord."

When she came within hearing range, he called, "Hello."

A soft smile touched her lips. "Hello."

Unsure what else to say, Mark blurted out. "I was just on

my way to see you."

"I wanted to see you, too." She held out a box to him. "I brought you something for Christmas."

Mark took the offered package. Her soft eyes studied his face.

"I'm sorry I've been so busy these last few weeks. I've been a little confused, too," she added, looking at the ground.

He wanted to reach out and touch the soft hair that escaped her hat. "I have something for you, too." To keep his hands away from her, he reached inside the wagon bed and pulled out the pot of honey. He straightened the card on it, said a silent prayer, and handed it to her.

"Can we sit down for a moment?" she asked.

"Of course." He took her hand and led her to the back of the wagon.

She handed the honey back to him and then climbed into the wagon. He hid a smile behind his hand. Peggy reminded him of a little girl as she found her seating and swung her legs over the edge. Once situated, she extended her hands for the honey. "Would you get your box? I'd like for you to open it, and then we can talk."

Mark did as she said. The smile on her face and warmth in her eyes gave him hope. He returned a few seconds later and hopped up beside her in the wagon.

"Go ahead and open it." She held her bottom lip between her teeth as she waited for him to do as she said.

He opened the box to find a fruitcake nestled in red and green paper, a little card resting on the top of the folds of the paper. Mark picked up the card and looked into Peggy's light-blue eyes. At her nod, he opened the card and read aloud, "I'm nutty for you."

A rumble built in his chest and tumbled out his lips. "That's a great play on words. I'm nutty for you, too." He leaned forward and brushed his nose with hers.

She scooted away from him. "I'm sorry I avoided you. I was scared." He started to speak, but she laid a gloved finger across his lips. "Please let me finish. I am allergic to bees, and I was afraid of being stung and dying. But now I'm not afraid anymore. I'm trusting in the Lord to take care of me, of us." She removed her finger.

Mark picked up her hand. "Will you open my card now?"

She nodded. He held his breath as he waited for her to read the card. Mark knew the words by heart; he'd rehearsed them many times in his head. *Honey, I'd rather spend every Christmas with you. I can do without the bees. Will you marry me?*

Peggy's eyes filled with tears, and she looked up at him. "Mark, I can't ask you to give up beekeeping for me."

"You didn't. I wanted to. I've always wanted to be a farmer, but my father and father-in-law were both bee men. I followed in their footsteps to make them happy. But, thanks to you, I bought a farm and now can live my dream." He took a deep breath and pressed on. "Please say you'll marry me."

Peggy realized that like her sisters before her, she'd found love on the Biltmore estate. "Yes. I'll marry you." Her eyes glistened with unshed happy tears as he reached out and kissed her.

Peggy's Christmas Fruitcake

Ingredients:
    2 cups butter
    2½ cups sugar
    2½ cups molasses
    8 cups flour
    2 cups sour milk
    8 eggs
    2 teaspoons soda
    3 pounds raisins
    3 pounds currants
    1 pound citron
    1 pound figs
    2 lemons (grate rind and squeeze juice)
    2 glasses jelly
    Cloves
    Mace
    Cinnamon
    Nutmeg
    Nuts

Instructions:
Mix flour, butter, sugar, molasses, sour milk, eggs, and soda together. Then layer flour mixture with fruit alternately. Bake 3½ hours at 250 degrees.

Rhonda Gibson resides in New Mexico with her husband. She writes romance because she is eager to share her love of the Lord. Besides writing, her interests are reading and scrapbooking recipes. Rhonda loves hearing from her readers! P.O. Box 835, Kirtland, NM 87417, rgib2001@yahoo.com, www.RhondaGibson.com

AN ACCIDENTAL CHRISTMAS

Diane T. Ashley with Aaron McCarver

Dedication

To my coauthor.
I could not do it without you.

Chapter 1

I wish I was a boy.

The familiar phrase ran through Melissa Bradford's head as her hands gripped the reins of the Vanderbilts' mare, and her vision centered on a farm wagon in the valley below her. The farmer was loading it with pumpkins, kale, and other winter vegetables in preparation for its end-of-week trip to Biltmore Village.

Weak late-November sunlight washed across the gentle hills of her employer's acreage, but it failed to warm her shoulders. With an impatient finger, she swiped at the tears dampening her cheeks. She refused to dwell on what could not be changed. She had been born a girl, and no matter how wrong it seemed to her, she would never be miraculously turned into a boy.

A sigh of resignation filled her. Another thing that could not be changed was the disaster in the brown laundry. She couldn't return there. Miss Bohburg, the Swedish laundress who oversaw the laundry maids, would not allow her to get near any of the Vanderbilts' clothing ever again, especially not the gowns belonging to the Vanderbilts' three-month-old daughter.

Melissa leaned forward and pressed her face against the neck of the horse she was supposed to be exercising. "You don't care whether I have skills, do you?"

The mare tossed its head as if impatient with her rider's self-pity. Melissa sat up and sighed once more before turning the horse's head north. Was there time to visit Mama Elsie at the orphanage?

Miss Bohburg had told her not to return to her domain today. And who could blame her? Melissa had destroyed one of the handmade gowns belonging to little Cornelia. But she had managed to make an adjustment to the wringer so it would never happen again to her or anyone else. It was so unfair. As a man, she could have put her mechanical solutions to work, and everyone would applaud her talents. As a female, all anyone saw were her mistakes.

She tightened her knees to encourage her mount into a faster pace. Together they galloped past the formal gardens and into the leafless winter woodland, but Melissa could not outrun the look of horror on the head laundress's face when she first saw the shredded garment. That moment seemed the culmination of her three months at Biltmore, a low point to haunt the rest of her life. How excited she had been to follow in her older sisters' footsteps. How thrilled to be chosen to work at the largest house in all of America. But that was before she realized she had no useful skills, or at least no useful *feminine* skills. If only she had been born—

Melissa's thoughts ended abruptly as she rounded the bend, coming face-to-face with a roaring, smoking beast. Death hurtled toward her with the speed of a bullet. Her horse reared, and she fought to keep her seat as her heart clenched in fear. Time seemed to slow as she pulled back on the reins. The huge specter hurtled toward her, turning away at the last possible instant. Tree limbs snapped, and startled birds left their shelter as the screaming monster plunged into the woods.

The front hooves of her frightened mare came down on the roadway, and Melissa pranced away from the snorting, snarling attacker she finally recognized as a horseless carriage. As she thought the words, a mighty crash rang through the woods, followed by a yell. She twisted her head to see the driver catapulted from the seat of his vehicle, following a wide arc before hitting the ground several feet away.

Was he dead? Melissa scrambled down from her saddle and ran toward the stranger, pushing back the accusing voice in her head as she knelt next to him. The accident was all her fault, but she didn't have time to think about that now.

The unconscious man was very pale, but his chest was moving up and down. At least he was alive.

Unsure of what to do, she lifted his head into her lap and gently brushed his jet-black hair away from his face. "Please wake up."

Round rubber goggles hid his eyes. Melissa removed them, hoping his eyelids would flutter. But they remained closed. Her fingers gently probed his head, pushing back the thick hair to encounter a lump the size of a hen's egg. No wonder he was unconscious.

The stranger had a handsome face—broad forehead, straight nose, and a square chin cleft by a deep dimple. She wondered where he had come from. And why was he here? Was he a friend of Mr. Vanderbilt's? Would he awaken?

She closed her eyes. *Lord, please send help. This stranger is hurt because I wasn't paying attention. Please don't make him suffer for my faults.*

A noise from the road behind her brought Melissa's head up. A pair of horses, pulling the laden farm wagon she had seen earlier, rounded the same curve she had recently traveled.

Carefully sliding from under the stranger's head, Melissa jumped to her feet and ran to the edge of the road. "Stop! Oh please stop."

The farmer, a burly man with broad shoulders and thick arms, pulled back on the reins. "Whoa, boys." The wagon rolled to a halt. "What's the matter?"

"There's been an accident." Melissa pointed to the stranger. "The driver was thrown from his horseless carriage. Can you help me get him to the hospital in the village?"

The older man climbed down and tied the horses' reins around a tree trunk. "Let's see what we have here." He walked to where the stranger lay still as death. "Here we go." He lifted the man over his shoulder, carried him to the wagon, and settled him onto the front bench. He turned back to Melissa. "Can you hold him here while I go to the other side?"

Melissa nodded and reached upward. He was heavy, but she managed to keep him from falling over for the short time it took the driver to climb into his seat.

The farmer leaned his passenger toward him and grabbed

for the reins before looking down at her with a frown. "I'm sorry there's no room for you up here. Are you hurt? Do you need me to come back and get you after I deliver this fellow to the hospital?"

With a shake of her head, Melissa looked around. The mare stood a few feet away. "I'll be right behind you."

The farmer must have seen the direction of her gaze because he nodded. "That's good then." He clucked at his horses, and the wagon trundled forward.

A convenient fallen log served as a mounting block. In a matter of seconds, she climbed into the saddle and headed toward town. The beauty of the woodland scenery was lost on her. Her whole focus centered on the stranger. Would he survive?

Her earlier problems were swallowed up in her concern for his recovery. But the voice of accusation grew louder with each yard she traveled. When would she learn to be more careful? More aware of her surroundings? More in control of her impulses? And how many others would have to bear the burden of her inadequacies?

❄

"It's not your fault." Robert Griffith's concerned gaze checked the tired mare for any sign of injury as he spoke to Melissa.

"How can you say that?" Melissa brushed the mare with long strokes. "If I'd been paying more attention to the road, I would have heard the motorcar coming."

"And done what?" Robert snorted. "Ridden the mare into a ravine? The river?"

Melissa stopped currying and focused her gaze on him. Blond curls framed his face and teased the tops of his ears. An impish grin turned his mouth upward as his blue gaze challenged her. Although he was a year younger, Robert had begun working at Biltmore almost three years ago. He was a stable hand, one of the young men who cared for the extensive stables kept by George and Edith Vanderbilt. But she had known him more than ten years.

She still remembered the day his widowed papa dropped him off at the orphanage. Robert had been a frightened, grieving little boy. Her heart was touched by his pain, and she took him under her wing. Some of the older children thought he would be an easy target because of his youth and head full of soft curls. But when they found out she was his champion, they left Robert alone. The two of them had become inseparable as they grew, pulling each other out of scrapes almost on a weekly basis. Although it always seemed Robert did most of the pulling, while she did most of the scraping.

The past faded away as her friend pointed a finger in her direction. "You have to stop blaming yourself for everything that goes wrong."

"I guess you're right." Dropping the currycomb into a bucket at her feet, Melissa sighed. "But bad luck follows me everywhere I go. I appreciate your letting me take the mare out to exercise her. I needed something to do. But instead of enjoying a calming ride, I had to run right into an automobile. How many other people experience two calamitous events in one day?"

"Plenty of other folks."

His answer made her eyebrows climb toward her hairline. "Name one."

"I don't know, Melissa. But you are not the only one who suffers, you know. You really ought to be counting your blessings. Seems to me the Good Lord was watching out for you today. After all, it could be you lying in a hospital bed, or worse."

Her conscience pricked her at his words. Robert was right. She should not be whining about her luck when a man lay in the hospital recuperating. And his beautiful machine lay broken in the woods. An idea popped into her head. She could feel a smile stretching her mouth as she glanced toward her friend.

He groaned. "What now?"

"I was thinking we could surprise the stranger by getting his vehicle brought here so I could take a look at it. Who knows? Maybe we could get it running by the time he gets out of the hospital."

Robert's eyes narrowed. "I suppose you think I should help you retrieve it."

"Oh, would you?" Melissa clasped her hands together and tried to assume an angelic appearance, but she knew her mud-splattered skirts and flyaway hair marred her attempt.

Throwing his hands in the air, Robert chuckled. "You can drop the act. I know you far too well."

Melissa couldn't stop the smile on her face. Robert was a good friend. "Do you think we could use the Percherons?" The huge draft horses were the best animals in the stable for the job ahead of them.

"I'll go ask *Signore* Ribet," he said, naming the Italian stableman. "You put the mare back in her stall." He walked to the stable door. "And make sure she gets plenty of food."

Chapter 2

The first thing Ned felt was pain. Pain in his right leg. Pain in his right arm. Pain in his head. He tried to move, groaning with the effort. Bright light made him put his hand in front of his eyes.

"I need to check your pupils." The accented voice held a note of authority, as though the woman it belonged to was used to giving orders. "That's right. Don't fight me."

Ned allowed the fingers to manipulate his eyelids as they pried open one lid, then the other.

"Where—" He coughed and started over. "Where am I?" His throat was dry. Like he'd swallowed cotton while he slept. He coughed again.

Immediately the woman's hands moved from his eyes. After a moment a cup touched his lips.

Ned opened his mouth, and sweet, cool water flowed down his throat. The cup moved away after a moment, and he breathed, the air coming easier than before.

"Is that better?" The woman's outline solidified as she removed the cup from his mouth. A frilly white cap outlined her kind face. His bewildered gaze took in her gray dress covered by a white pinafore.

"Where am I?" His voice was not as raspy as before.

"Biltmore Village."

The two words brought a flood of memories. Traveling across steep mountains, looking for fuel, tinkering with the complex engine of his brand-new machine. He remembered the jubilation when he caught his first glimpse of Biltmore, the palatial home of George and Edith Vanderbilt. Then. . . nothing. He reached a hand toward his head, his aching head. "Who are you?"

She patted his hand. "I'm Sarah, your nurse. You're lucky your accident occurred so near our hospital. Who knows what might have happened to you if little Melissa Bradford hadn't brought you to us."

Little Melissa Bradford? Who was she talking about? A child had brought him to the hospital? The words made no sense.

As Ned was trying to formulate a question, the door to his room opened and a middle-aged man with thinning brown hair stepped inside. "How is your newest patient?"

Sarah straightened and turned her back to Ned. "Good afternoon, Brother Martin. He's just awakened, but I believe he'll recover his full health."

Ned didn't feel very healthy right now. His head throbbed and even though the ache in his arm had eased somewhat, his leg still hurt.

"The doctor said he shouldn't have any lasting effects from his concussion, and the rest of his aches and pains are bumps and sprains." The nurse patted his shoulder and glanced down at him as though she expected him to applaud her optimistic appraisal.

Ned pushed against the bed, trying to raise himself to

a sitting position. The nurse's hand, however, applied some force to keep him pressed against the bed. He should have been able to overcome her gesture, but he was as weak as a newborn pup.

"You don't have to sit up because the pastor is here." Her voice was a mixture of sternness and understanding. "He knows you were in an accident."

"That's right. I'm Martin Thomas, Brother Martin to most of the folks around here." The pastor stepped to the end of his bed. "It's a blessing to see you awake."

He stopped struggling for now. As soon as Sarah the nurse moved away, he would sit up on his own. "How long have I been asleep?"

"Let's see." Sarah glanced toward the window. "It's Monday, December 3. You've been here three days."

Ned's gaze followed hers to the window. He could see the slopes of mountains in the distance, their ridges softening as the sun disappeared behind them. Had he really been asleep for three days? He glanced to the pastor for confirmation and saw the man's nod.

"The Lord blessed you with some needed rest while your body healed."

"Yes, sir. But now I need to get up and resume my life."

"Not so fast, young man." Sarah's grip tightened on his shoulder. "You still need a few days of recuperation."

"I cannot afford a few days." Ned turned on his side, the only movement her hand would allow. "I probably can't even afford the care already lavished on me."

"From the look of your clothes when Melissa brought

you to us, I'd guess you're not penniless, Mister. . ." The nurse's voice trailed off in an obvious request for his name.

He searched his memory for a minute, relieved to find the answer. "Robinson. Ned Robinson."

"Mr. Robinson." The hand patted his shoulder once again. "And you were driving an expensive vehicle on your way to visit our wealthy patrons, the Vanderbilts."

"My motorcar!" Concern flooded him. "Please don't tell me it's been exposed to vandals and the weather for three days."

The nurse rolled her eyes and left the two men alone in the room.

The pastor stepped forward. "That's one reason I came by to see you. We're not exactly sure what's happened to your motorcar."

"What do you mean?"

"A couple of local boys went up to see it, but they came back saying they couldn't find it."

Ned shook his head. "It can't be true. They must have looked in the wrong place."

"They searched the whole length of Approach Road." Brother Martin sighed. "They found broken limbs and some deep ruts in one spot. But no sign of your vehicle."

"You don't seem to understand." Ned's hand gripped the edge of his mattress. "This is a disaster. Everything I have is tied up in that machine. If I can't recover it, all my dreams will be lost."

"Perhaps this is God's way of guiding you onto another pathway."

"I don't want another path. I want my motorcar, or what's left of it, anyway." Ned heard the belligerence in his voice and paused for a moment to rein in his anger. It wasn't the pastor's fault his vehicle was missing. "If I have to look behind every tree in George Vanderbilt's forest, I will get it back."

The older man looked at him, his blue eyes radiating understanding. "Although I admire your enthusiasm, Ned, perhaps there's another way."

Ned's anger dissipated under the calm gaze and reassuring words. He pushed himself up and swung his legs over the edge of his bed. "I'll be glad to listen to any suggestions you have, sir."

"You were brought in by a young woman, Melissa Bradford."

"Melissa Bradford? The nurse mentioned her earlier. Who is she?"

"She was on the horse you nearly ran over."

Splinters of memory pierced the fog in his mind—a rearing horse, tree branches, fighting to control his vehicle, and the smell of lilacs. Everything fell into place. "She's the reason for this disaster." Ned took a deep breath and launched himself out of the bed. The room swayed as though in a breeze but quickly settled back to normalcy. His legs were rather shaky, but they held him up. That's all he needed. He spied his trousers lying across the top of a chair in one corner of his room and limped toward them.

"I don't think you're supposed to be up yet."

"I've wasted enough time as it is." Ned drew a shaky

breath as he pulled on his trousers and tucked his shirt into them. He had a direction now, a goal to pursue. He felt better already. "I can't wait to talk to Miss Bradford. After all, she's the reason I'm in this fix. If she hadn't been cavorting through the woods on a horse she could not control, I wouldn't have had to run my motorcar off the road. I wouldn't have been injured. I could have already met with Mr. Vanderbilt and received his blessing." He buttoned his shirt with stiff fingers, but the rush of blood made him feel better. All he had to do was continue fanning the flame of his anger. "The sooner I get hold of Miss Bad News Bradford, the better off I'll be. She'd better—"

His words were cut off as the door to his room swung open and an auburn-haired young woman stepped inside. "I came today to check on your health, Mr. Robinson. But it seems I should not have wasted my time."

Lightning seemed to crackle between them. Who was she? He was struck by the intensity of her gaze and the way she stood up to him, even though she barely reached the height of his shoulder. Admiration filled him. This was no simpering young woman like the ones his family often promoted as bridal candidates.

Brother Martin cleared his throat. "Good morning, Miss Melissa."

Melissa? Melissa Bradford? He groaned. Why hadn't anyone mentioned how beautiful his albatross was? Her features were delicate—a pair of wide-set eyes as green as blades of grass, a pert little nose, and a wide, generous mouth currently pulled into a tight line. She tilted her chin up and stared at him, her eyes throwing angry sparks.

Why was she still single? Perhaps her heart was cold as a blizzard, or maybe she had a string of men chasing her and she was taking her time choosing one. "Where is my horseless carriage?"

"Is that what it is? I've read some call it a quadricycle." Her tone was cool, even though her glare practically singed him.

Ned could feel his neck growing hot. "It's my property, and I call it a horseless carriage or a motorcar."

"I suppose that's fair." The fire died out of her gaze. Now her eyes reminded him of summertime, a shady forest. The more he stared into them, the more they seemed to change—greens and grays and browns swirled together, drawing him further in.

For a moment Ned forgot what they were talking about. His heart accelerated. He had never seen eyes like hers.

Brother Martin stepped between them. "I trust everything is going well at Biltmore."

Ned put a brake on the rhythm of his heart as she turned her green gaze toward the pastor. "Not especially."

The pastor nodded. "I heard you had a problem in the laundry."

"I guess I wasn't paying attention." Her cheeks reddened and she glanced at the floor.

Ned couldn't stop the harsh laughter that filled his throat. "So it's a normal occurrence for you, then."

The lightning returned to her eyes. Ned wondered why he was baiting her. No one had ever accused him of being mean. But he'd rather see her angry than downhearted. "Do you know where my motorcar is?"

"As a matter of fact, I do. I have it. And you ought to thank me for taking care of it instead of casting aspersions on my character." She looked at him as though he were a slug and, truth to tell, he felt a bit slimy. But her words wiped his conscience clear. She'd stolen his motorcar.

Ned pointed a finger at her. "Don't touch my motorcar. I won't hear of it." A sudden weakness swept him. He supposed it was relief at knowing his vehicle—his plan for the future—wasn't gone for good. He sank back to his bed. "Don't do anything to it." Was that puny sound his voice?

Brother Martin put a hand on Ned's forehead. "Why don't you lie down."

He allowed the gentle man to pull the cover over him "Don't. . .hurt. . .my motorcar." Someone held a cup to his lips, and he was enveloped once again in the scent of lilacs. Green eyes chased him into an uneasy rest.

Chapter 3

Melissa stormed out of the hospital and marched back to Biltmore. How dare Mr. Robinson tell her not to touch his precious motorcar? If it weren't for her, the vehicle would have sat out in the weather. She had only been trying to do him a favor. And what did she get for her trouble? Insults and suspicion.

Besides, she probably knew more about his horseless carriage than he did. She had studied it carefully and understood exactly how it ran. Well, maybe not exactly. But she had a very good idea.

Her anger cooled as a yawn stretched her mouth. Melissa should have refused Robert's advice to visit the driver and reassure him about his vehicle. But her friend had been very patient with her the past two nights. He had even ignored the maid he was sweet on to help her work on the stranger's vehicle.

They had spent the first night cleaning mud, dirt, and debris from the vehicle. Of course she splashed a liberal amount onto her dress and apron. On the second day, she had donned her oldest clothes and appropriated a leather apron from the carpenter's shed with a promise to return it as soon as she finished her work. Although the apron was heavy, it did protect her clothing from oil and grime as she slid under the horseless carriage and studied its workings.

Its engine was a marvel, as beautiful as any of the artwork inside the Vanderbilts' house. She understood instinctively that every part of the engine had to be in balance or it could not perform properly.

Melissa stopped and swung back toward the village. How could she have forgotten to stop by the mercantile when she left the hospital? She had planned to purchase a monkey wrench to continue her repairs. But that was before the infuriating Mr. Robinson had forbidden her to touch his precious machine. She kicked a pinecone that lay on the path and watched as it tumbled into the woods.

Sighing, she turned her face toward Biltmore and resumed her trek, eventually arriving at the palatial house that never failed to amaze her. Gargoyles watched her progress silently from the many levels of roofline and turrets, their malevolent expressions a contrast to the graceful lines of Vanderbilt's castle.

Robert met her at the stable entrance. "They've been looking for you."

"Who?"

"Nora came out here awhile back." His face turned ruddy, and he kicked at a bit of straw at his feet.

Melissa knew her friend was infatuated with the young chambermaid and would normally have teased him about whether or not he had enjoyed her visit, but his next words took away her breath.

"Mrs. King wants you to come see her as soon as you get back."

She put a hand to her heart. Was she about to lose her employment? What would she do? Where would she go? Back to the orphanage? She couldn't do that to Mama Elsie. The warmhearted woman who had raised her and her three sisters could not afford to house and clothe her anymore. Melissa had to keep her job here.

Turning to go inside the main house, she felt her friend's worried gaze on her. She whispered a prayer for help as she made her way to Mrs. King's parlor. Here and there maids worked industriously, but not one of them spoke to her. Melissa's heart thudded painfully as she knocked on the parlor door.

"Enter." Mrs. King's British accent was evident even in the short command.

"You wanted to see me?" She caught a glimpse of herself in the mirror above the mantel as she entered the large room and wished she had taken time to rinse her face. It wouldn't make a good impression on Mrs. King if her chin was dirty. She pushed back a loose curl with a nervous hand.

"Miss Bradford, what have I been hearing about you?" Mrs. King sat behind a large desk, a pile of receipts and an open ledger in front of her. She closed the leather book and pushed her chair back. She stood and turned her back to Melissa, staring out a tall window at the mountains. "Is it true you ruined one of Baby Cornelia's irreplaceable gowns?"

Melissa cleared her throat. "Yes, ma'am, it's true, but I—"

"You fixed the wringer so it won't catch fabric in the future."

"Yes, ma'am." This time Melissa limited her response.

"Miss Bohburg is quite excited about your modification." Mrs. King turned around, her brown eyes calm. "This is not the first time you've improved something here at Biltmore."

Not knowing what to say, Melissa remained silent. There had been a pendulum clock in one of the guest bedrooms in the west wing, a room she had been assigned to dust during her first week at Biltmore. The clock was supposed to chime every quarter hour, but the clunking noise that issued from it was not at all pleasant. So Melissa retrieved her tools from her bedroom and worked on the clock.

After studying its workings, she understood the basic problem. Soon the clock was chiming again, but as she closed the casement and backed away, she had tripped over the edge of a rug. To stop herself from falling, Melissa had reached out and grabbed at the nearest surface, an English rosewood table with spindle legs. The table overturned and an expensive Tiffany lamp crashed to the floor and shattered. She had immediately been removed from the west wing.

"It seems you have a propensity for fixing things. An ability Mr. Burdette and I feel should be put to better use."

Her heart thumped. Mrs. King and the butler had been discussing her? And it sounded as though they were not planning to let her go, at least not for now. She breathed easier and untwisted her hands. "I would be glad to work wherever you feel is proper."

The older woman nodded. "Your three sisters gave such excellent service in the time they were here. And I don't doubt you will do the same. I have spoken to both Chef

Anderson and Monsieur Ceperlean about placing you in the kitchen where your sister Peggy worked."

The kitchen? She was going to cook? Melissa closed her eyes for a moment as myriad possible disasters came to mind. How she wished Peggy was still living in the area. Her oldest sister had done so well in the kitchens when she came to Biltmore. She had visited all of them at the orphanage from time to time with wondrous stories of the masterpieces being created by the culinary experts. Perhaps Melissa could write to her and ask for tips on how to please her new task-masters. And yet she knew how to do so—avoid any more catastrophes.

"You will help with the more menial tasks in the kitchens, but do not let that upset you, Melissa." Mrs. King's kindly voice brought her back to the present. "I am certain you will soon rise to the rank of assistant chef."

"Yes, ma'am." Melissa dropped into a curtsy. "When do I begin?"

The housekeeper smiled. "Such willingness is a good trait. You are to report to Monsieur Ceperlean immediately. But please try to stay out of trouble. I don't know where we will place you if you are not successful in the kitchens."

"Thank you, Mrs. King." Melissa made her escape from the housekeeper's sitting room. She hurried down the back stairs to the basement level of the sprawling mansion, her shoes tapping on the wide steps.

Please, God, please let me do well in the kitchens. Keep me out of trouble, and help me to perform every task I'm given by the chefs. I don't know what I'll do if I lose my job here. . . . Please help me stay out of trouble.

Chapter 4

Ned was more than ready to leave the hospital. He had been well cared for, but after a week of convalescing, he was eager to resume his life. And eager to make an apology to Melissa Bradford. Shame overcame him as he remembered blaming her for his troubles. Brother Martin had told him about the young girl's part in rescuing him, as well as her sterling reputation in Biltmore Village. He needed to rectify his mistake.

The sun warmed his back as he walked to the main gate of the Biltmore estate. The gatekeeper, a tall, thin man with sharp eyes, recognized him, of course. He supposed most of the people in Biltmore Village had heard of his accident. Once he explained his errand to retrieve his horseless carriage from the Biltmore stables, the gatekeeper allowed him to pass.

He traipsed up the macadam path, glad his leg no longer caused him pain. The ankle was perhaps not quite as sturdy as before, but that seemed the only lasting consequence from the accident. He only hoped his horseless carriage was in half as good a shape.

The sound of a river gained his attention, and he stopped to enjoy the clear water rushing between steep banks alongside the road. A moss-covered bridge ahead drew him forward. He nearly forgot his errand as he absorbed the peacefulness of his surroundings. But concern for his vehicle and for reaching his goal soon had him moving forward again.

When he had first read about Biltmore Village and George Vanderbilt's dream of encouraging businessmen to move to the area, Ned had been inspired. He had decided right then to visit North Carolina and petition Mr. Vanderbilt to support his own dream of manufacturing horseless carriages. A manufactory at Biltmore Village would be a perfect solution for both of them.

Ned believed horseless carriages were the future of transportation, and he wanted to be a part of that future. His father thought he was crazy and would not advance him the money to open a manufactory, but Ned hoped George Vanderbilt would understand his vision.

He topped a hill and gasped as the enormous home of the Vanderbilts came into view. It was a castle! No other word could be used to describe it. His wondering gaze traveled from one side to the other, taking in the long roofline punctuated by crenellated turrets and tall spires. The main door was in the center of the building, flanked by a line of arched doors and windows. He could see the slanted outline of what must be the main staircase to the left of the central tower and the glass roof of an indoor garden to its right.

Realizing he was gaping at the overwhelming sight, Ned snapped his mouth shut. A carriage was being led from the double doors of a stable, a building larger than the home he'd grown up in. Ned turned his footsteps in that direction.

He'd better find out what condition his vehicle was in before asking to see Mr. Vanderbilt.

A blond stable hand met him inside the entrance.

Ned looked around and pointed to a stall in the back where he could make out the familiar lines of his vehicle's back fender. "I'm Ned Robinson, the owner of that horseless carriage."

The young man in front of him chewed on a piece of straw and watched him through cold blue eyes. "So you're the fancy gent who nearly killed poor Melissa."

Ned opened his mouth to protest but closed it again. No sense in further antagonizing the fellow. From the muscular contours of his arms and chest, he could easily toss Ned out of the stable. "It was an accident. And I'm very sorry for any pain I may have caused."

"You ought to tell her that, not me."

"I plan to as soon as I check my vehicle."

"I guess you can see it." The young man watched him for a minute more, then shrugged and moved out of the way. "But it would be in a lot better shape if you hadn't told Melissa to stay away from it. She nearly had it running before she went to the hospital to check on you. After that, she hasn't touched it at all."

Ned left the girl's defender behind as he stepped into the stall and began examining his vehicle. He winced at the scrapes and scratches along its side, but he knew those could be remedied and would not affect the operation of his horseless carriage. He dropped to his knees and pushed against the cylinder with one hand. It seemed unharmed, but he wouldn't know for sure until he could take it apart and check its operation. He pushed himself up.

The stable hand was waiting for him. "Well?"

Ned reached for a rag lying across the top of the windshield. "It looks okay, but I need some gasoline to see if I can crank it."

"If it runs at all, the credit goes to Melissa. She gave up two nights of sleep to work on your contraption."

Ned's sigh was resigned. He knew Melissa's champion had a point, but he had other matters to consider. "And I'll be certain to thank her. You have my word on that." He stuck out his right hand.

The stable hand looked surprised at the gesture but grabbed his hand after a brief hesitation and shook it firmly. "Good."

Ned left the stable wondering if he would ever break through the fellow's distrust and suspicion. He hoped so. He had the feeling he was going to need all the allies he could muster to succeed.

Checking his hands for any sign of grease or dirt, he strode to the front door of the main house with more confidence than he felt. A black-suited butler answered his knock and accepted his card after ushering him into the entrance hall. The proper servant disappeared, leaving Ned to wait.

Light flooded into a winter garden from arched windows, making him feel he had entered a tropical retreat. At the center of the large glass-roofed room was an exquisite fountain topped by a statue of a boy feeding several geese. The whimsical sculpture brought a smile to Ned's face. He

stepped down into the garden room, marveling at the tower-
ing palm trees and green plants.

"Mr. Robinson."

Ned started at the sound of his name and turned to see
the butler standing beneath one of the arched entrances to
the garden.

"Mr. Vanderbilt is entertaining guests in the billiards
room, but he will take a few moments to meet with you,
since you have come such a long distance." The butler waited
for him to retrace his steps to the entrance hall before leading the way around the sides of the winter garden to the
billiards room.

As the door opened, Ned heard the distinctive clack of
ball striking ball. Several men stood around holding long,
smooth cue sticks or bending over one of the two tables in
the room.

Which of these gentlemen was the host? The tall, bois-
terous blond man in the far corner who was congratulating
one of the players? Or was he the one leaning over a table,
lining up his cue with a ball before making a play?

In the far corner of the room, a man sat next to a table, a
book in his hand. When Ned stepped into the room, he put
his book facedown on the table and rose. "Good morning,
Mr. Robinson. It's a pleasure to make your acquaintance."

Ned took the man's hand in his own and shook it.
George Vanderbilt's hair was as black as his and matched his
thick brows and mustache. His eyes were also dark, almost
black, and bright with intelligence. Ned liked him instantly.
"Mr. Vanderbilt. The pleasure is mine."

His host indicated the table where he'd been sitting. "I hope you will excuse me for not meeting with you in my study, but as you can see, these fellows need a chaperone."

The other men in the room laughed. Mr. Vanderbilt introduced him around, but Ned could not have remembered a single name if his life depended upon it. He was much too concerned about winning Mr. Vanderbilt's approval of his plans.

Once the other guests returned to their games, his host sat and indicated the chair on the far side of the table. "Now tell me why you've come all the way from New York to meet me, Mr. Robinson."

This was it. The moment he'd been working toward for nearly two months. His mouth was as dry as a desert. He cleared his throat. "I have an idea I think you'll appreciate since your family has earned its wealth through transportation."

George nodded but said nothing.

"I've purchased a fine self-propelled vehicle manufactured by the Duryea brothers. You may have heard of them. A Duryea vehicle has either won or placed in every motorcar race in the United States for the past five years."

Mr. Vanderbilt seemed to have turned into a statue. What would cause such a change? Ned looked at his hands rather than at his host, trying to gather his thoughts. "My idea is to use this vehicle to start a manufactory right here in Biltmore Village." Now the words came faster and faster. "I'll start by building one motorcar, and as soon as it sells, I'll use the money to buy parts for another. Since the parts are much less expensive than the assembled vehicle, I should be able to build two or perhaps even three. I hope to one day employ as many as twelve people in my manufactory and perhaps a salesperson as well. I believe if you will help me get started, you and your town will reap the benefits for years to come."

He finally ran out of words, so Ned sat back in his chair and looked at the other man. He wished he knew Mr. Vanderbilt well enough to read his expression.

A few tense moments passed. The other men in the room seemed oblivious to the drama playing out in this corner of the billiards room. They laughed and continued their game while Ned waited to see if his dreams were about to be dashed.

Vanderbilt frowned. "I don't much like these horseless carriages. I prefer the grace and safety of a well-trained team of horses."

Ned's heart fell at the other man's words. Weight seemed to fall on his shoulders. His ankle throbbed. "I see." He forced the words out through a tight throat. He refused to let his emotions out. He still had his dream. All he had to do was convince someone to take a chance on him. He stood.

One of the men to whom he'd been introduced walked over to the table. "Excuse me for intruding on your conversation, but I have to say, George, I'm shocked by your attitude."

Surprise froze Ned in his tracks. Who was this man to talk so to his host?

"Why is that, Horace?"

"You're a man of vision. I have never seen you reject an idea without giving it due consideration. What if this young man's right? What if his vehicle is to become the future of transportation? Why don't you give him a chance to show what his motorcar can do?"

George frowned. "You have a point." He stood and faced Ned. "How soon can you give me a demonstration?"

Ned gulped. "There was a slight problem upon my arrival."

"Something is wrong with your horseless carriage?"

Unable to lie to the man but unable to admit the truth, Ned nodded. "But I can have it ready by the end of the year."

George looked from Horace back to Ned. "You have exactly two weeks. I'll let you use the stables since I understand your vehicle was brought here after it nearly ran down one of my mares. But I want you to be finished and out of here before the rest of my holiday guests arrive in two weeks' time."

"But I don't—"

Horace put a heavy hand on his shoulder. "I'd say yes, young man. I can hardly convince George you have a reliable product unless you can take us all for a drive."

Another gulp preceded his nod. Somehow he would have to repair his vehicle. He would have to find out what had been damaged in the accident and order replacement parts as soon as possible. Then he would have to put everything back together and pray it would perform well. "Two weeks."

"If you can take Horace and me on a tour of the grounds in a fortnight, I'll consider your proposal. If not, I will hold to my original decision."

"Thank you, sir." He nodded to both men and turned to go. He had a lot to do and very little time to get it done. Perhaps if he could hire someone to help him. But where would he find the extra funds?

Chapter 5

"Where are those potatoes?" Vivian Anderson, the English chef, frowned at Melissa. "I need to add them to the venison stew, or the staff shall not enjoy their dinner this evening."

Melissa nodded and wiped her forehead with one hand, being careful not to slice open her forehead with the razor-sharp knife she held. "I am going as fast as I can."

"Humph." One of the other kitchen workers, a young girl named Annette, flounced across the kitchen holding two cans of peaches. "You're courting disaster to hurry her."

A frown pulled Melissa's brows together. She had not heard as many taunts as when she first began working in the kitchens, but some of the maids still did not trust her.

"You leave her alone, Annette." The chef shook a finger at the girl. "I don't recall the butler coming down here to congratulate you on a job well done."

"*Oui.*" Monsieur Ceperlean added his support as he took the peaches from Annette. "Melissa saved *le déjeuner*. You have only brought some fruit. Now go to find some eggs from the refrigerator."

Annette turned on her heel and retraced her steps across the pastry kitchen. The look she tossed at Melissa would have done more damage than any knife could.

Melissa blushed and returned her attention to the potatoes. Last Sunday night one of the dumbwaiters had stuck between the kitchen and the butler's pantry. No matter how much pressure was applied to the electric button, the box would not move.

Climbing into the shaft with a lantern, Melissa investigated the situation. She found a cracked box that had deposited a mass of splinters as it moved up and down the walls of the shaft. She had managed to push the box free so it could finish its journey upward, and then she had removed the splinters before climbing out to resume her duties.

When the English butler, Mr. Burdette, came to find her the following day, he had heaped praise on her, calling her an angel in disguise. The fuss he created had embarrassed her, but Melissa appreciated the compliments.

The English chef took the bowl of peeled potatoes from her and walked toward the main kitchen. "I want you to finish those before I return."

Melissa nodded and reapplied herself to her task.

Monsieur Ceperlean whipped his special dessert, a soufflé filled with peaches and spices. He slid it into the large oven behind Melissa and nodded emphatically. "Now we wait. How go your potatoes?"

"Slowly." Melissa grimaced. "I am afraid I won't finish in time."

The chef frowned and sat down on the other side of the table. "Do you want Annette to help?"

"No, monsieur." She stopped peeling. "Thank you, but Annette and I do not always see eye to eye."

A chuckle answered her. "Then you must hurry, little one. Here, let me show you." He picked up one of the unpeeled potatoes and took the knife from her hand. He held it at an angle and whipped it back and forth, moving the potato between nimble fingers. The peel seemed to disappear magically. "This is the way to peel a potato." He held it up for her inspection before dropping it into the bowl with the others she had managed to complete. "Now let me see you do it."

She peeled it the way he showed her, slowly at first, and then faster as she grew more confident. "I see."

The chef rose and went to the stove to check his soufflé. "It is done."

Melissa continued peeling as she turned to see the chef's masterpiece. It looked like a cake or a tall pie. The crust had risen above the edge of its pan and was lightly browned. "Very nice." She took one last swipe at the potato in her hand and watched as a long piece of brown peel flew away from the vegetable.

She tried to stop it, tried to catch it, but all she managed was to knock over the bowl of peeled potatoes. Water sluiced across the planks of the table, and potatoes rolled everywhere. But Melissa didn't see them.

As if guided with the accuracy of a hunter's arrow, the length of brown peel sailed upward in an arc and down again toward the soufflé, landing with an audible *plop* right in the center of the dessert. For a second she thought it was going to be okay, that she had not done any damage to Monsieur's soufflé. Then a slight hissing sound became audible, and the top sank. Slowly at first but then faster. The sides caved in toward the potato peel and wilted like a punctured balloon.

Melissa dropped the knife and put a hand to her mouth. "Oh no."

Her moan was echoed by Monsieur. "My soufflé. It is gone." He turned toward her, and Melissa saw tears in his eyes. "What have you done?"

Horrified, Melissa stood and backed away from the table. "I—I am so sorry."

A potato hit the floor with a wet *splat*, and she bent over to pick it up and return it to the now-empty bowl. Water was everywhere—dripping from the table, puddled on the floor. One by one she began picking up the vegetables and returning them to their proper places, wishing she could say something to make things right. When she finished she looked toward the Frenchman.

"Leave me." His mouth drooped downward, and his voice broke, like someone trying to hold grief at bay.

Melissa's heart dropped to her toes as she ran from the room. She would never succeed, no matter how hard she tried. She wasn't fit to work at Biltmore.

She left the house by the nearest doorway and headed to the stables. Robert would understand. Maybe he could even offer some hope. As she ran, tears filled her eyes. She stumbled once but managed to keep her balance. Cold air brushed her but brought no relief to her hot, tear-streaked cheeks.

The stable appeared empty when she entered. "Ro. . . bert." She ran to the back stalls when she saw the dim shape of his head through her tears.

She barreled into him at full tilt. "I–I've done s–something terrible."

"What?"

Sobs shook her. "I've r–ruined everything."

His hands alternately patted and rubbed her back as he held her close. His whispered words offered comfort and understanding, eventually slowing the flood of tears. That's when she realized something wasn't right.

Robert's shoulders were too tall, and the arms around her were strong but not as thick. And his hands. . .his hands were larger. Horror replaced her anguish. This was not Robert!

She pushed at his chest with balled fists. "Who. . .what?" She looked up at him in the shadowy room. Instead of the blond hair and kind eyes of her childhood friend, she encountered a stranger's face.

The man stood at least half a foot taller than her friend. His hair was as dark as midnight, brushing across his forehead in a thick wave. His eyes were as dark as his hair, his nose was narrower than Robert's, and his lips were fuller, wider as they stretched into a tentative smile.

"I'm Ned Robinson." He bowed at the waist, moving slowly as if hurt. "I don't know what's happened, but it cannot be as terrible as you think right now. God is in control, and I'm certain a good night's sleep will help you regain your perspective."

Melissa gasped. The driver of the horseless carriage! What was he doing here? "How dare you. Why didn't you tell me right away you weren't Robert?"

His smile widened. "You didn't give me much opportunity."

She sniffed.

He reached in his pocket, withdrew a handkerchief, and offered it to her.

She took it and mopped her face. Her innate fairness made her admit to herself he was right. He hadn't asked her to come running blindly into the stable. And he had been chivalrous enough to offer comfort when she needed it.

"What's going on here?" Now Robert made an appearance.

Melissa whirled around to watch him march toward them. He held a lantern up high, shedding light into the dark corner of the stall. She dropped her gaze to the straw at her feet.

"Did he hurt you, Melissa?"

The question brought her head up. "Oh no. He was— he let me cry on his shoulder."

Mr. Robinson stepped forward. "She was a bit distraught and came looking for you. I have a sister. I know how it can be."

Melissa wanted to take offense at the look that passed between the two men. Was he saying she was overly emotional? And was Robert agreeing with him?

"I heard what happened in the pastry kitchen." Robert lowered his lantern and glanced toward her. "Why were you peeling potatoes in there instead of the main kitchen?"

"Too many people were working in the main kitchen." She twisted Mr. Robinson's handkerchief around one hand. "The chef sent me to work in the pastry kitchen. I didn't mean for the peel to land in the soufflé."

Robert whistled. "You ruined Monsieur's dessert."

Hot tears pressed against her eyes once more. Would she never exhaust her supply? She sniffed and pulled harder on the handkerchief. "He sent me away—" Her voice broke. "I–I'm sure they'll sack me this time."

"Because of an accident?" Mr. Robinson's face showed disbelief. "I cannot imagine you'd be dismissed for such a small thing."

She glanced at him and nodded.

Robert sighed. "You don't know how many 'accidents' Melissa has caused since she was hired." He briefly described the laundry accident and the broken Tiffany lamp, taking care to include the improvements she'd made in both cases. He finished with the repairs she had made to the dumb-waiter.

A frown appeared on Mr. Robinson's face. "I don't understand. It seems to me she's an asset to the Vanderbilts."

Feeling like she had received an unexpected Christmas gift, Melissa looked at the tall, dark man with gratitude. Never had she dreamed he would champion her. Not after he blamed her for his accident. The threat of renewed tears receded. "I wish Mrs. King shared your views."

The smile he gave her warmed Melissa to her toes. The low opinion she'd held of him disappeared like the Christmas cookies Selma used to make before she left the orphanage. Her heart fluttered as his smile widened. Dimples appeared in his cheeks, and she suddenly realized how handsome this newcomer was.

Warm blood rushed to her cheeks, and she looked away.

Seeing Robert's knowing smirk, her cheeks then went from warm to blazing in an instant. With a hasty curtsy, she backed away from both of them and made her escape.

The cool air felt good on her overheated skin as she made her way back to the main house. Perhaps things were not as bleak as she'd thought.

Chapter 6

The sky outside Melissa's window blushed pink, reminding her of her reaction the evening before when Ned Robinson smiled at her. Melissa splashed cold water on her face and gasped, her thoughts of the man temporarily banished as she reached for a clean towel. She ought to be able to stop thinking about him, anyway. Stop thinking about the gentle way he had soothed her while she cried. No man as handsome and debonair as Ned would glance at her a second time. The only reason he'd paid any attention to her at all was because she had thrown herself at him.

Her stomach grumbled as she dressed for the day, unhappy with her decision to avoid dinner the night before. But she had been unable to bear the thought of the accusing faces gathered around the servants' table. She sighed as she made her way toward that same table. It was time to face the music. She couldn't skip a second meal.

As she entered the room, all conversation stopped. Melissa squared her shoulders and tilted her chin. She would not retreat now. She walked toward the sideboard and selected a piece of toast and a slice of ham. By the time she gathered the necessary utensils and some fresh butter, laughter and talking had resumed. She sat stiffly in a chair between two maids whose names escaped her and closed her eyes to bless the food on her plate. When she opened them, no one sat on either side of her. Did they think her contagious?

A knot formed in her stomach, and her appetite disappeared. Melissa broke off a piece of the toast and put it in her mouth, nearly choking as she tried to force the dry morsel past her tight throat. After another equally difficult bite, she gave up. Picking up her plate, she set it on a tray and exited the dining room.

Not sure what to do next, she returned to her room and sat on the bed she'd made up when she first arose. The Bible her sister Selma had given her last year rested on the small table beside her bed. Melissa picked it up, her fingers caressing the raised lettering on the stylish cover, and wished her sister still lived in the area. Or either of her other sisters, Charity and Peggy. But she was the last one here.

A noise brought Melissa's head up. A note appeared under her door. A notice of dismissal? Her heart throbbed slowly as she rose and walked toward it. She bent over and grabbed it between shaking fingers. What would she do?

She perched once again on the edge of her bed and opened the heavy vellum sheet. Her eyes dropped down to the signature. *Mrs. King.* Her gaze flew to the top.

Melissa,

I regret your position in the kitchen did not work out well. Mr. Burdette and I have put our heads together and decided to give you duties more suited to your abilities. We are aware of your enjoyment of the out-of-doors, so we have settled on tasking you with gathering the greenery for decorating the hearths, tables, and doorways of Biltmore for the Christmas holiday season. You may acquire the necessary tools from the estate gardener, Mr. Arthur, who has been apprised of your new duties. After gathering the greenery, you will work in the stable to craft eye-pleasing decorations. You may look at the current arrangements before beginning as long as you do not disturb the family or any of the guests. Mr. Burdette and I trust you will excel with this assignment. If not, I fear we may have no further choice in the matter of continuing your employment at Biltmore.

Clutching the note, Melissa flew downstairs and out to the stable. She could not believe this turn of events and wanted to share her excitement with Robert. The fact that she might see Mr. Robinson again had absolutely nothing to do with the way her heart pounded.

"Robert!" She ran into the stable and took a deep breath, enjoying the smell of fresh hay. "Where are you? I have something to tell you!"

"I'm in here." His voice came from the tack room.

Melissa hurried toward it and found him mending a harness. She thrust the note at him. "Look at this."

Robert's lips moved as he read the words. When he finished, he smiled up at her. "This sounds perfect. Miss Elsie always says you've an eye for decorating."

"I know." She twirled around in her excitement, her arms

303

spread wide. "I can hardly believe it."

"Careful."

Melissa's whirl came to an abrupt halt at the unexpected voice. Her eyes flew open and met the ebony gaze of the newcomer. "What are you doing here?"

Mr. Robinson chuckled at her blunt question, but Robert did not.

"Melissa!" Her friend's voice held censure. "Mind your manners. Ned's staying here until he gets his horseless carriage running again."

Ned's dimples appeared once more, as intriguing as they'd been the evening before. "And what, may I ask, are you doing here? Have you been banished to the stable for your misdemeanors?"

Melissa shook her head. "I'm going to be in charge of the Christmas decorations inside the house."

He stroked his chin as he considered her words, his dark gaze focused on her face. "All by yourself? Isn't that a rather large job for a single girl to accomplish?"

Doubt flooded her at his words. Her elation faded a little as she considered the enormity of her task. She turned to Robert. "I'm sure you'll be able to help some, won't you?"

A shout from the main entrance interrupted his answer.

Robert shook his head. "I have to go." He put down the harness and hurried out of the tack room, leaving Melissa with the tall stranger.

"I don't suppose you would consider letting me help you."

Melissa glanced at him, caught again by his intense gaze.

Was there humor lurking in his dark eyes? "I—I don't know."

His mouth turned up in a smile. "I have a proposal I think will benefit both of us."

"What is that?"

"I noticed the work you did on my carriage—"

Her jaw tightened and her chin went up. "I haven't touched it since my trip to the hospital."

He nodded. "I know. And I truly regret my impulsive words that day. I realize how wrong I was. In fact, I need your help if I'm going to get my vehicle in good working order by the deadline Mr. Vanderbilt gave me. And you'll need someone with a strong back to help you harvest and carry limbs from the woodland to the stable."

A shiver of anticipation raced through her. She would love to work on his horseless carriage, so she nodded without further consideration. "I accept your proposal." As soon as the words were out, she began to wonder if she'd made a terrible mistake. But she couldn't go back on her promise now.

"Good." He captured her hand in his. "Let's get started then, shall we?"

Chapter 7

I think that's got it." Ned couldn't keep the excitement from his voice as he tightened the final bolt. His motorcar would crank now. It had to. He and Melissa had spent a whole week taking the engine apart, cleaning each piece before carefully fitting it back into its proper seating. It looked better than when he'd first bought it.

"Do you want me to crank it?" Melissa brushed her hair back with one arm.

Ned's heart thumped. She was so adorable, standing next to him, her eyes sparkling with anticipation. He wanted to grab her in a hug and swing her around until she was breathless. No. He wanted to embrace her and tell her how much he owed her for her help. And then he wanted to kiss her until she was breathless.

"Ned?" Her innocent gaze questioned his lack of response.

He cleared his throat and shoved his rag into the back pocket of his trousers. "No, you get inside and push in the clutch while I turn the crank. The engine will likely need a flood of gasoline and oil as soon as it fires up, so be sure to use your right foot to keep the accelerator pressed down."

She rubbed her hands against her apron, liberally streaking it with grease. "Are you sure? What if the vehicle starts moving?"

"The gears are not engaged, so it can't move much." He motioned her toward the seat. "And I'll be here to stop it if it starts rolling."

Ned waited a moment for her to get settled. "Are you ready?"

She nodded, but he noticed how her fingers gripped the steering wheel. "Don't worry, Melissa. You'll do great."

He bent over and inserted the crank into its slot. As he began to turn it, he prayed for God's help. So much depended on their ability to get the car going. On the first rotation, nothing happened, but Ned was not discouraged. It often took two or more rotations for the motor to fire up. He pushed against the crank again. Still nothing. Again. And again. He was about to give up, when he felt a vibration. It was working!

With renewed vigor he turned the crank, hoping God could hear his prayer. The next sound he heard was a cough. And then all at once, the engine roared to life. He straightened and looked toward Melissa. She was beaming her excitement. Ned grinned. Success was a heady feeling.

As he had suspected, the hay in the barn kept the wheels from moving at all. Melissa was in no danger, as long as she did not engage the gears.

Ned strode toward where she was sitting and pulled open the door. "We did it!"

"I know." Melissa nodded. "What do I do now?"

Before he could give her any instructions, the engine began to cough. It stuttered and shook before stopping with a choked sound.

Ned watched as black smoke billowed upward from the engine. His shoulders drooped. All that work and nothing to show for it. "What am I going to do?"

Her hand took his limp one and squeezed it. "*We* are going to find out what is causing all that smoke. And then *we* are going to fix it. It shouldn't take us long. After all, the engine cranked and ran smoothly for a few moments." Her voice was filled with optimism.

Ned glanced down at her upturned face. How could he resist such fervor? Such faith? The expression on her face filled him with hope. He felt ten feet tall. As long as Melissa was at his side, he could do anything. "That's true."

"Come on. Let's find out what went wrong." She tugged him forward.

"Wait a minute." He planted his feet in the hay and pulled her back toward him.

Melissa had started the morning with a scarf tied around her auburn hair to protect it from grease and grime, but she must have pulled it off while she was sitting inside his vehicle. A shaft of winter sunlight shone through the stable window and landed on the thick tresses. Caught in the golden light, her hair almost seemed to catch fire. His fingers twitched as he imagined combing through the glorious mane. Standing there looking at him, she was the most beautiful, beguiling woman he had ever met. From what well did her fountain of optimism flow?

Melissa had grown up without the love or memory of her parents. Yet she never seemed to let circumstances keep her down. Her joy and pleasure for every task had infected him. She had infected him. And he wasn't sure he wanted to be cured.

Her brows drew together over her beautiful green eyes. "Is something wrong?"

Ned cleared his throat. How could he confess the tenderness flooding him when he didn't understand it himself? He reached for his handkerchief with his free hand. "Nothing that cannot be remedied." He gently rubbed at a streak of oil on her cheek. "You're not like any other woman I've ever met."

Her mouth formed an *O* of surprise or shock, and he could see her cheek reddening where he had wiped it clean. To be such an optimist, Melissa had very little confidence in herself.

Ned had no idea why this should be so. He wished he could do more to help her understand how special she was. Perhaps in time he could convince her of the truth.

He stepped back and returned his handkerchief to his pocket. "That's better. Now let's see what we can do about my horseless carriage."

❄

"I've brought dinner." Robert's voice brought Melissa's head out from the hood of Ned's vehicle.

Only Ned's legs were visible as he worked underneath the engine mount. They had not yet discovered what had caused the motor to stall earlier.

"Is it already dinnertime?" Melissa had become so engrossed in finding the problem, she lost track of the time. She glanced at the line of windows above the stall, surprised to see how dark the sky had become.

With a series of grunts, Ned dragged himself out from under the engine mount. "If the rumbling in my stomach is any indication, it certainly is."

"I need to wash up." Melissa held up her grimy hands. "I'll be right back." She hurried to the lavatory, still amazed Mr. Vanderbilt had installed running water even out here in the stables. The small room looked much like the wash-rooms in the main house, with its white-tiled floor and walls. It even had a wooden washtub for bathing. Biltmore was certainly a modern house, outfitted with every convenience anyone could dream up.

Ned was awaiting his turn as she emerged. "Don't start until I get back." He winked at her.

Why did her cheeks have to get so warm when he teased her? If Robert had said the same thing, she was sure it wouldn't have caused her to blush. What was the matter with her? She had spent nearly every waking hour with Ned Robinson the past week. She ought to be over her shyness around the man. She shook her head and went back to help Robert set out the food.

By the time Ned returned, everything was ready. They sat around the small table. Melissa folded her hands and bowed her head, and then Robert and Ned did the same. Silence fell in the room, broken only by the snorting of one of the horses.

She opened one eye. "Isn't someone going to bless the meal?"

Robert looked up. "I thought you were going to."

"I'll do it." Ned cocked an eyebrow in Robert's direction before smiling at her and bowing his head once more. "Lord, thank You for the many blessings You shower on us daily. Help us to be ever mindful of Your Word and to follow Your lead in every decision. Bless this food and the hands that prepared it. Bless the three of us as we enjoy Your bounty and each other's company. Amen."

All three of them fell on the food as if they had not eaten for days. Melissa had not realized how hungry she was. Thick slices of roast beef quickly disappeared, as did the stewed carrots and potatoes Robert had brought. When he uncovered half of a pecan pie, she eagerly held out her plate for a slice, not slowing down until the last morsel of golden crust vanished.

"That was outstanding." She sat back with a contented sigh.

Robert nodded his agreement. "Are you sure you don't want another piece of pie?"

"No, I'm full." Melissa smiled at Ned. "Why don't you take it?"

"I don't want to be a glutton, but I must admit I've never tasted anything half so delicious."

"Do you mean to say you've never had pecan pie before?" Melissa could not keep the surprise from her voice.

Ned shook his head. "But I plan on taking the recipe back to my mother and sisters when I return."

"Return?" Melissa put a hand on her stomach to quell the sudden queasiness there. Had she eaten too much? Or was it the thought of Ned going back to New York? "I thought you wanted to set up a business here in Biltmore Village."

Pushing his chair back from the little table, Ned stretched. "I do. I'd love to live here. It's a beautiful part of the country." He glanced at her, and his dimples made an appearance. "And the people here are special."

She blushed again. Ned was going to think something was wrong with her if she didn't quit acting so silly.

Robert tossed his napkin over his empty plate. "What's it like where you're from, Ned?"

His rough voice caused Melissa to look at her friend more closely. Why was he acting so strange? She thought Robert and Ned got along well. As Ned answered the question, she pondered the sudden tension in the room. Was Robert feeling peevish because she had spent so much time working on Ned's motorcar? She needed to do something special for him right away. She couldn't afford to lose her one true friend.

"My papa is a boot maker. I can remember people coming from miles around to get their feet measured. Everyone says walking in his boots is like walking on a cloud. Mama is a wonderful woman. She is a great cook, and she's going to love that recipe when I go home *to visit*."

His emphasis on the last two words made Melissa's heart flutter a tiny bit. So he was planning to stay in North Carolina. She stacked the empty plates into the basket Robert had used to bring the food to the stable. "I'd better get these back inside. I'll see you two in the morning."

"Let me carry that for you." Robert took the basket. "No reason for you to overtire yourself. I know how hard you've been working."

Melissa smiled at him. Robert was always thinking of others. She wondered why he had not been caught by some young lady. He was handsome, kind, and he made a good living. She shook her head at the way Nora ignored him. That young lady had better be careful, or she might wake up and find he had transferred his affection to some other girl.

"Good night, Melissa."

She looked over her shoulder at Ned and nearly stumbled. Was that loneliness she saw in his eyes? Or was he simply tired?

"Good night, Ned." She let Robert take her arm. "Don't forget to meet me at the toolshed next to the Italian garden in the morning. We have a lot of Christmas greenery to gather."

Ned bowed as she turned away. She felt his gaze boring into her back as Robert led her to the main house. A part of her wanted to turn back, but what could she say to erase the pain she'd seen in his eyes? If only she had the same intuition her sisters had always demonstrated, she would know the right words. But she wasn't them. She had no feminine traits at all.

She glanced up at Robert's tight jaw and wondered what was wrong with him. Had both men lost their minds? Or was she too tired to understand the undercurrent swirling around tonight? Perhaps a good night's sleep would bring clearer vision.

❄

"Perhaps we should wait until tomorrow." Ned leaned over and brushed snow out of his hair. "It looks like we're in for a real storm."

Melissa turned from her discussion with the gardener's assistant and watched as Ned stomped his feet to rid them of wet flakes. "We cannot go tomorrow. It's Sunday. We'll be in church most of the day." She handed him an empty basket and picked up an identical one for herself. "We have to fill these with evergreen boughs before the storm grows worse." She wrapped a wool scarf around her neck.

"Your lips will get chapped if you don't cover them." He put down his basket long enough to tug the scratchy material over her nose.

Of course she blushed. At least he couldn't see her pink cheeks, but from the look in Ned's eyes, she had the feeling he knew the effect he was having on her.

The assistant drew their attention by clearing his throat. He had wooden-handled shears for each of them to use. Melissa thanked him and headed toward the door. "Let's get started."

Ned shut the toolshed door and followed her across the large rectangle of the Italian garden. "It's like being in a snow globe."

Melissa stopped and looked at the sky. Light gray clouds bumped into each other, filling the air with huge flakes. "We'll need to hurry. The limbs will be frozen soon."

Ned caught up with her, and they walked side by side for several minutes. They walked for what seemed like miles, neither speaking. Once she looked back over her shoulder and realized she could no longer see the mansion for the thick curtain of snow. Mist was rolling down from the higher slopes, too, cutting them off from all civilization. It was quiet in the forest, peaceful. They seemed to be the only creatures around.

She pointed to a group of trees with short, blue-gray needles. "Let's start here." She set her basket down and began lopping off the branches she could reach.

Ned moved to a taller tree and did the same.

She noticed the branches he cut were much thicker than hers. She hoped they would not be too heavy for his basket. "Did you get your vehicle to crank again after I retired last night?"

He shook his head. "Not yet." He stopped his work and smiled at her. "Do you think we have enough for now?"

Melissa looked at their overloaded baskets and nodded. "This should be sufficient to start. I saw some winterberry and holly bushes on our way out here, however. I'd like to stop and gather berries from them to add some color to the arrangements."

"What about kissing balls? There seems to be plenty of mistletoe around." He pointed to a clump of greenery high on the limbs of a nearby oak.

"We'd need a ladder for that." Her voice was muffled, so Melissa pushed down her scarf to repeat her statement. "We don't have a ladder today."

He raised an eyebrow at her. "No ladder is going to reach that high. I'll see if I can borrow a rifle and shoot some down for you."

"Won't that destroy the plant?"

"I'm a decent shot. I think I can manage to gather enough for our needs."

She liked the way he included himself in the plans. Although their bargain had been to help each other, she had imagined he would only help with the gathering part and leave the crafting part to her while he went back to the repair of his horseless carriage.

"Let's get back to the stables." He rubbed his gloved hands together. "I could use a nice cup of apple cider or hot chocolate."

Melissa picked up her basket, surprised at how heavy it had grown.

"Here, let me take that." Ned held out his shears. "You can carry our tools back."

She allowed him to pull the basket from her hand. For the first time in her life, Melissa felt. . .feminine. And she liked it. She liked having his warm, solid presence beside her. On the way back to Biltmore, her feet seemed to skip along the pathway. Perhaps being a girl wasn't all bad.

Chapter 8

Ned removed his hat and coat as he entered the graceful church.

Brother Martin greeted him warmly, as did several of the local villagers, making him feel like he was already a part of the community. It was amazing how warm and open these people were. Their kindness reinforced his desire to make North Carolina his permanent home. If only he could convince Mr. Vanderbilt to share his vision.

He took a seat toward the back of the church, where he could see each new arrival. Where was Melissa? A group of female servants from Biltmore came in, whispering and giggling as they made their way to a pew up front. His gaze searched in vain for a glimpse of her auburn hair and sparkling green eyes, but she was not part of their group. The next arrivals were the senior members of the staff. Although most of them were strangers to him, Ned did recognize the butler who had announced him to Mr. Vanderbilt a few weeks earlier.

Heads turned and the general murmur of voices came to a halt as Mr. and Mrs. Vanderbilt arrived. He carried a bundle—their infant daughter Cornelia—while Mrs. Vanderbilt floated down the aisle at his right elbow. They were followed by several of their guests, who smiled and nodded as the Vanderbilts slowly made their way to the front pew, stopping every few feet to speak to one or another of the churchgoers.

Ned was so engrossed in watching them, he almost missed Melissa's arrival. The scent of lilacs as her skirt brushed past his pew alerted him to her presence. The scent suited her so well—sweet and fresh, a reminder of the coming of spring. He stood with the intention of inviting her to sit next to him, but when he did, his gaze clashed with the blue gaze of Robert, her escort. Robert shook his head slightly, warning him away. Ned felt his heart hammering in his chest. When had the stable hand become so possessive of Melissa? And why?

Ned had thought Robert and Melissa were friends. Were the other man's feelings warmer than friendship? Or was he simply trying to protect the girl from someone he did not trust? Ned had thought he and Robert were friends, but perhaps he had misread the other man's motives. He sat back down and pondered the questions in his mind until the pastor began his sermon.

He tried to concentrate on Brother Martin's message but found his gaze straying again and again to Melissa's auburn hair leaning toward Robert's blond curls. Then something Brother Martin said did snag Ned's attention. Something about the trust of a man in the woman he loved. Never before had Joseph's story of faith touched him. How had the man managed to put aside his own doubts to accept Mary's story of Immaculate Conception?

The jealousy Ned felt seemed petty and mean in comparison.

Do you love Melissa?

The question made his breath catch. It seemed to come from outside him, but his heart answered with a resounding affirmative: *yes, yes, yes.* The words repeated in his mind with every thud. They filled him with hope, excitement, anticipation.

When the congregation stood to sing a hymn, he joined in with a booming voice. Hallelujah! He was in love. He could hardly wait to get Melissa alone and tell her about his feelings. He didn't care if she had walked in with Robert. He was going to invite her to lunch with him.

He would take her to the picturesque café he had seen when he first arrived in Biltmore Village. The building sat on the banks of the Swannanoa River. It would be the perfect setting to hint to Melissa of the romance in his heart.

As soon as the pastor released them, he made his way to the front door. He would catch Melissa there and pull her away from Robert. She had to agree to go with him. He couldn't wait another minute to tell her how he felt. Robert would be fine. They were friends, that's all. If he loved Melissa, he would have told her before now.

They came out of the church together. Robert had tucked her hand in the crook of his arm, and he was leaning over her, whispering something into her ear.

Ned refused to let jealousy consume him again. Instead, he stepped forward and bowed to both of them. "Brother Martin really knows how to bring the scriptures alive, doesn't he?"

"Yes." Melissa smiled at him.

Robert sketched a bow, but remained silent.

What was he supposed to say next? His mind seemed to freeze. *Freeze.* "Do you think the snow will last until Christmas?"

Robert looked at the bright sunlight. "I doubt it." He tugged on Melissa's hand. "We need to leave."

"Are you walking back to Biltmore?"

"No." Melissa frowned toward Robert and stood her ground. "The lady who runs the orphanage, Miss Elsie, was not at church this morning. We heard she has fallen ill, so we wanted to go check on her."

Robert tugged on her arm again. "She's the only mother either of us has ever had."

"Please let me know how she's doing," Ned spoke to their retreating figures.

Melissa looked back at him over her shoulder and waved her hand in farewell. But that was little comfort. Not when he'd been imagining a romantic meal with her. He could not fault her for wanting to check on the lady at the orphanage. It spoke of her warm heart and generous spirit—two of the reasons he'd fallen in love with her in the first place. But now that he'd realized his feelings, he was anxious to secure her affections. And to make sure she felt the same way about him.

He nodded at the nurse who had cared for him after the accident and tipped his hat to Mr. and Mrs. Vanderbilt as they climbed into the carriage that would take them back to their home. Then he began the solitary walk back to the Biltmore stables.

He passed by the little café without a second glance, all

thought of food banished as he considered what he would do if Melissa did not return his affection.

❄

"How did it go?" Melissa put down the kissing ball she had been working on when Ned walked into the stable.

"Mr. Vanderbilt gave me until the end of this week." Ned walked to where she sat and dropped to one knee. He took her hands in his and chafed them. "As long as we can get the part to repair the fuel line by then, everything will work out fine."

"But I thought you said the man in Asheville wasn't sure—" Her words were cut off when Ned placed a finger on her lips. His touch made her tingle and forget all about what they had been discussing. She knew she ought to move away, but she could not find the will.

"Everything is going to be okay, Melissa. God would not have led me here if He didn't have a plan for me." He brushed his finger over the hot color in her cheeks. "Don't worry."

He stood and looked at the table covered with all sorts of greenery, as well as berries, vines, and cones. "Why don't you show me what we're doing this afternoon."

Melissa was glad no one else was in the stable. Especially not Robert. Yesterday, as they walked to the orphanage to check on Mama Elsie, he had warned her about listening to Ned's glib words. He thought Ned was toying with her emotions while he waited for Mr. Vanderbilt's approval. Robert had lectured her the whole time they were together, reminding her Ned was a stranger who might leave Biltmore at anytime.

She shook her head to rid it of Robert's warnings and turned to the table. "We'll be using these potatoes to form the hearts of our kissing balls." She picked up the one she'd been working on and showed him how to poke holes to hold the mistletoe he'd brought to her as promised. "Secure the mistletoe with one of the vines. Then you add color and texture with the berries and cones. When the potato is completely hidden, you take a ribbon and go around the ball like this." She twined the ribbon around her creation and secured it at the bottom with a hat pin. "Be careful to leave enough ribbon so we can hang it later."

The only sound in the stable came from the horses as she and Ned concentrated on their task. She finished two more as he struggled to wind a vine around his potato. "Let me see how you're doing."

Ned held up his potato. It looked more like a demented porcupine than a kissing ball. A giggle escaped her, and his brows lowered. "It's awful, isn't it?"

Melissa assumed a serious expression. "You should have seen my first one." She took his ball from him and began to work with the greenery. "It takes a little practice." She added a clump of mistletoe to round out the arrangement before handing it back to him. "See? Now get some ribbon and one of the hat pins."

His next effort was much better, and she made sure to compliment his artistry.

He held the ball up and stared at it for a moment. Then he looked at her oddly before returning his gaze to the kissing ball.

"Is something wrong?"

"I've always wondered if these work." His lazy smile made her heart skip a beat.

Melissa didn't know what to say. Was Ned flirting with her? Impossible. She concentrated on the potato in her hand. "We have a lot of work to do."

She held her breath, but he didn't say anything else before placing his kissing ball into the basket. After a little while, she decided the incident must have been a misunderstanding. No man could be interested in a girl without any feminine talents.

When all the potatoes had been festooned with mistletoe, berries, and colorful ribbons, she took a moment to admire their handiwork. Melissa could hardly wait to go to the house and begin hanging them in the doorways and halls.

"Where should we start?" Ned grabbed a hammer, nails, and a ladder at Melissa's direction.

Melissa pointed the way to the music room. "I never dreamed this job would be so easy or so much fun."

"I hope part of your pleasure comes from working with me." Ned set up the ladder in the arched doorway and picked up one of the kissing balls.

How she wished he really found her attractive, but Melissa knew better than to harbor such hopes. Only last night she had read again the scriptures in Proverbs that described a "virtuous woman." Although she did work hard, she made too many mistakes to be a successful housewife. She couldn't cook or clean or even do the laundry without creating a mess.

No, Robert must be right. Ned was only spending time with her because he needed her help. He would never tie himself to someone like her. And who could blame him? Any other female would be a better choice.

Chapter 9

Ned let out a howl as he scraped his knuckles on a brass fitting. This most important day was not beginning well. Would he be able to convince Vanderbilt to help him build a manufactory?

"What's wrong?" Melissa's concerned voice came from above his horseless carriage.

He slid out from under the vehicle, shaking his hand to relieve the pain, and pushed himself to his feet. "I'm ashamed to show you how minor my wound is." He put aside his concerns and held out his hand.

She came around the front side of the vehicle and took his hand in hers. "There should be some liniment around here."

Ned allowed her to fuss over him for a few moments, enjoying the feeling of being coddled. He watched as she spread a thin paste over his knuckles and wound a soft, clean cloth around his finger. "Thank you."

Melissa looked up at him and blushed. "You're welcome."

Quiet pervaded the stable this morning, as if they were the only two people around. She was so close he wanted to sweep her into his arms and kiss her. But after he had recovered from his euphoria last Sunday afternoon, Ned had realized he should wait until he secured a future for the two of them before asking her to marry him. He stepped back and turned toward his motorcar. "Let's see if we can crank it."

She clambered into the seat while he went around to the front and pulled on the crank. It only took two revolutions before the engine turned over, coughed, and roared into life. Ned cheered and Melissa squealed her excitement.

He walked to where she sat and draped an arm behind her back. "Do you want to drive?"

Her eyes widened. "May I?"

Ned grinned and nodded. "Put on your scarf and coat, though. The wind is going to be quite cold." He maneuvered the carriage so it faced the stable doors while she grabbed her coat from a nearby hook and wrapped her scarf around her neck and lower face. She also picked up his coat and handed it to him while she waited for him to scoot past the steering lever.

He cupped his hands around his mouth to be heard over the noisy engine. "Do you understand how to work the clutch and the fuel pedal?"

The look she tossed at him was full of disdain. He should have known better than to ask her. Melissa probably understood better than he did. When he'd first purchased the carriage, he had spent nearly an hour learning how to manage both pedals and the steering lever at the same time. She was sure to master the skills with much less effort. He moved to the right side of the seat.

Melissa climbed up and pulled on her gloves before grabbing hold of the steering lever that curved up from the floor of the vehicle. She released the clutch, and they began rolling forward.

Ned knew he should be watching out for possible hazards, but he could not tear his gaze away from her eager face. Even bundled up as she was, he could almost feel her exhilaration. It brought back his own thrill when he'd first mastered the powerful vehicle. Driving a motorcar was nothing like guiding a horse-drawn carriage.

They followed a horse path toward the back of the estate grounds, gaining speed. Soon they were rushing along at more than five miles per hour, so he turned his attention to their progress through the rolling landscape. The recent snow had melted and caused muddy ruts, making Ned glad he had purchased the optional fenders for his vehicle. Otherwise, both of them would be covered with mud.

"This is the most wonderful experience of my life." Melissa's voice brought him back to her.

He put his hand over hers as it rested on the steering lever and squeezed gently before letting go. "I'm honored to be part of it."

"You're the most important part. If not for you, I wouldn't be driving at all."

Her words were the sweetest he'd ever heard. She must feel the same way he did. He didn't have to wait to ask for her hand in marriage. As soon as they were back at Biltmore, he would ask her to be his wife. His heart nearly exploded from happiness.

Melissa turned the vehicle with ease when they reached a level spot, and they raced back to the stable. She parked it and turned off the motor. "That was so. . .so. . .I can't think of any words to describe it. Thank you, Ned."

He took a deep breath. This was the moment. He knew it in his heart. Vanderbilt would surely help him get started. His future was secure. He could admit his feelings. "Melissa, I have something I've wanted to say to you."

Her green gaze sobered. "What is it?"

He took both of her hands in his. "In the past weeks, working with you, I've come to realize what a special person you are."

Melissa's fingers fluttered inside his. Her gaze dropped to the seat. "Don't—"

He overrode her protest. He had to get the words out to let her know how he felt. "I love you, Melissa. Will you be my wife?"

Silence greeted his question. He waited for her to say something, do something, look at him. "Melissa?"

"I. . .Ned, you don't know the real me." When she finally looked at him, her eyes were filled with tears. "I can't." She jerked her hands away and slid out of the horseless carriage.

"Melissa, stop."

She shook her head and ran into the side entrance to the main house. He thought he heard a sob just before the door slammed shut behind her.

"What's going on out here?" As Ned got out of the motorcar, Robert appeared at the stable entrance. "Did you and Melissa finally succeed? Where is she?"

"She went inside." Ned stalked past him without further explanation. He'd been an idiot to ask her today. He had shocked her. He should have kept his mind on Vanderbilt and the motorcar. Once he'd secured their future, Ned could spend whatever time it took to convince Melissa to marry him.

❄

"This lever turns the front wheels." Ned demonstrated the maneuverability of his vehicle to Mr. Vanderbilt as his motorcar sped along the road toward the hills behind Biltmore. He had wanted to take his passengers to the village, but Mr. Vanderbilt had insisted they go in the opposite direction. Somewhat concerned about putting such a strain on his engine by negotiating the steep back roads, he prayed the recent repairs would hold.

"May I try it?" Vanderbilt reached a hand toward the steering lever.

Ned slowed the vehicle some and nodded, hoping the man would not steer them off the road. After several minutes he relaxed. If the smile on his face was an indication, Vanderbilt was pleased.

"How does it feel?" Horace, the man who'd convinced Vanderbilt to give Ned a chance, lounged in the backseat.

"It's rather exhilarating."

Ned breathed a thankful prayer and glanced over his shoulder to smile at Horace. A sudden jerk made his stomach clench. He twisted back around in time to see one of the front tires run over a boulder. Ned took his foot completely off the accelerator, but the vehicle was already moving too fast. Mr. Vanderbilt lost control of the steering lever and the vehicle careened off the road, running over bushes and small trees as it headed down the slope of a hill. Ned grabbed the steering lever with both hands, pushed down on the clutch with his left foot, and applied pressure to the brake pedal with his right. But still his vehicle plunged forward, jostling all three of the men as it bounced across the uneven terrain.

Death loomed in the form of the rushing river at the bottom of the hill. Ned didn't know if he could stop the vehicle in time. "Jump!"

"What?" Vanderbilt's voice was filled with horror.

"Jump. Both of you. Get out of the motorcar!" He shouted the instructions as he fought for control. The carriage was picking up speed. If they didn't jump soon, it would be too late.

Vanderbilt went first, landing in a clump of bushes. Horace was right behind him, his body rolling with the impact. As soon as he knew both men were free of the vehicle, Ned let go of the steering column and jumped, tucking his head and shoulders. As soon as he stopped rolling, Ned sprang to his feet, paying no heed to the scrapes on his hands and legs. His motorcar had already splashed into the river and now bobbed like a piece of cork as it was swept away in the strong current. Ignoring it, he ran back up the hill toward the other men. "Are you all right?"

Horace's coat had torn and his hat was missing, but he didn't seem to have any broken bones. Mr. Vanderbilt also seemed miraculously free of serious injury, but the anger on his face did not bode well.

"I'm so sorry—"

Mr. Vanderbilt raised a hand to silence him. "I don't want to hear a word from you. In fact I want you off my land immediately."

Ned opened his mouth to argue, but he could see by the look on the other man's face that Mr. Vanderbilt was not going to change his mind. His heart stuttered.

Vanderbilt turned to his friend. "I lay part of the blame for this at your door, Horace. I should never have let you cajole me into ignoring my instincts. It's a wonder we didn't all lose our lives today. Horseless carriages are far too dangerous. I will not have them on my land. Ever." Having finished his words, the angry man stomped away from them.

"George, wait for me," Horace called to his friend. Then he turned to Ned. "I'm sorry, son, but I doubt you'll ever convince him to change his mind now."

Ned watched as the two men walked away and wondered what he would do now. He'd started the day with such high hopes. Where would he turn? What could he do?

Chapter 10

The moment she stepped into the stable, Melissa knew something was wrong. From the way Robert was waving his hands and shaking his head, it appeared he was arguing with the head coachman.

"I don't care—" The head coachman broke off his statement as soon as he saw her. "Miss Melissa, is there something we can do for you?"

Silence filled the large space. "I—I was looking for Mr. Robinson."

Neither man answered her. The coachman exhaled loudly and looked up toward the ceiling. Robert kicked at a bit of straw with one foot and shook his head.

"Robert?" Dread seeped into her chest. "What's going on?"

He grabbed her arm and led her away from the other man. "Let's go outside. We need to talk."

Wondering what could have happened, she looked around and noticed Ned's horseless carriage was no longer in the stall they had used while repairing it. Nor had it been outside where she parked it earlier. "Is it Ned?"

A brief nod answered her. Robert looked grim. He led her to a wide bench looking out over the front lawn. "Sit down."

She complied and twisted her hands in her lap, huddling into the folds of her cloak. Even though the sun had risen several hours earlier, the air was still fairly cold. At least the wind was quiet this morning.

Robert sat next to her and took one of her hands in his. "There was an accident."

Melissa gasped. "Accident? W-was Ned hurt again?"

"No. Nor Mr. Vanderbilt or the other guest who rode with them." Robert glanced away from her as though considering how much to tell her.

"Go on."

"Somehow the horseless carriage left the road. All three men had to jump free. It fell into the river, and someone said they fished it out down below the village. Mr. Vanderbilt is so angry he's forbidden any horseless vehicles at Biltmore. I guess he's worried someone will get hurt."

She grabbed his sleeve with her free hand. "Where is Ned now?"

"He's gone."

"Gone? He can't be gone." Disbelief turned to grief as she saw the truth in her friend's gaze. Tears pressed at her eyes. She sniffed once and turned away from him.

Robert put an arm around her. "I was afraid something like this was going to happen. Ned is from a different part of the world. He was bound to leave one day."

His words brought her head up. Her temper flared. How dare he malign Ned when he wasn't here to defend himself? "Ned *was* planning to stay. He even asked me to marry him." She clapped a hand over her mouth, wishing she had not already said too much.

Robert's arm dropped from her shoulders and gripped her elbow. "He did?" He drew her farther into the recesses of the stable so no one else would hear their discussion. "Did you accept?"

"No." She forced the answer past her clogged throat. The tears had returned. They overflowed her eyes and ran down her cheeks.

"No wonder he left, then." Robert's blue eyes softened, and he held out his arms. "I didn't realize how you really felt. I'm beginning to think you gave him the wrong answer."

Everything inside her seemed to melt. She allowed Robert to hold her while she cried into his chest. It took awhile, but finally the tears were spent. She raised her head. "What else could I do? I'm not womanly enough for any man, especially not someone like Ned."

"What are you talking about?"

"I can't do anything without making a mess." She sniffed and accepted the handkerchief he offered. It reminded her of the time Ned had done the same, and she nearly fell apart again. But she knew she was right. "I don't have the slightest idea how to make him a comfortable home like the woman in Proverbs."

Robert's smile was gentle. "We all have God-given talents. Did you ever think yours might be perfect for a man interested in manufacturing horseless carriages?"

Could he be right? Melissa shook her head, rejecting his idea. "It doesn't matter, anyway. He's gone. Without Mr. Vanderbilt's help, he'll never open a shop in Biltmore

Village. I doubt we'll ever see him again." She hoped Robert would have an answer for her, but he simply shrugged.

She handed him his handkerchief and returned to the main house, her heart heavy. She knew it would be hard to work on the holiday decorations without Ned alternately helping and teasing her, but somehow she would have to complete her task.

She prayed for strength as she climbed the steps to the third floor to begin hanging the greenery she and Ned had put together the day before. Christmas was only a few days away, and she had loads of work to do. Other servants would be involved, but not the one person Melissa wanted to have at her side. She might as well be doing her job alone.

❈

Ned didn't know where to turn. He considered his options as he walked the three miles to Biltmore Village. Who would help him there? Would word already have reached the village he no longer had George Vanderbilt's support? He passed through the main gate and looked around. His gaze rested on the tall church tower. Perhaps the pastor could guide him. He strode to the large building and pushed the door open. "Brother Martin?" His voice echoed in the empty chamber.

Ned stepped inside and waited a moment for his vision to adjust. Sunlight, filtered by the stained glass windows, streaked the aisle, and washed his clothing with color as he moved toward the altar. A door opened and closed toward the back of the room, and Brother Martin appeared, a smile on his face and a Bible in his hand. "Welcome, Mr. Robinson. How may I be of service?"

Emotion welled up inside him. Ned wanted to cry like a child. But he could not. He was a grown man. So he swallowed hard and clenched his jaw. "I've messed up everything."

"I doubt that." Brother Martin sat down on the front pew and invited him to do the same with a gesture. "Why don't you tell me what's happened."

Ned told his story, haltingly at first. He described the accident and Mr. Vanderbilt's ire. He even talked about Melissa and her refusal to marry him. When he finished, he felt drained but a little more peaceful. "What should I do?"

Brother Martin patted his shoulder. "You must trust God."

"Of course I trust God." He frowned at the pastor.

"It seems to me you are depending on your own strengths to see you through. Are you putting your faith in Him? Or in your own abilities?"

The questions struck him with the force of physical blows. He thought of the time and effort he had put into making his dream of manufacturing horseless carriages a reality. But had he asked God if that was what he should be doing?

"God works in amazing ways." Brother Martin opened his Bible, taking a moment to find the scripture he sought. " 'Some trust in chariots, and some in horses: but we will remember the name of the Lord our God.' "

Ned bent forward as the pastor read, feeling the conviction of the words sink deep into his soul. Suddenly he could see how far he'd strayed from his faith. Instead of relying on God to lead him, he'd followed the path he wanted to take. And look where it had led him. Heartbroken. Lost. Uncertain of the future. He needed to return to the basics. . . to God's Word.

"The Lord led me to this psalm this morning." Brother Martin regained his attention. "I have to believe it was so He could speak to you, son."

"Yes, sir, you're right. I needed to hear that." He could hear the shame in his voice. "What can I do to make it right?"

The other man's smile warmed him. "Let's pray and see what the Lord has in mind."

Ned prayed humbly for forgiveness. He could see how willful he'd become over the past weeks, even months. Was he supposed to be here? Should he return home? What about Melissa? Was he supposed to forget his feelings for her? The questions ran round and round in his mind. Eventually the peace of Christ filled him, and he let go of his shame and fear. As he opened his heart and mind to the Lord, ideas began to flow once more. Ideas he believed would lead to a brighter future.

When they finished praying, Brother Martin invited him to take tea in his parlor. Ned accepted, and the two men left the church together, discussing possible solutions. The hot tea and cookies Brother Martin's housekeeper served them made him feel better, too. He was about to take his leave when a knock sounded at the pastor's front door.

"I wonder who that can be." Brother Martin looked out the nearby window. "It looks like one of the horses from Mr. Vanderbilt's stable."

Ned wondered if Vanderbilt had sent someone to find

him and make sure he left the village. He had certainly been angry enough to make the idea plausible. A sense of dread filled him as he recognized the familiar face of the Biltmore stable hand. Had Robert come looking for him?

Chapter 11

The church was noisy, and nearly every pew was filled when Melissa entered on Christmas morning. She should have gotten up earlier, but she had not slept well, which made it hard to rise with the sun.

Mama Elsie waved her to an empty spot in her pew. "I was afraid you were sick."

Melissa shook her head. "I'm glad to see you're feeling better."

Brother Martin stepped to the pulpit and waited for the stragglers to find places to sit. Slowly the room quieted. "Stand with me as we welcome the Lord with stanzas from 'O Come All Ye Faithful.'"

As she stood, Melissa allowed her gaze to wander across the congregation. Something about the tilt of one man's head and shoulders drew her attention. *Ned.* He was here! He hadn't left, after all. Her heart seemed to take flight as the rest of the people in the room began singing. Why was Ned still in Biltmore Village? His dream of starting a business was over. So what business did he still have here?

The hymn ended, and Melissa willed herself to pay attention to the beautiful story of Christ's birth as Brother Martin read from the Gospel of Luke. The words came alive to her, carried her back almost two thousand years to a frightened young couple and their newborn child.

"We are here to celebrate the birth of our Lord, as Christians have done for hundreds of years." Brother Martin motioned for everyone to sit as he began his sermon. "This morning I want to talk a little about Jesus' mother. She was a woman of practicality, a talent we don't spend much time thinking about. But consider how lost she must have felt, far from home and family, when she and Joseph could not find an open inn or home in Bethlehem. I wonder if she wasn't the one who suggested they spend the night in a stable. When Christ was born, I like to imagine her looking around and seeing the manger. She may have asked Joseph to place fresh straw in it while she wrapped the newborn babe in swaddling clothes."

Melissa had never considered practicality a talent. Was it true? Had God gifted her with the ability to engineer practical solutions? A hint of hope brightened her morning. She could feel her lips bending upward. The future did not seem as dark and dreary as she had thought when she dragged herself out of bed.

As Melissa considered the idea that she, too, had talents, Brother Martin drew his sermon on Mary to a close. "We've spent the last two Sundays concentrating on Christ's earthly parents, and I hope it's helped you see them with new eyes. As you spend your day feasting and enjoying the company of your loved ones, stop and think a few minutes about Mary and Joseph. Their trust in God's plan saw them through hardship and trials. It can do the same for us."

The organist took his cue from the pastor, and the

strains of "Hark the Herald Angels Sing" filled the church sanctuary. Melissa sang along with the others, her heart lighter than it had been in days. She could hardly wait to talk to Ned. As soon as the hymn was over, she gathered her bonnet and cloak, hugged Mama Elsie, and slid out of the pew.

Where was he? She looked all around at the people still inside the church but could see no sign of him. Where had he gone? Had she imagined him? No. She was certain it had been Ned. Was he avoiding her? Her heart pounded. Whatever the reason, Ned obviously no longer wanted to have anything to do with her. She sighed and plodded down the aisle, her earlier joy dimmed by his disappearance.

She tried to move closer to the front door, but the crowd slowed her progress. Step by step she moved forward, trying to force a smile as people pressed against her. Finally she stepped across the threshold. Dozens of people still milled about at the corner. At first she couldn't see why, but then a break in the crowd allowed her to catch a glimpse of something shiny on the road—a horseless carriage. Melissa's breath caught. Could it be?

Ned was talking to a group of men, his arms waving about as he described something.

She moved closer to listen.

". . .in Asheville. We'll soon be producing motorcars like mine. Purchasing one will change your life. You won't have to rely on slow, jaw-cracking rides on the back of some old nag. This morning I drove my carriage over here from Asheville in a matter of minutes."

One of the men whistled. "I thought your horseless carriage was wrecked."

"Not a bit. It runs like a dream. It just got a good washing in the river."

The men laughed at that, and one of them slapped him on the back. "Glad to hear you'll be staying near." The others nodded.

"Thank you, gentlemen." He turned back toward the church as the men sauntered away.

Melissa caught her breath when their gazes met. "Happy Christmas."

"Happy Christmas to you, too." His smile was so dear, more familiar to her than her own. "I'm glad to see you this morning. I have a proposition for you."

The happiness welling up inside her brought a giggle. "Do you need help with your horseless carriage?"

"No." He shook his head. "It's all repaired, and I'm about to sell it."

Surprise drowned her mirth. "Why?"

"Remember the man in Asheville who helped me get the part we needed?"

She nodded.

"I went to him after the accident and talked to him about opening a manufactory. We're going into business together. My investment will come from the proceeds of my sale."

"I see. I'm happy for you." She started to turn away.

"Melissa, don't leave. I have something to ask you. Right after the accident, Robert came to see me and explained why you refused my proposal."

She stopped and looked over her shoulder. "Why would he do that?"

"Because he cares about your happiness."

They had discussed her? Embarrassment made her cheeks flood with color.

Ned took a step toward her and turned her around to face him. "I need you in my life, Melissa. You are the help-meet God created to make my future rich."

She stared at his shoes. She might have a talent for practicality, but it wasn't enough to make her a good candidate for him. She didn't want to hinder his success. "I'm a disaster. Catastrophe follows me wherever I go."

"Hmmm. I wonder if I can purchase wife insurance to cover any contingencies."

Her gaze flew upward at his words. He was teasing her? About this most serious issue? Couldn't he see she was trying to save him from making a big mistake? "But I can't do any of the things wives should—"

Her words were cut off when he put a finger across her lips. "Don't you see, Melissa? I don't need someone who can cook or clean. Once we get the manufactory running, we'll be able to hire those services. What I need is a woman who can fix things, like motorcars, for example."

Her gaze searched his face. "You want a mechanic?"

He threw back his head and laughed. "I suppose that's one way to look at it. But what I really want is to marry you, to love you, to spend the rest of my days with you. When I was thrown off the estate, I thought my dreams had ended. But the past few days have been filled with unbelievable things. First Brother Martin helped me see how I'd driven away from my faith. As soon as I surrendered to Him once more, God took over. He's opened so many opportunities I can hardly believe it. The only piece missing is you."

She tried once more to make him see reason. "But I don't want to hold you back, Ned."

Ned put his hand under her arm and helped her into the horseless carriage. "I have something to show you." He cranked the motor and climbed into the front seat. She watched the road as he drove out of the village. He pulled over beside a sunny field overlooking a bend in the Swannanoa River. "Are you cold?"

Melissa shook her head. The air was cool, but the warmth of the sun counteracted any discomfort.

Ned reached under the seat and pulled out his Bible. "When Robert told me how you felt, I turned to God's Word. Do you want to hear what I found?"

He opened the book without waiting for her answer. "I didn't have to look far. 'But for Adam there was not found an help meet for him. And the Lord God caused a deep sleep to fall upon Adam, and he slept: and he took one of his ribs, and closed up the flesh instead thereof; And the rib, which the Lord God had taken from man, made he a woman, and brought her unto the man. And Adam said, This is now bone of my bones, and flesh of my flesh: she shall be called Woman, because she was taken out of Man.'"

As soon as he stopped reading, Melissa felt like a curtain had been lifted away, allowing the warm sunlight to flood her soul. Was Ned right? Was she the helpmeet God had created for him? Was that why she had a talent for practicality and an ability to fix mechanical things? Could it be so simple?

"Melissa, I love you so much, and I want you to share your future with me. Please say you'll marry me."

She had missed him desperately when she thought he was gone from her life. She could not bear to consider losing him again. Suddenly she knew what answer she had to give. "Yes, I'll marry you."

The joy her words brought to his face was a wonder to behold. As Ned pulled her into his embrace, she realized God had not made a mistake when he'd made her a woman. He'd known exactly what He was doing.

Diane Ashley, a "town girl" born and raised in Mississippi, has worked more than twenty years for the House of Representatives. She rediscovered a thirst for writing, was led to a class taught by Aaron McCarver, and became a founding member of the Bards of Faith. Visit her at www.bardsoffaith.homestead.com.

Aaron McCarver is a transplanted Mississippian who was raised in the mountains near Dunlap, Tennessee. He loves his jobs of teaching at Belhaven University and editing for Barbour Publishing and Summerside Press. A member of ACFW, he is coauthor with Gilbert Morris of the bestselling series, The Spirit of Appalachia. He now coauthors with Diane Ashley on several historical series.

A Letter to Our Readers

Dear Readers:

In order that we might better contribute to your reading enjoyment, we would appreciate your taking a few minutes to respond to the following questions. When completed, please return to the following: Fiction Editor, Barbour Publishing, Inc., P.O. Box 719, Uhrichsville, OH 44683.

1. Did you enjoy reading *A Biltmore Christmas* by Jeri Odell, Sylvia Barnes, Rhonda Gibson, and Diane T. Ashley with Aaron McCarver?
   ❏ Very much—I would like to see more books like this.
   ❏ Moderately—I would have enjoyed it more if _____

   _____

   _____

2. What influenced your decision to purchase this book?
   (Check those that apply.)
   ❏ Cover   ❏ Back cover copy   ❏ Title   ❏ Price
   ❏ Friends   ❏ Publicity   ❏ Other

3. Which story was your favorite?
   ❏ *A Carolina Christmas*   ❏ *A Honey of a Christmas*
   ❏ *A Proper Christmas*   ❏ *An Accidental Christmas*

4. Please check your age range:
   ❏ Under 18   ❏ 18–24   ❏ 25–34
   ❏ 35–45   ❏ 46–55   ❏ Over 55

5. How many hours per week do you read? _____

Name _____

Occupation _____

Address _____

City_____ State_____ Zip_____

E-mail_____

A QUAKER CHRISTMAS

by Lauralee Bliss, Ramona K. Cecil,
Rachael Phillips, and Claire Sanders

Christmas is a simple matter among the
Quakers of the historic Ohio River Valley,
but can it be time to welcome love into
four households?

Christmas, paperback, 352 pages, 5.1875" x 8"

Please send me _____ copies of *A Quaker Christmas*. I am enclosing $7.99 for each.
(Please add $4.00 to cover postage and handling per order. OH add 7% tax.
If outside the U.S. please call 740-922-7280 for shipping charges.)

Name _____

Address _____

City, State, Zip_____

To place a credit card order, call 1-740-922-7280.
Send to: Heartsong Presents Readers' Service, PO Box 721, Uhrichsville, OH 44683